NEW YORK TIMES AND USA TODAY BESTSELLING AUTHOR

MELANIE MORELAND

Van - Vested Interest #5 by Melanie Moreland
Copyright © 2019 Moreland Books Inc.
Registration # 1157176
eBook ISBN # 978-1-988610-21-4
Print ISBN # 978-1-988610-20-7
All rights reserved

MORELAND BOOKS INC.

Edited by Lisa Hollett—Silently Correcting Your Grammar
Cover design by Melissa Ringuette, Monark Design Services

❀ Created with Vellum

DEDICATION

To My Matthew
Because your love is the reason
for all that I am and all I am able to do.

Always

ONE

Van

I sat down heavily, my chair squeaking under me in protest. Dust swirled from my clothes, and I ran a tired hand through my messy hair, grimacing when my fingers got stuck in some drywall compound that had splattered.

It had been a long, hard day.

A low groan left my mouth as I rotated my shoulders and flexed my sore hands. The left side of my body ached the most, my leg stiff and sore, adding another layer of discomfort to the day. To top it off, I was hungry, and unfortunately, the café at the front of the building was closed this time of night.

My office was located at the back of the main floor of the BAM building. BAM had been founded by Bentley Ridge and was a highly successful, diversified company. Along with his two best friends, Aiden Callaghan and Maddox Riley, they had turned Bentley's vision of a land development business into a multibillion-dollar conglomerate. Huge land development deals, vast holdings, and investment opportunities were only a few of the things BAM was involved in. Bentley's first passion for flipping houses was what kept me busy. I made sure his profit margin stayed high. I loved what I did —and the company I worked for. All the owners of BAM believed in one simple rule: treat your employees well and reward them for their hard work. It worked. I had never known another company that ran as smoothly as this one did.

The small café in the building was popular with the staff,

1

especially Aiden and me. Although the public had access, it was BAM that kept the business as successful as it was—the baked goods were stellar, the sandwiches top-notch, and the couple that ran it knew us all by name, and our likes. Mine was basically everything on the menu.

Tonight, though, I would have to settle for pizza.

For a moment, I let my head fall back against the headrest and shut my eyes, enjoying the quiet.

I shared my space with Jordan Hayes, who oversaw all the details of the larger builds and projects BAM handled. Our office was filled with plans, blueprints, and models. The shelves overflowed with books and documents, and the cupboards held a lot of tools and equipment I liked to keep safe. In one end of the office was a large table we used for meetings—if we remembered not to pile junk on it. The door to the back loading dock was convenient and a great place to park my large truck.

Across the hall was the area various crews used when they needed some office space, and the rest of the floor held the design team, headed up by Olivia Rourke, who'd joined the firm over a year ago, filling a much-needed void for a designer. She handled all aspects of the final look of the houses, condos, and apartments Bentley liked to buy and flip. That end of the business kept us both busy with crews constantly working on a new project. On occasion, we were brought in on some aspects of the larger projects, but those were usually left in the capable hands of Jordan and his vast network of contractors and trades.

A twinge shot through my arm, and with a groan, I reached for the Tylenol, swallowing a couple of tablets with some warm water from a bottle on my desk. The compact refrigerator was too far away to get a cold bottle.

I dropped my head to my chest, and I inhaled long, slow, deep breaths. I centered my thoughts and focused on the air that entered and exited my lungs. I worked my way through the pain and let the medication take the edge off.

I flexed my left hand, wondering if I needed to go see the doctor again, or if it was a simple case of working too much. This job involved a lot of demolition and moving of walls, heavy lifting, and long hours. All work I loved and excelled at, but I was tired.

Maybe I was getting too old for this shit. Sometimes thirty-nine felt ancient.

The sound of a throat clearing startled me, and as my eyes flew open, I knocked over the empty bottle on the edge of my desk. In my doorway stood Liv. The light from the hall highlighted the bright glints in her light brown hair, creating a halo around her face. Short and curvy, she was dressed in her usual work clothes. A long, loose shirt over dark leggings. Her hair was always up in a knot or a long braid flung over one shoulder, the way it was tonight. Without looking, I knew her feet would be encased in either flat shoes or high-top sneakers. When we were on working job sites, she wore steel-toed boots on her small feet, which, along with the hard hat perched on top of her hair, I found incredibly sexy.

A fact I never shared.

Our relationship was strictly professional.

"Sorry," she apologized. "I didn't mean to startle you."

"I thought I was alone," I admitted. "You're here late. Everything okay?"

She hesitated in the doorway until I waved her in.

"Catching up on a few things. Did you see Bentley's earlier email?" she asked.

"No, I've been demolishing the Randall place all day. I haven't checked email." I grinned. "What's he got his eye on now?"

She slid into a chair in front of my desk, folding her legs under her. She reminded me of a cat curling into a basket the way she tucked herself into the large chair. I knew she did it due to the fact that her feet didn't hit the floor when she sat in that chair. I also knew it was her favorite in the office. It was comfortable. God knew I'd dozed off in it more than once.

"He found a cabin on the Niagara River. It's on a bluff—the view is astounding, but the cabin is in bad shape. He wants us to look at it. He isn't sure if it should be demolished or redone."

"How did he find it?"

"He spotted it from a boat they were on this past weekend. He tracked down the owner. Apparently, it's been deserted for a while and needs, in his words, some TLC."

I chuckled. "Only Bentley would notice a run-down cabin and get interested while out with his wife. I bet Emmy was impressed. He probably started searching immediately."

Liv smiled, the action transforming her features. She was quietly pretty, with wide eyes that were an unusual golden-brown color with a black ring on the outside of the iris, making them stand out. Her creamy skin had a wide expanse of freckles across the bridge of her nose and cheeks. Her lips were plump and full, a deep pink in color— a fact I found intriguing. I always wanted to know if her lips would stay that color after being kissed or go an even deeper hue.

I shook my head to clear my thoughts, concentrating on her smile. It lit up her face, crinkled her eyes, and caused two deep dimples to appear in her cheeks. It didn't happen often, but it was a thing of beauty to witness.

"He said in his email he took pictures and had Aiden and Reid start digging into the history. The owner inherited the cabin from his grandfather and has no interest in it. He lives in the States and only remembers how difficult it was to get to the cabin and how boring it was to stay there when he was a kid. He had a few renos done and rented it out in the summers for a few years, but he found it too much trouble, and it's sat empty for the past while."

"Huh. It must be worth a lot with the land."

"No doubt Bentley made him a fair offer. Once BAM develops the whole concept, it'll be worth more."

I groaned. "He already bought it? Sight unseen?"

"Yep."

"So, either way, we have another job." I looked at the various folders on my desk. "Is it a priority?"

"No. But he wants us to go with him to see it in a couple of weeks and give him our thoughts."

I grabbed a piece of paper and scribbled a note to myself. Liv snickered as I turned, looking for a tack to add it to the various other notes pinned to the bulletin board behind me.

"Your computer could keep better track for you." She shook her head. "I have a terrible memory at times. My mom always swore I would forget my head if it weren't screwed on. I forget things all the time if I don't put them in my calendar or use notes on my phone."

I shook my head. "I hate them. I have to use one here for things, but I prefer my own system."

"You call that a system?"

"It works."

"Reid must hate coming in here."

It was my turn to laugh. Reid was the IT genius of BAM—his brilliant mind was ten steps ahead of everyone else, and our systems were incredible thanks to him.

"Reid and I get along fine. I use what I have to use for all the business stuff. And I'll add it to my notes in my phone, but I prefer the old-fashioned ways of doing things. I have a laptop at home I rarely open."

"No social media stuff?"

"Nope. Nothing. No Facebook, Twitter, Instagram. None of it."

"I get that. I hate texting, although everyone does it." Her brow furrowed. "What about your gigs?"

I lifted my shoulder, trying not to wince. It still ached. "One of the other guys posts stuff. I go to play and enjoy the music. I let them handle it. When I do a solo gig, if there is someone I want there, I let them know. Otherwise, I just play. It's not about the crowds or the money..."

"It's about the music," she finished for me.

"Yeah."

She frowned, looking worried. "Are you okay? You keep wincing."

"Little stiff, that's all. Long day."

"Are you overdoing it?"

I was touched by her concern. "I'm fine, Liv. I have an old injury that flares up at times if I push too hard. We were drywalling a ceiling today and I was a man short, so more lifting. It'll be fine tomorrow."

"Massage."

"Pardon?"

"Massage would help. Some simple yoga stretches would keep the muscles loose too."

I cleared my throat. "Ah, yoga?"

I was gifted another one of her smiles and quiet laughter. "I know you work out a lot with Aiden. But yoga does wonders for your body. It helps me a great deal."

I tried not to imagine her doing yoga. In my mind, the loose shirt and leggings were replaced with a tight shirt and shorts. I had seen her once in a dress. It had hugged the curves she kept hidden and showed off her shapely legs, emphasized her heavy breasts and hourglass figure. It had been the first time I had noticed how incredibly attractive she was and made me wonder why she kept her beauty hidden. The thought of her body stretching and bending while doing yoga was enough to set my imagination flying and allow the thoughts I kept locked away to escape. Watching her bend and stretch, her body arching. Seeing her skin glisten with moisture. Joining her on the mat and showing her a whole new workout routine that ended up with me inside her and my name falling from her lips.

"Van?"

I startled, realizing my head had fallen back and my eyes had drifted shut. I was fantasizing about Liv's body and fucking her.

What the hell was going on with me tonight?

I sat up, shaking my head and fumbling for words.

"Yeah, ah, sorry. Guess I'm more tired than I thought."

"I have the name of a great masseuse if you decide you want to try it. Eve is awesome."

6

"I'll keep it in mind."

There was a pause before she spoke. "You look really tired."

"This project is a lot of work." I chuckled as I tugged on my hair, and a piece of drywall compound hit my desk. "And messy."

She laughed, the sound melodic. "Part of the job. Last week, I was painting a room with Kim. I bent over to get a spot I missed, and she bumped into me. I went around the rest of the day with deep turquoise all over the top of my head. Took me forever to scrub it out. Sammy wanted me to leave it in. She thought it was cool."

I caught the undercurrent of affection when she mentioned her five-year-old daughter. I had only met her once, but she was a cute kid. Polite and quiet. She looked like Liv, except her eyes were dark. I knew nothing about Sammy's father, other than he was out of the picture and Liv raised her on her own. Her mother helped her out a lot and was close to them both, but aside from some humorous stories Liv would share, that was all I knew.

"I bet she did."

"I had to tell her my boss preferred me without turquoise hair."

"Bummer."

Laughing, she stood and slid her hands down the front of her shirt to smooth the wrinkles. I tried not to imagine what her curves would feel like under my hands.

"You should head home and get some rest. I need to go too," she stated.

"Big plans?" I asked, trying to sound casual.

She shook her head. "I have to pick up Sammy soon. Mom took her to a birthday party that involved pizza and the early movie, so I took advantage and caught up with some work."

"Ah."

I didn't ask her any questions. Liv was intensely private, much like myself, so I never pried.

Our relationship was, after all, strictly professional.

She smiled. "At least it's the weekend. You can rest."

"Yeah, thank goodness for that."

She walked toward the door, pausing. "Voltaren cream works really well on joints."

I didn't bother telling her I had a cupboard full of medications and creams to try to help with the aches. "Thanks."

Her phone slipped from her hand, and she bent over to grab it. The action caused her shirt to ride up, giving me a long glimpse of her ass. Her spectacular, full, round ass.

Suddenly I wanted to jump out of my chair and cross the room. Grab her ass and stroke it. Bite it. Lift her into my arms and use my desk as a place to sit her sweet ass on while I fucked her.

She stood, the movement interrupting my lust-filled thoughts. Her brow furrowed as she took in my expression, then she lifted her hand with a quick wave.

"Have a good weekend, Van. I hope your shoulder feels better."

I returned her wave with one of my own, unable to speak, confused at the sudden onslaught of sex-driven thoughts when it came to Liv.

Thoughts I would never act on.

I yanked on my hair in frustration. I needed to get laid. That was the problem. It had been a while. A long while. I frowned as I tried to remember. The last woman I had been with was...

Fuck. I couldn't even remember. I stared at the ceiling, trying to recall. It had been last year. Early last year. Sometime before Liv started with BAM.

What the coincidence had to do with it, I had no idea, but somehow the fact stuck in my mind.

Liv.

Pretty, funny, caring, and untouchable.

She was a coworker. Younger than me by seven years. A mother. Sweet, kind, and thoughtful. The kind of woman you didn't mess around with. She was a forever, not a right now.

And I didn't do forever. I tried it once and it failed.

Our relationship would stay professional.

It was the way it had to be.

I felt another ache start as memories of the past began to surface. The dark ones that pulled me in and reminded me why I chose to be alone.

Why I would never allow my heart to dictate my life.

TWO

Van

I couldn't sleep. No matter what I tried, nothing helped. The long, hot shower I took after I got home barely took the edge off the constant ache. I had rubbed the pain-relief ointment into my shoulders and legs, swallowed more medication, but still, the throbbing persisted. Although I didn't usually like being touched by strangers, the thought of someone working out the kinks in my neck and shoulders tempted me. Giving up on sleep, I sat up in bed, swinging my legs out and sitting on the edge of the mattress.

I would text Liv and ask for the number.

Liv.

She had been on my mind all night. Why I had no idea, but for some reason, the past couple of months, she'd slipped into my thoughts more than I cared to admit.

I liked working with her. She was bright and creative. She had a way of studying a room, or a drawing, and then with a few strokes of her hands, transforming a plain space into something beautiful. She could take the darkest spot and bring light into it. Change the feel and composition of an area with color and material. Her visions were incredible. She was patient and quiet—and a good listener. Clients loved her. Bentley trusted her completely, always accepting her vision of any project without question. We were lucky to have her at BAM. Her staff thought highly of her, and she treated them well. Level-headed and tolerant, she treated everyone around her with courtesy and respect. We had a great working relationship, one of mutual admiration. Our interactions were easy and filled with humor.

Yet lately, I had been wanting something different. I wanted to get to know her. Delve into the private person behind the loose clothing, extraordinary eyes, and brilliant mind and find Liv. It was an odd sensation—one I had never thought I would experience again. Something I wasn't sure I should allow myself to attempt. Yet, the feeling persisted. There was something about her that drew me to her, and it had only grown in the months I had known her, no matter how I tried to fight it—or deny it. Maybe I was tired of fighting it. Or maybe I was finally ready to try again. All I knew was that for the first time in years, I wanted something more. I wanted her. She was sweet, intelligent, and articulate. Sexy as hell with an understated beauty I found intriguing. It was a wicked combination.

In the bathroom mirror, I studied my face. I looked tired, the lines around my eyes more prominent than usual. The long scar across my shoulder and arm was puckered and twisted—a reminder of why getting close to someone wasn't a good idea. I scrubbed at my face, too exhausted to bother trying to shave, and stepped into the shower, adjusting the water as hot as I could stand it, hoping another shower would help dispel the aches. Bracing my arms against the tile, I rolled my shoulders, letting the heat soak in and loosen my muscles. I stood there until the water became tepid, then quickly washed and shut off the tap. The room was steamy, the condensation running down the glass, endless rivulets of water going nowhere.

Sort of like my life.

Too restless to stay home, I went into the office. As usual this early on a Saturday, Toronto was quieter, traffic thinner, and I arrived quickly. I parked my truck by the loading dock, somehow not surprised to see Jordan's SUV parked in its spot. Grateful the café in the building opened early, even on a Saturday, I went directly there, grabbing coffee and a box of the pastries we devoured on a regular basis. Rhonda, the owner, grinned at me as she handed me the box.

"Fueling up for a busy day, Van?"

"They're not *all* for me." I winked.

Her husband, Bob, chuckled as he passed me the tray with four coffees. "And these aren't all yours?"

"Jordan's around somewhere. I'm sure some of the crew will wander in, and I never know when Aiden is going to show up."

Rhonda laughed, tucking a strand of white hair behind her ear. "That man and his lemon Danish. I put three in the box in case."

I slid the coffee tray on top of the box of pastries. "Thanks, Rhonda."

"Anytime."

I cut through the back of the hall, using my pass to get through the door that led to the private part of the BAM building. In our office, Jordan had his head bent over a stack of paperwork, the pile of completed documents beside him as large as the one he was currently working on. I hated paperwork, but Jordan excelled at it, making sure we were covered for permits, licenses, agreements, anything we needed to complete a job and stay on track. He handled it all with his exacting attention to detail and calm attitude.

"You look like you need this as much as I do." I interrupted him.

He glanced up, his green eyes tired behind his glasses. But his smile was warm and approachable, and he greeted me with his usual affability.

"You are a life-saver."

I handed him a coffee and popped open the box of pastries. He took a cherry Danish and bit into it with a groan. "Manna from heaven."

I snagged a lemon, my favorite as well as Aiden's, and chewed the fresh, sweet pastry with appreciation. I sat at my desk, sipped my coffee, and ate two pastries.

"What you are working on?"

"More Ridge Towers. Phase Two. Plus going over the new plans for Ridge Estates." He chuckled and finished his Danish, wiping his mouth. "The boys are keeping me busy."

"They always do."

He sorted through his pile of folders and handed me a gray-colored stack. Every person had their own color. "These are yours for the next few flips you'll be working on. Everything is in order."

I took the files. "Awesome."

"I haven't had a chance to delve into Bentley's new acquisition."

"The deserted cabin?"

"Yes." He shook his head. "Only Bentley."

"Exactly what I said."

He picked up his pen, laughing. "Great job security."

I turned to my desk, flipping open the first file. "That it is."

I worked for the next while, sorting and listing the projects, making notes and entering information into my laptop and adding it to my calendar. Despite my teasing with Liv, I did use the technology to my advantage for work. I still preferred my handwritten notes, but only I saw those. My crew and Jordan could access the details when needed on the shared drive. Jordan worked for another hour, then left, although he grabbed a croissant before heading out.

Sitting in the corner at the drafting table, I studied the plan for a house BAM had recently purchased. It was in a great area, large and well built, but it'd had nothing done to it in years. The rooms were small and chopped up, and Liv wanted to open walls and move rooms, switching the kitchen to the other end of the house, adding a sunroom, and master bedroom on the main floor, as well as more changes to the second story. It would be a massive renovation, and although the end result would be stunning, it was my job to determine if the changes could happen, and if, cost-wise, they were a good investment. I liked seeing Liv's designs and her notes and ideas, then making them a reality. She was intelligent and knowledgeable and rarely asked for impossible tasks. She understood load-bearing walls and structure, and her designs were always sympathetic to the limits we had to work within.

This time, however, her requests were long and complex. I began my list, room by room, of the changes she wanted, jotting notes and foreseeable problems.

A noise caught my attention, and I sat up, looking around, shocked to see I had been hunched over the table for two hours, engrossed in the plans in front of me. I heard the noise again, recognizing Liv's voice and the high-pitched reply of a child. Sliding from my chair, I crossed the office, glancing down the hall. Listening, I heard Liv's soft-toned voice.

"Soon, Sammy. Mommy needs to do a little more work."

"I'm bored!"

"I know, baby. Why don't you draw Mommy another picture?"

"I already drawed you three. Why can't I go stay with Grammie?"

"Grammie isn't feeling well today, Sammy. Mommy has to get this work done, and I have to do it here. I'll be done soon, and we can go to the park."

"Can I have ice cream?"

"May I," Liv corrected gently. "Remember your manners, Samantha."

"May I have ice cream, please?"

"Yes. Be good for Mommy and let her work for a while, then we'll go to the park and get ice cream."

"Okay."

I walked down the hall and leaned on the doorframe, studying the picture in front of me. Liv was at her desk, surrounded by drawing pads and sketches. Sammy was stretched out on the floor, dolls and papers scattered everywhere. They had obviously been here a while, but I had been so absorbed, I never heard them. Liv was in a sweatshirt, long and dark, the sleeves rolled up to her elbows. Her hair was down today—something I rarely saw. It fell in long waves over her shoulders and down her back, the light catching the golden glints, making it shine. Her fingers were covered in dabs of color as she worked on a design, bringing it to life.

Sammy's head was bent over a piece of paper, her hair the same shade as her mothers, except it was curly and wild, moving freely as she concentrated on her drawing.

Sammy noticed me first. She sprang to her feet, looking excited. "Hi!"

Liv looked up. Her beautiful eyes were round and startled, but she smiled when she saw it was me. "Hey, Van. I didn't know you were here. Your door wasn't open."

I had pushed it shut for privacy after Jordan left. Often if a crew member dropped in, I lost hours of work as they chatted. I had wanted to concentrate.

"Liv. I was so busy I only now realized you were here."

Sammy hurried to the door. "Hi. I'm Sammy."

I hunched down, taking her tiny hand in mine. "Hi, Sammy. We met a long time ago. You've grown so much, I hardly knew it was you."

She grinned wide. "I remember you. You're Mr. Van. You work with my mommy and build stuff!"

I laughed. "That's me."

She edged closer. "I want a new shelf for my dolls. Could you build that?"

"Sammy!" Liv admonished.

I shook my head, holding up my hand. "It's fine, Liv." I addressed Sammy. "What kind of shelf do you want?"

She held her arms wide. "A big one!"

"You must have lots of dolls."

"Books too."

"Ah—books are good."

Her responding nod was fast, making her curls swirl around her chubby cheeks. Aside from her dark eyes, she looked exactly like Liv, right down to the row of freckles across her nose. She was an enchanting child.

"Mommy reads to me every night." Her eyes became round. "Do you like to read, Mr. Van?"

"Yep."

"Mommy is teaching me. I can read a lot too, but I like it when she reads to me." She leaned forward, her voice becoming secretive. "Grammie reads to me too, but she talks too fast and she doesn't do the voices. Mommy does funny voices. I like them."

I met Liv's glance over Sammy's head. She was watching us with a look of patience and exasperation. I grinned and threw her a wink to let her know it was all good.

"I bet she does."

I stood, smiling down at Sammy. Her head tilted back on her neck as she peered up at me.

"Are you a giant?"

"Sammy!" Liv groaned.

"He's taller than anyone I ever met, Mommy! You said the only way I would learn stuff was to ask questions."

I waved my hand, chuckling at her response "It's fine, Liv. No, Sammy, I'm not a giant." I studied Sammy. "Although, you're so tiny, *you* could be a mouse."

A grin split her face, showing a small gap in her teeth. "I'm a girl, not a mouse."

I stroked my chin. "Nope. I think you're a mouse."

She giggled.

I glanced at Liv, noting the fact that she looked tired. The need to help her in some small way was suddenly paramount. "How about I take this little mouse to my office and we can plan out her bookshelf while you work?"

Liv began to shake her head, but Sammy clapped her hands. "Oh, yes! Please, Mommy? I'll be so good for Mr. Van!"

"You don't need to do that, Van."

"I'm not doing it because I have to, Liv. I want to. Mouse and I can stay busy, and you finish what you need to get done." I met her gaze. "We're ten feet down the hall. She'll be perfectly safe."

Sammy looked delighted. "Mommy, I have a new nickname!"

Liv's lips quirked. "Yes, it seems you do. Mr. Van and Mouse."

I smiled down at Sammy. "Sounds good, right, kiddo?"

Sammy beamed. "I love it!"

"That's settled, then." I glanced at Liv. "How about that drawing?"

Sammy's tiny hand snuck into mine. "Please?" She beseeched Liv.

Liv grinned, clearly defeated. "Okay." She wagged her finger at Sammy. "You be good."

Sammy tugged on my hand. "I will. Come on, Mr. Van! Let's go!"

Laughing, I let her lead me to my office.

Sammy tapped the paper with a sticky, impatient finger. "More of these."

I had to bite back another chuckle. I wasn't Liv, but I could render fairly accurate drawings. A bookshelf seemed pretty simple. I'd thought I could keep Sammy busy for a while and let Liv work. Sketch out a bookshelf and be entertained by her stories. I knew kids liked to talk. They loved a captive audience, and I found her easy to listen to. She was a bright, happy kid.

But this wasn't just any kid, and it certainly wasn't just any bookshelf.

This one had a top shaped like a castle. Nooks and cubbyholes as well as shelves for all her stuffed friends. It had to be pink. With glitter.

Lots of glitter.

"More turrets, Mouse?" I asked.

Her curls bobbed wildly. "Yes," she hissed slightly, finishing off the Danish I had let her have. There were bits of icing all over the drawing, my lap, and her fingers and face, but she had loved it, and I wasn't able to say no to her. She had been very polite and very excited when she spied the pastry box and asked if there was anything in it.

"I'm hungry, Mr. Van."

I flipped open the lid and let her choose. Little minx took the last lemon Danish, then proceeded to devour it after she climbed up on my lap and continued to describe the bookcase of her dreams.

I huffed, my breath moving her curls around her head.

"We have two. Where could I put more?"

She scrunched up her face, looking so much like Liv when she concentrated, I grinned.

She tapped the paper again, leaving a smear of icing. "On the side." Her eyes widened. "Oh! Both sides, Mr. Van!"

I leaned back, snagging a wet wipe from the dish beside me. It held an assortment of condiment packets we kept on hand, and I remembered we had a few of the wipes in the dish too. Judging by the smears on the paper, I needed to clean her hands.

"Hands up, Mouse. Show me those sticky fingers."

Immediately, she lifted them, and I gently wiped at the tiny digits on her hands, removing the traces of sticky icing clinging to her fingers.

"Let me see your face."

She tilted up her chin, facing my direction. Icing was stuck to her cheeks and lips, and I grabbed another wipe and cleaned it off.

"Good thing I did that before Mommy saw you."

"Before Mommy saw what?"

I looked at the door. Liv leaned against the jamb, smirking knowingly. It was sexy.

"I had a treat, Mommy!"

One eyebrow rose on Liv's face. Her gaze was direct. "I see."

"She said she was hungry."

Liv shook her head. "She's always hungry if there is something sweet around."

"Sorry, I didn't want to bother you asking. I guess I should have done so."

She waved her hand. "It's fine. We're going to the park, so she can run off the sugar. I'll get her a decent lunch."

"And ice cream," Sammy interjected.

Liv sighed. "Yes. As a special treat."

Sammy clapped her hands. "Mommy, come see my bookshelf!"

Liv crossed the room, staring down at the paper. "That's, ah, quite the shelf."

"Pink," I informed her.

"Ah."

Sammy patted the paper. "With glitter here. And here."

"Wow."

"Glitter, I have been informed, is mandatory for castle bookshelves."

"Makes sense." Liv tapped Sammy's head. "Go get your coat and stuff, baby. Mommy's done."

Sammy slid from my knee. Without prompting, she peeked up at me. "Thank you for the treat, Mr. Van. And drawing my bookshelf."

"You're welcome."

She patted my hand, wrapping her fingers around one of mine. "You can come to the park with us. I could show you my slide and where I hang upside down on the bars." She leaned closer. "Mommy doesn't like that part, but I'm good at it."

"I think Mr. Van has other plans," Liv said quietly. "Maybe another time."

Sammy's face fell, but she didn't argue. "Okay." She paused at the door, looking back. "You can come to the park anytime, Mr. Van. It's a happy place."

She hurried to Liv's office, the sound of her rushed footsteps making me chuckle.

"She's amazing," I said to Liv.

She smiled and indicated the paper. "May I take that?"

I frowned. "How will I know what I'm supposed to build?"

She looked confused. "I don't expect you to build it, Van. Neither does she. It's a drawing. I like to keep her ideas in a book so I can show her one day."

I stood and took the paper to the copy machine and scanned it. I handed Liv the original. "I'm building it for her."

"I can't ask you…"

"You didn't. She did. I told her I would, and I never break my promises."

"I'll pay—"

I interrupted her. "No, you won't. This is between my new little friend and me."

Her eyes were filled with wonder. "How can I thank you?"

Words I never thought I would utter came from my mouth.

"Can I go with you to the park? I like happy places."

THREE

Van

Somehow, as we headed to my truck, Sammy's hand slipped into mine, a tiny fist nestled against the callused skin of my palm. She chatted the entire way down the hall, telling me about her favorite grilled cheese sandwich at the diner we were headed to before the park.

"Do you like ketchup with your grilled cheese sandwich, Mr. Van?" she asked.

I found the way she addressed me amusing. It made me smile. "I don't think you can legally eat it without ketchup. Or bacon."

She peered up at me, her eyes round. "Bacon? I never had bacon on mine. I love bacon!"

"Well, we'll have to change that today."

Liv laughed quietly, shaking her head and mumbling about the two of us being trouble.

When we reached my truck, she paused. "Um, we should walk."

I opened the back door. "I know what you're thinking, Liv. I've got it." With a few simple tugs and adjustments, I stood back, grinning proudly. "Voila! Instant child seat."

"Wow."

"It was a built-in feature. Surprisingly, it's come in handy at times."

A strange look flitted across her face. "Oh."

"I've gone fishing with a buddy and his son a few times. Jesse is the same age as Sammy."

"Oh," Liv repeated, this time with a smile. "Handy."

"Yep." Leaning down, I picked up Sammy, lifting her into the seat, and strapping her in. She giggled as I made sure she was safe, tugging on the straps and ensuring her hair wasn't caught in the restraint. Once she was settled, I opened the door for Liv. "Madam, your chariot awaits."

She peered at the truck with uncertainty. I tried not to laugh at the look of trepidation on her face as she eyed the distance between the ground and the door. Without thinking, I looped my arm around her waist and lifted her into the cab. She squealed and grabbed my arm as I hoisted her up, settling her into the passenger seat. She was a small, warm weight in my arms. Close enough I could smell the scent of her floral perfume. Her hand looked minute clutching my biceps, and somehow, I liked the feeling of the way my size dwarfed her.

As though I were protecting her.

Our gazes locked momentarily as I hunched over her. Her beautiful golden eyes had flecks of brown and green that caught the light. The dark circle around her irises made them stand out. They were unique. A strand of her tawny hair drifted across her cheek, and without a thought, I tucked it behind her ear, my fingers drifting over the silkiness of her cheek.

"Do you need help with your seat belt?" I murmured, my voice pitched low.

Wordlessly, she shook her head.

My gaze dropped to her mouth, the rosy tone of her lips tempting me. Her teeth sank into the plump flesh of her bottom lip, and I tugged gently, freeing it from the attack. When my finger touched her mouth, she gasped quietly, the action causing her tongue to flick against my skin.

Instantly, the thoughts of what her tongue would feel like pressed to mine filled my head. How her mouth would taste as I kissed her. The way her hair would feel grasped in my fist as I explored her.

It was only when Sammy clapped her hands, giggling at the way I had lifted her mom into the truck that I realized how close I was bent over Liv. How rapid her breathing had become, mine matching her fast inhales. Had I dropped a mere few inches, our mouths would have fused together.

With a start, I realized how much I wanted that to happen.

Blinking, I stepped back, shaking my head to clear it. Liv's gaze was shocked, confused, perhaps even a little disappointed as I met her eyes, then shut the truck door. I adjusted myself as I walked around the back of the truck to the driver's side, wondering if this was, after all, a good idea. Spending more time with Liv and Sammy —it could prove to be complicated.

I hated complicated.

Yet, despite my misgivings, I found I wanted it anyway.

When we reached the diner, Liv scrambled out of the truck before I could get out and help her. Sammy raised her arms, letting me lift her from the truck. Once again, her tiny hand rested in mine as we walked into the restaurant. Her other hand was clutched in Liv's as she chatted away. Her dialogue never ceased the entire meal, filling the silence that had fallen between Liv and me.

Our eyes met several times, holding briefly, then skittering away. I felt the occasional press of Liv's knees against mine under the table as she would shift or turn to help Sammy with her meal. I observed her carefully as I sipped my coffee and devoured two grilled cheese and bacon sandwiches, plus a salad, and most of Sammy's fries. Liv was an attentive mother, smiling and responding to Sammy's never-ending questions and queries.

"Where does bacon come from, Mommy?"

"How come ketchup is red?"

"Can you push me on the swing, Mr. Van, when we get to the park?"

I startled hearing my name, but I quickly agreed.

"I can do that."

"Will you catch me when I slide?"

"Sure."

"Maybe you could come on the monkey bars with me."

I had been to the park before, and I knew the playground. It wasn't far from my house, and I liked to run through it during my spare time, often sitting on a bench and watching families together and imagining having one of my own. At times, I fought down the swell of sadness at my thoughts.

"I think I'm too big for the monkey bars, Mouse. But I'll watch you."

"Okay," she agreed easily, finishing her sandwich, or at least most of it. Crusts, she informed me, were *yuck*. She giggled loudly when I shook my head in disagreement and made a point of eating mine first, telling her they were the best part. Liv laughed quietly when Sammy nibbled at the crisp edges, testing them out. Liv rolled her eyes at me as we shared the quiet joke of watching Sammy.

It was an oddly intimate moment.

At the park, I caught Sammy as she hurtled down the slide. Pushed her as high as I dared on the swing, listening to her squeals of delight. Made her and Liv laugh as I hung from the monkey bars, holding my legs as high as they would go, my feet still hitting the ground. I made funny monkey noises, then chased Sammy around the trees, threatening to catch and tickle her until she begged for mercy.

Finally, we grabbed ice cream cones and sat on the bench eating them. Sammy still had lots to tell me, although she had talked nonstop the entire afternoon.

"Sammy, take a breath," Liv admonished her. "Stop talking Van's ear off, and eat your ice cream."

Sammy frowned, tilting her head from side to side to study me.

"He still has both ears, Mommy. I can't be talking that much," she replied.

My laughter was loud, making Liv jump and causing Sammy to giggle.

"It's all good, Liv. I like hearing Mouse talk."

Sammy finished her ice cream and jumped to her feet. "Can I go back on the swings?"

"Yes," Liv said. "Make sure I can see you at all times."

"Okay. Watch me, Mr. Van!"

"I will, kiddo."

I slid over on the bench closer to Liv. I finished my ice cream and stretched, letting my arm rest on the back of the bench. We watched Sammy soar high, leaning back so her hair trailed low into the dust of the sand below her.

"Oh God, she is gonna need a bath *and* a shower tonight," Liv muttered.

"Is she always this full of energy?"

"Feels like it. She's a busy little girl."

"She's awesome."

Liv smiled, looking downward. I noticed she did that a lot when she smiled. As if she didn't want to share her smile. I wanted her to share it with me.

I stretched, stifling a groan at the effort.

"Are you still in pain?" she asked quietly.

"I always am. Some days are worse than others. I'll survive."

"You shouldn't have played on the monkey bars," she scolded. "Sammy is old enough to understand the word no and why you couldn't have done so."

I waved my hand, dismissing her concern. "It's fine, Liv. I try not to let it affect my life. If I give in, I'm done for. Swinging a little on the monkey bars didn't harm me. Mouse got a kick out of it, and I enjoyed it."

She pursed her lips and stayed silent. She finished her cone and wiped her fingers. "Thank you for being so kind today, Van."

"Not a problem. It was fun."

Liv made a strange noise in the back of her throat but didn't say anything else.

I watched Sammy for a few more minutes. She jumped from the swing over to the monkey bars, chatting with another little girl. Both of them hung upside down, swinging and talking as if it was normal. I had to chuckle.

Liv groaned. "I hate it when she does that, but she does it anyway."

"She's being a kid."

"Hmm." She leaned back and crossed her legs. Her hair brushed against my arm, the strands soft. I had to resist bunching it in my hand.

I cleared my throat. "Her dad around?"

Liv scoffed. "No."

"I'm sorry."

"Don't be. We're better off without him. Both of us."

The bitterness and pain in her voice were blatant.

"Then I'm glad he's out of the picture. How long ago did you divorce?"

Liv shifted, turning toward me. "We were never married. I was young when I met Chris. Looking for myself, for love. He seemed great—charming and nice. Interested."

"But?" I asked.

"It took me a while to see the real him. He was very good at hiding it. He was anything but nice underneath. Demanding, exacting, controlling. Mean."

My hands curled into fists. "Did he lay hands on you, Liv?"

"No. He used words to hurt." Her eyes focused on something behind me as she gathered her thoughts. "My mom said I was following in her footsteps. My father was the same way, and it took her a long time to walk away. When I discovered I was pregnant, I told Chris. He wasn't happy."

"So you split?"

"Yes. He walked out." She laughed, the sound bitter. "When I found out it was a girl, I went to see him. I thought he would see the ultrasound picture, realize what he was missing, and we'd try again. I was still in denial about his real self."

"I assume that wasn't what happened."

"No. When I told him, showed him the picture, he informed me he didn't need another weak, clingy female to look after. He told me to get rid of it." Liv's voice shook. "He looked at a picture of his daughter, a tiny little being growing inside me, and called her an *it*. As if she was nothing. As if *I* was nothing. Right then, I realized how stupid I was being even wanting to give him a chance. I walked away and never looked back. My lawyer sent him papers, and he signed away his rights." She wiped at her cheek. "Last I had heard, he left town. I have no idea where he is, and I hope never to see him again."

"Bastard," I growled, looking over at Sammy. How could anyone walk away from their child? It was inconceivable to me.

"I can't believe I told you my sob story. I'm sorry."

"Don't be. I asked." I wrapped my hand around hers, holding it tight. "I think you're amazing, Liv. Sammy is a great kid."

She stared down at our hands. "What are you doing here, Van?"

Our eyes locked.

"I don't know," I admitted.

"I can't-I can't do this. I don't date." Liv slid her hand from mine. "I like you, Van. I think you're wonderful. But only as a friend."

I felt a frisson of sadness at her words. I heard the pain and finality in her voice.

I also heard regret. Somehow, it made her words easier to take and made me push a little more.

"I don't date, either, Liv. But we can be friends, right? Maybe grab a sandwich and an ice cream with Mouse on occasion?"

"I don't want to confuse Sammy." She moved her fingers restlessly on her lap. "She likes you, and she tends to become attached."

"I like her. I don't plan on going anywhere, Liv. We're friends already, and we can stay friends. The occasional sandwich or ice cream isn't going to confuse her." I played the best card I could think of at the moment. "Men and women can be friends. Hang out on occasion. Surely, you want her to understand that?"

She paused.

"I love kids," I admitted. "I like her. I would enjoy seeing her every so often, if you wouldn't mind."

"I sense there's a story there."

I nodded, not meeting her eyes. "Maybe one day I'll tell you."

She was quiet for a moment, seemingly contemplative. "Maybe one day you will."

She turned and faced Sammy again, ever watchful. I copied her posture, my head filled with thoughts, swirling with odd emotions.

All of them stemmed from the pretty woman beside me and the child laughing across the playground.

I knew Liv knew how to drive but didn't own a car, so I drove them home, the feeling of regret pulsating in my chest as I pulled up in front of her building. I had enjoyed the simplicity of the afternoon and their company. Both of them. I didn't want it to end, even though I knew it was for the best.

Liv was cautious. She had to consider Sammy, and I understood her trepidation. I understood that more than my own desire to spend time with her. Get to know what made Liv tick. It made no sense. I wasn't in the market for a relationship, but somehow my heart hadn't gotten that message.

I was more confused than ever.

Liv

I watched Van drive away, still unable to believe we'd spent the day with him. It didn't seem real. *He* didn't seem real.

From the moment I met Van, he was larger than life. And not only his size. Tall and broad, he was a wall of muscle. All his shirts stretched tight over his wide biceps. His preferred denim overalls hugged his torso and showed off his tight ass. His waist was thick, his long legs powerful. The first time I had seen him, I'd stepped back as a shot of alarm tore through me. Then I met his gaze. Warm, kind, and calm, his deep brown eyes showed the compassionate soul that lurked under the massive build. His handshake was gentle and his voice soothing. He put me at ease right away and had never given me any concern to be wary of him.

I had never seen him lose his cool. He handled every problem or issue that occurred with the same patient mind-set he had shown Sammy earlier.

The longer we worked together, the more my admiration for him grew. He was thoughtful, concise, and could build or create anything. His talent was endless. He treated his crews with respect, and they worked hard in return. He expected nothing less than the best, and he led by example. He wasn't the kind of manager who sat back and let others do the work. He toiled as hard as his crews, if not harder. He was a great listener, and a supportive coworker. Working with him was a pleasure, and I enjoyed our interactions.

Another added layer to his talent was his music. I had gone with some people from the office to hear him play at a bar one night. Watching the way his fingers coaxed the haunting notes from his guitar was enthralling. I felt his passion as he played, lost in the nuances and scope of the song. He stayed in the background, seemingly content to let others take the spotlight, but I was unable to take my eyes off him. The lights cast shadows on his face and highlighted the glints of silver in his hair and scruff. His muscles rippled as he played. A small, sexy grin curled his lips.

And when he sang...

I thought my heart would explode in my chest. Low, raspy, and sensual. Filled with passion and desire, his voice made me feel things I hadn't felt in years. It created a sense of longing that left me breathless.

Now, when I could, I went to see him. I never told anyone, and he didn't know I was there. I would sit in the back, cloaked by the darkness and listen, filled with my own longing I knew would never be resolved.

I would never risk myself that way again.

Sammy tugged on my hand. "Come on, Mommy!"

We walked into the apartment building, and Sammy ran to her room. I heard her talking to her dolls, telling them about the park, lunch, and the bookshelf Mr. Van had drawn for her. I made a cup of coffee and sat at the small kitchen table, sipping the brew and thinking more about the day.

Lunch had been fun, Sammy, of course, being her usual direct self when talking to Van. He was wonderful with her, always answering her questions, and responding with humor.

He had leaned forward at one point, asking me if I was okay since I had been quiet. I was surprised he had noticed, but I hastened to assure him I was fine.

"Yes, of course. I was, ah, thinking about the design I had been working on."

"Well, lunch will be here any moment. Forget about work and enjoy the day."

"Then we go to the park!" Sammy exclaimed, grinning as she *lifted her head from the place mat she was coloring with the crayons the waitress had given her.*

Van grinned at her, his eyes twinkling. "The happy place."

The waitress slid my grilled chicken salad in front of me and handed Sammy her new favorite—a bacon and grilled cheese sandwich. My eyes grew round as Van's lunch appeared in front of him. Two double grilled cheese and bacon sandwiches along with French fries, a salad, and coleslaw filled his plate.

"Are you gonna eat all that?" Sammy asked, her eyes wide with awe.

"Sammy!" I admonished her.

Van only laughed as he lifted his sandwich. "I eat a lot, Sammy. I'm a big guy."

She lifted her sandwich, biting into it, looking thoughtful. "I'm just a little girl."

He threw me a wink. "Yep. A little mouse."

She giggled, dipping her sandwich into the ketchup I added to her plate. "Mommy says I eat like a horse sometimes. They are way bigger than a mouse."

He winked. "That they are, Sammy. Do you like horses?"

She nodded enthusiastically. "Mommy took me to ride one once. It was awesome!"

He chewed slowly, then wiped his mouth. "Maybe we'll go one day."

Sammy's face lit up. "Yeah!"

I sighed remembering how happy those words made her. I thought about his remarks as we sat on the bench. How nice it had felt to sit beside him—his sheer size made me feel safe, and his gentle demeanor was both appealing and sexy. My body had responded to him when he lifted me into the truck as if I weighed nothing. Being in his arms, even for a moment, had felt so amazing. I thought of the way he hovered over me, his warm breath drifting across my face as he tucked a strand of hair behind my ear. Despite the fact that Sammy was behind me, I wanted him to kiss me. I wanted to feel his mouth on mine and taste him. To know how it would feel to be in his arms for longer than a minute. Sammy's giggle had broken the moment, which was a good thing. Another second pressed so close to Van, and I might have lost my head and kissed *him*. We both would have been embarrassed.

In the park, the way he spoke, how he kept an eye on Sammy while talking to me was unexpected. His quiet words and the flash of anger when he asked about Sammy's father surprised me.

I still couldn't believe I had told him about Chris. Only a few people knew my history. I was a very private person, especially at the office, yet with Van, I opened up. He made me feel as if it was okay to tell him.

He was a good man, but what I had said was true. We could be friends and nothing more. He seemed fine with it, and it was for the best. I could work with him, admire his talent from the dark corner of a bar, and stay focused on what was important.

Giving Sammy a stable home and keeping her happy.

Still, my heart ached a little as I stood and dumped my cold coffee in the sink. I ignored the little voice in my head that asked what would make me happy.

In the grand scheme of things, I didn't really matter. Only she did.

FOUR

Liv

"Fine," I said into the phone, frustrated. "I'll be there as soon as possible."

"Make it fast. I need a decision," Ben Campbell snapped and hung up.

I dropped my head into my hands, overwhelmed. I felt the stirrings of panic begin, but I had to shake them off. I ran through my list of options in my head, and as much as I hated to do it, I knew I had no choice. I stood, grabbed my purse and laptop, and hurried out of my office, strategizing as I rushed down the hall. I was so deep in thought I never saw the person headed toward me until I ran straight into him.

A hard, thick torso that belonged to Van Morrison stopped me in my tracks. I gasped an apology as I slammed into him, my purse and laptop clutched to my chest. His arms snaked around me, keeping me from falling.

"Whoa, Liv. Where's the fire?"

I had to tilt my head back to meet his gaze. His deep brown stare was amused and curious. He frowned as he took in my expression, his voice changing, becoming concerned.

"Hey, what's the matter?"

The urge to drop my purse and laptop and fling my arms around his neck was so strong it shocked me. To seek his comfort and feel the sense of safety he invoked when close. With a sigh, I shook my head.

"I'm sorry, Van. I didn't see you."

He chuckled. "That in itself is telling, Liv. I'm sort of hard to miss."

I had to chuckle at his words. He was correct.

"I need to go get Sammy then head to the Miller place. There's a huge issue, and the foreman is insisting I go in person before they proceed."

He furrowed his brow, confused. "And Sammy is going with you because...?"

I stepped back, realizing I was still in his arms. I felt the loss of his warmth right away, my panic beginning to seep in again.

"My mom is unwell again. She has chronic migraines and is in the middle of a bad run. She called me a while ago to let me know she couldn't get Sammy from day care. I was going to head there and get her, when the foreman called, demanding my presence." I passed a weary hand over my face. "I have to get Sammy, and I have to get to the house."

"Hold up," Van said, reaching into his pocket. "Campbell is the foreman, right?"

"Yes."

"Stay here."

He disappeared into his office. I shifted on my feet, looking at my watch. With traffic, I was going to be late getting Sammy. The day care by my place was good, but she was a stickler for pickup times. Then I had to get across town to the house and sort out the problem. I would also need to stop and get Sammy something to eat.

Ben Campbell was a crusty, demanding foreman, and he wasn't going to be happy about being delayed. Sammy wasn't going to be happy about being dragged around, and I wasn't happy about the constant migraines my mom kept getting. I needed to convince her to go back to her doctor. It had been getting worse lately, and her meds no longer helped.

I slung my purse over my shoulder and began to hurry down the hall. Whatever Van was up to would have to wait.

"Hey!" Van's voice bellowed.

I turned, shaking my head, still walking. "I have to go. I'm sorry."

His long legs covered the distance between us easily. He wrapped his hand around my arm, stopping me. "You're going the wrong way, Liv."

"I need to get a cab. The main road is out front."

"My truck is out back."

"I'm sorry?"

He stopped, gently ceasing my steps.

"I called Campbell and told him to chill. I'll drive you to get Sammy, drop you at the house, then I can take her home and look after her while you deal with him."

I gaped at him.

"No, you can't."

"Yes, actually, I can." He tugged me with him down the hall toward the back of the building.

"I-I can't ask you to do that, Van."

He flashed me a grin. A wide, wicked grin that told me he wasn't going to listen to any of my arguments.

"You didn't. I offered."

"But—"

He stopped. "Do you trust me with Mouse?"

There was no hesitation. I had seen the way he acted with her on Saturday. I knew his responsible nature from the length of time I had worked with him. I trusted him completely.

"Yes."

"Then let me do this. You can give me all the instructions on the way. If you need references, you can call my buddy AJ, and he'll tell you how often I take his son, Jesse, for the night. I'm good with kids, Liv. Sammy will be fine, and you can take care of whatever you need to."

Shocked at his plan, I let him guide me to the truck. He opened the door, and before I could move, lifted me into the cab again, and handed me the seat belt.

"I was going to give you my truck, but given your, ah, height restriction, I decided this was the best option."

Without thinking, I cupped his cheek. "Thank you."

He smiled, warmth and kindness spilling from his eyes. He turned his face, pressing a kiss to my palm.

"Sure, Liv. Anytime."

I watched him hurry to the driver's side.

Somehow, I knew he meant those words.

"That puts us three days behind schedule."

I looked at Ben Campbell, trying to be patient. "I realize. There isn't anything else I can do. These cupboards are the wrong style and color. They screwed up the order and are express shipping the correct one." I dug deep, trying to find my patience. "Surely, we can work on something else and come back to the cupboards in three days?"

He grunted, flipping through his file. "The tiles arrived for the master bath. I guess I can switch around some guys to work there and start the framing for the laundry room downstairs. But I need those cabinets ASAP."

"They assured me they would be on the truck and here by ten a.m."

"And the fixtures?"

"Will arrive tomorrow."

He huffed a sigh. "Fine." He snapped the file closed. "I guess it's all we can do." He crossed his arms. "You can talk to Mrs. Miller. I've dealt with her enough today."

This was a rare job for us. Usually, BAM bought a place, Van and his crew did the demo and rebuild, I decorated it, and it was sold. This time, a client was involved in the flip and had her own ideas of what she wanted. It was proving to be difficult on many levels. She was demanding and exact. Bentley had assured me he would never allow this to happen again, but in the meantime, we had to finish the project.

"I'll call her right away."

His tense expression loosened. "Sorry, Liv. I was out of line earlier. She was here when the cupboards and fixtures showed up and went off on us big-time. She ranted for a good fifteen minutes. Nothing I said worked, and I lost my cool."

"I know," I soothed. "She is very difficult at times. I'll talk to her, and we'll get back on track."

He huffed a sigh. "Okay. I'll go and rearrange the guys."

He left and I pulled out my phone, dialing Mrs. Miller. Once I spoke with her, I could go home and relieve Van of his babysitting duties.

I was shocked by his offer—not only that he made it, but the fact that he seemed excited at the thought of spending some time with Sammy. I had tried dating a few times since she was born but found, to my disappointment, the men I went out with either stopped calling once they knew I had a child or were content to say hi then whisk me away, not at all interested in Sammy. After one particularly disastrous experience, I decided that part of my life was over until Sammy had grown. She was my priority.

Van was different. That much was obvious, yet I was still nervous about what could happen between us. If anything.

After a conversation of soothing and promising, I requested an Uber. Mrs. Miller had been surprisingly understanding, assuring me she knew how hard we were working and "glitches happen."

"I'm so glad I have you and Mr. Campbell to deal with the details," she gushed. "You're both so amazing!"

I had pulled my phone away from my ear, convinced I was being punked. Her next words made the picture a little clearer.

"Your boss, Mr. Morrison, also called. He told me of the lengths you are going to in order to make sure I got exactly what I wanted. He told me you and Campbell are his best and I was in great hands. He even gave me his number in case I needed it in an emergency. I love the personal attention."

I was going to have to speak to Van. Although I appreciated his kind words, he didn't have to smooth over angry clients for me. That was my job, not his, even if this was an odd situation for us to deal with.

I dealt with some emails and messages on the car ride home. When I arrived, I hurried up the stairs, knowing I had to get dinner for Sammy, follow up with the cabinet people, and finish the design I had been working on. I also wanted to go over and check on my mom, to make sure she was all right. I sighed, already weary. It was going to be a long night.

I opened the apartment door, two things hitting me. Something smelled wonderful, making my stomach growl. The second was the sound of laughter coming from the back of the apartment where Sammy's room was located.

I set down my bag and wandered down the hall, pausing in the doorway. I had figured Van would bring Sammy home, give her some cheese and crackers, and let her play. Maybe put in a movie. I had told him where everything was located.

I didn't expect this.

They were sitting in her room, her in a small chair, holding up her teapot, asking if Van wanted more tea. Between them, her tea set was arranged on the table, many of her stuffed animals gathered around it. As usual, she was dressed up while having a tea party. A hat, gloves, and one of her princess dresses.

Van sat on the floor, his legs crossed, a few animals on his lap. A blue boa was draped around his neck, and a tiara sat askew on his head, the plastic gems glittering in the light. He held out his cup, his pinkie extended, no doubt having been schooled in proper tea party etiquette by Sammy, murmuring his thanks for more "tea."

Sammy filled his cup with water and held out the plate of Oreos. I frowned. I never bought Oreos.

"More cookies, Prince Van? I made them myself."

Prince Van?

He lifted his chin royally and accepted a cookie. "They are delicious. You must give me the recipe. I'll have my cook at the castle make them."

Never had I wished for a camera more than I did at that moment. Unable to contain myself, I giggled. They both turned to the door, excited to see me home. Sammy clapped her hands, demanding I join them.

I expected embarrassment from Van, but he simply tossed his boa around his neck and indicated the floor beside him with a wide grin.

"Liv, you're home. Join us for tea? Sammy has made the most divine cookies."

How could I resist?

Van

Liv had a lot of responsibilities, and as I was discovering, she carried a huge load on her shoulders all of the time. She was always friendly and polite, but her real smiles were rare. The ones which lit up her eyes and curled her lips into a perfect bow. I had determined on Saturday I loved Liv's real smile. I especially loved being the one to make her smile.

Seeing her reaction to the accessories Sammy insisted I had to wear made it all worthwhile. Liv's golden eyes were lit with amusement, her expression filled with levity. The giggles that escaped her mouth were endearing. She glowed.

She was so beautiful.

"I like the tiara," she deadpanned. "And the boa suits you."

"It's blue because he's a boy, Mommy. Van said he couldn't wear a fancy hat because he isn't a girl, so I let him borrow my tiara and he says that made him a prince."

"I see." Liv cut her gaze in my direction. "Funny, I don't remember having Oreos in the cupboard."

I grinned unabashedly. "You didn't. We got them at the store."

"We made supper, Mommy!"

Liv looked surprised. "You did?"

"Mr. Van and me made it together! It's his special thing!"

Liv looked confused. "Special thing?"

I chuckled. "My specialty. A little mouse told me your favorite comfort food was mac and cheese. It happens to be one of my signature casseroles."

Liv's eyes grew wide. "You-you didn't have to do that," she sputtered. "You've done so much—"

I cut off her protests with a wave of my hand. "Nonsense. I was hungry and so was Mouse, so we made dinner. We ate and I have yours ready to heat up."

Her expression morphed into something soft. Grateful. Sweet. Her eyes shimmered like liquid gold, and she blinked, dropping her gaze.

Was she crying over macaroni?

She laid her hand on my arm, her voice quiet. "Thank you, Van. Having dinner, my favorite dinner, made for me is a treat. What you did for me today—I can't even begin to say thank you."

I looked at her hand resting against my bicep. Small and delicate, her fingers clutched at the material of my shirt as if she needed something to hold on to. I had to refrain from telling her she could hold on to me anytime she wanted. Instead, I covered her hand with mine and squeezed her fingers.

"Anytime, Liv. Mouse and I had a great time together." I winked at her. "And I was good. I made her eat dinner, including carrot sticks, before we had tea and cookies."

She raised her eyebrows in surprise. "Well then, you did well. She never eats carrot sticks for me."

"Mr. Van's taste better, Mom."

"Oh?"

"I think it's the ranch dressing we dipped them in," I confessed. I unfurled my legs and stood, holding out my hand in invitation. "Why don't you come, eat your dinner, and tell us about what happened. Mouse has lots to tell you about her day."

She accepted my hand, letting me help her up from the floor. "I want to check in on my mom."

"Oh, ah, well, she called about twenty minutes ago. Mouse spoke to her, then I did. Her head was feeling a little better, but she was going to bed. I gave her the name of the pain clinic I go to. There's a guy there who does wonders with migraines. I told her she should go see him."

"She's been trying to get into one, but so many aren't accepting patients."

"I know. I know Phil really well, and I sent him a text telling him to expect her call. He promised to see her as a personal favor."

Liv stared up at me, silent.

"Was that okay?"

Her voice was thick when she spoke. "More than okay."

"So how about dinner?"

Mouse jumped up. "I'll go push the button on the microwave!"

I looked at Liv. "Coming?"

She launched herself at me, catching me by surprise. Her hug was hard, her arms tight around my neck. I embraced her, holding her snug, enjoying having her close.

"Thank you," she breathed out. Her lips pressed on my cheek, once, twice. "Thank you."

She hurried away, rushing down the hall. I could hear the emotion in her voice, and I knew she was crying. I wanted to go after her and hold her some more, but I knew I needed to take things slow. Instead, I headed to the kitchen to help Mouse heat up Liv's dinner.

"This is delicious," Liv mumbled around a mouthful. "I can't believe you cook. Is there anything you can't do?"

I chuckled while trying not to stare. When Liv had reappeared, her hair was loose and hung down her back in a long, silken wave. It was gorgeous and I wanted to touch it. I had to stop myself from doing so by staying busy and getting her a drink. "I cook simple. My mom taught me casseroles, and I do a mean barbeque. I can't create meals the way she does."

Liv kept eating, obviously hungry. I had put extra effort into dinner since I knew she liked Sammy to eat healthy. I added carrot and celery sticks, sliced cucumber, and red pepper pieces to the plate. Sammy had gobbled them up, especially after I told her she only got Oreos if she ate everything, vegetables included, on her plate. Liv laughed when I told her the same thing.

But they both polished off their dinner.

It felt good knowing I had helped Liv. The look of exhaustion and panic on her face when she bumped into me in the hall made the need to do something, *anything*, for her, paramount. Her hesitancy had been easy to override, and I knew she was at her limit today. Mouse had been thrilled to find out we were spending some time together. Shopping with her was fun, although I quickly realized she played the cute factor often. I only allowed her to add two items to the cart.

Oreos for the tea party she was desperately wanting, and a KitKat bar we shared in the truck.

Once she was strapped in, I broke off a wafer and handed it to her. "You were very good in the store, Mouse. But this treat is just between us, okay? Don't tell Mommy. I'm not sure she'd approve of cookies and a chocolate bar."

She giggled. "Okay. But you get some too, Mr. Van!"

I broke off another wafer and bit into it. I ruffled her hair, the golden strands wild and soft. "You're a good kid, Mouse. You share well."

"Mommy says you should always share and be nice."

"Mommy is right."

She grinned at me, looking so much like Liv, it made me smile.

"Okay, let's go home and make supper."

She bobbed her head. "I can help!"

I ruffled her hair again and gave her another wafer. "I'm counting on it, Mouse."

Liv set down her fork. "Thank you, Van. I can't remember the last time I enjoyed dinner so much."

I frowned. "Then you need some serious spoiling, Liv."

She smiled, looking down at her plate, running her finger around the rim.

"You do that a lot," I observed.

She glanced up, confused. "Do what?"

"You look down when you smile." Without thinking, I laid my hand on top of hers. "You have such a beautiful smile. You need to let people see it."

"Oh," she breathed out.

Sammy giggled, looking up from the picture she was coloring. "Grammie says my smile is just like Mommy's. Does that mean it's beautiful too?"

"Yep." I nodded. "It is."

"I like *your* smile," Sammy stated. "It's nice. And your eyes get all wrinkly. I like that."

Liv looked horrified, but I was amused by her honesty. "That's what happens when you get old, Sammy. You get wrinkly."

"You're not old," Liv objected. "I'm thirty-two."

"I'm seven years older than you."

She shrugged. "It's a number."

Her easy acceptance somehow made me feel better. It also made me feel as if perhaps she wasn't as set against the possibility of a date as I feared. Or a relationship.

Both of which, I realized, I wanted with her.

"She's out like a light," Liv murmured, stroking Sammy's hair. She peeked up at me with a grin. "I would have thought with all the sugar you fed her, she'd be wired."

"A couple of cookies isn't bad," I scoffed.

"Add in a chocolate bar, and it's a lot."

I grimaced. Obviously, I was busted. "She told you?"

Liv smiled. It was gentle and soft, filled with love as she looked down at Sammy. "She saved me part of one wafer. She didn't want me to miss out on the treat."

Aw, hell.

If I wasn't already fond of the kid, that did it for me.

"It was melted and stuck to the inside of her knapsack pouch, but I ate it," Liv said. "She was so proud of herself for sharing."

My voice sounded oddly thick when I spoke. "She's an awesome kid, Liv."

"Thanks. I think so."

With a final stroke to Sammy's head, she bent low and kissed her brow. Watching the two of them together did something to my chest. The love Liv had for Sammy, and the way Sammy adored her mother, hanging on her every word, saving a piece of chocolate for her. They were an amazing little family.

I followed Liv from the room, resisting the urge to kiss Sammy's head myself. I had already been given hugs and "smooches." And she demanded I come listen to Liv read to her. As I had discovered, when Sammy asked me to do something, I was powerless to resist, so I had sat on the floor listening to Liv's quiet voice as she read to her daughter. A yearning I had kept under wraps for years stirred as I watched them. The need to protect them. The desire to have them in my life. The longing to be part of their world.

It brought me up short, and my footsteps faltered behind Liv.

She turned. "Are you okay?"

"Yeah, I'm good."

In her living room, I hesitated. "I should go. You must be tired."

She sat down, curling her legs underneath her. "Not as tired as I would have been without your help." She indicated the chair beside her. "I would like to talk to you, though."

I sank into the chair. "What's wrong?"

"Nothing. Except, you didn't have to call Mrs. Miller. Or Ben," she scolded gently. "I don't expect you to fight my battles for me, Van. You can't do that."

"I didn't. Ben is a great foreman, but he goes off the rails at times with his demands. He doesn't deal well, and I stepped in to tell him to back off. I would have, regardless of the person he was dealing with," I assured her. "And Mrs. Miller is a handful. Bentley promised me this is the only time he will ever take on a project like this. I only smoothed her ruffled feathers. Again, nothing I wouldn't have done for any of the staff."

She gave me a challenging look but let it pass. "I still don't know why he took it on. We don't usually do builds for people. We buy, flip, and sell."

"She wanted this house, but Bentley outbid her. She told him the house used to be her grandparents' and she wanted it for sentimental reasons. She asked him to let her be the one who purchased it when it was complete and to be involved in the renos. She even offered him more than he felt it would be worth when it was done." I chuckled dryly. "He had no idea what he was getting us into. Last week, he offered to sell it to her for what he paid plus expenses, walk away, and allow her to finish, but she was adamant she loved our work and she didn't want that to happen."

"She is very particular, but she has a good eye. We're about two-thirds done. The rest is mostly cosmetic things," Liv informed me. "Once the cabinets and fixtures are in place, the rest will happen fast, and we'll be free."

"Yeah, another couple of weeks, and it's done," I agreed.

"Let me handle her and Ben, Van. It's important to me."

"All right," I said begrudgingly. I knew she was right. She was strong, capable, and smart. She didn't need me to fix things usually, yet today, I had to step in.

She reached over and touched my hand. "But thank you. For that, taking care of Sammy, dinner—everything."

Our eyes met and held. The room filled with a strange feeling—taking on a life of its own. One which contained only her and me.

Once again, Liv asked me a question.

"What are you doing here, Van?"

"Spending time with you and Sammy. I like it."

"To what end?"

I shrugged. "I don't know," I replied honestly. "I only know I enjoy it. I like both of you." I studied her for a moment. "Would it be so awful, Liv? To see each other on occasion? Maybe dinner out?"

She hesitated, looking torn. There was obviously a story behind her worry.

"Tell me," I urged.

A long sigh left her mouth. "Not long after Sammy's third birthday, I met a guy—Evan. He seemed nice. I told him about Sammy, and he was fine. He was great with her. He was great with me. We dated, and I got comfortable with him. Sammy saw him as part of our lives. We both did."

"But?" I let the question hang in the air, already knowing the answer.

"Nine months into the relationship, Evan decided a ready-made family wasn't for him. It was too much. *We* were too much. He walked away. Sammy suffered terribly. She missed him so much, and you can't make a three-year-old understand why the person they loved was simply gone. I couldn't tell her he didn't love us enough."

"What an asshole," I growled.

"We saw him about a year later. With his pregnant girlfriend. He had the audacity to tell me he had decided he liked being a dad figure, but he could never love Sammy fully since she wasn't his. So he had decided to move on and make his own family." She sucked in a deep breath. "I have never wanted to hit a person as much as I wanted to hit him that day. He basically told me my daughter wasn't good enough for him to love. The same as her biological father."

"Jesus," I muttered. No wonder she was gun-shy. I couldn't blame her, given her history. But I had to try.

"I'm not them, Liv. I'm not built to walk away. If I didn't think we had a shot together, I wouldn't put you or Sammy at risk."

"Why?"

"Pardon?"

"Why do you think we have a shot?"

"I've always liked you, Liv," I admitted. "But I made you off-limits because of my own history, the fact that we work together, and you're a single mom. But I find you highly attractive. Sexy. Smart. An awesome mother. A beautiful woman. I've been holding back, but I'd like to see you."

A smile curled her lips, and she dropped her gaze. I slid my finger under her chin. "What did I tell you about hiding your smile? I love to see it. I love knowing I caused it."

This time, her smile lit her face. For a moment I basked in it, until she became serious.

"It scares me," she admitted.

I decided to be honest. "It scares me too, Liv. I have my own history, and to be honest, I wasn't sure I'd ever want a relationship again. But there's something between us, and I want to explore it."

She tilted her head. "Will you tell me?"

"Yes. Soon." I took her hand in mine. "I'll tell you anything you want to know. If you want to try this with me, you deserve to know my story too."

She was quiet for a moment, then slowly nodded. "All right."

"We can take it slow, Liv. Dinner. Another visit to the park. Please don't say no to the idea and shut the door."

She bit her lip, looking undecided.

"I play this weekend at the Troup. Why don't you come see me and have a drink after? We're pretty good."

"I know," she said. "I always enjoy your show."

I smirked at her. "*Always?* I know you saw me once. You've been other times?"

Streaks of color highlighted her cheeks. "My friend, Judy, and I take turns once a month taking each other's kids on the weekend. We get a break and the kids get along so well. Whenever I have Saturday night to myself and you're playing, I come see you."

I found myself on the floor in front of her, resting my hands on her thighs, gazing up at her. "Are you stalking me, Ms. Rourke?" I quirked my eyebrow suggestively. "Because I find it rather hot."

"Maybe a little," she whispered. "I've always liked you too, Van."

I rose up on my knees, towering over her. "Then I suggest you call your friend and stalk me this weekend, Liv. I'll play just for you."

She whimpered, low and deep in her throat. Our gazes locked, feelings we were both admitting to simmering between us. Her golden eyes glimmered in the low light, and her soft scent surrounded me. My gaze fell to her mouth. Her tongue peeked out, moistening the plump bottom lip. Her breathing hitched, and mine deepened.

"I think I need to kiss you," I murmured.

"Think or know?" she retorted.

"Know," I groaned and pulled her into my arms, hauling her up tight to my chest. Our lips touched, separated, then joined again. Pressing, moving, learning.

When her tongue traced my bottom lip, I was lost. With a low growl, I pulled her closer and deepened the kiss.

She was everything I knew she would be and more. Sweet, giving, passionate. Our tongues stroked and tasted, our mouths melded as we discovered each other. She slid her hands into the hair at the nape of my neck, playing with the strands, her touch making me shiver. I caressed her everywhere. The length of her back, the bends and bows of her spine. The rounded slope of her shoulders. I ghosted my fingers along the delicate arch of her neck and wound them into her heavy hair. It was soft and silky under my touch. Her body aligned to mine perfectly. The quiet noises she made turned me on.

I wanted more. More of her.

I wanted to lay her out on her sofa and discover every hidden dip and curve of her body. Taste her everywhere. Find out what I could do to make her whimper. Gasp my name. I wanted to bury myself inside her and claim her.

Except... I had promised her slow. I knew I had already crossed every line with her, and I didn't want to scare her by moving too fast. Regretfully, I tempered my kisses. Eased back the passion. Nuzzled her lips before drawing away.

She was a vision. Her hair a tangled mess from my hands. Her lips pink, wet, and swollen from my mouth. Her breathing rapid, the fast pants causing her breasts to rise and fall, her nipples hard under her sweater. I had to push myself away. I stood slowly, never breaking our gaze, letting her see the regret and lingering desire.

"You stopped," she whispered.

I stooped and kissed her gently. "I'm not going to start our relationship off with a lie, Livvy. I said we'd go slow, and we will. You set the pace and I'll follow."

"Livvy?" she asked.

"Yeah, it's how I think of you—if that's okay."

She slipped her hand into mine. "Yeah. It's okay."

I squeezed her fingers. "I have to go." If I didn't, she'd be under me on the sofa in five minutes, and regardless of the fact that Sammy was down the hall, I wouldn't be able to stop.

Liv stood and walked me to the door. I was unable to resist tucking her into my arms again. She nestled against my chest as if she had always belonged there. I kissed the top of her head. "Lock the door and get some sleep."

She looked up at me. "This is going to be complicated."

"No, it won't. It'll be us, and we'll figure out what that is as we go. Okay?"

She stretched up on her toes and kissed me.

"Okay."

FIVE

Van

I leaned back in my chair, tugging a hand through my hair. I shook my head in regret. "We're stretched as it is, Bentley. I have no one I can put on another project."

He grimaced. "We need to figure this out. I want this one done." He looked at Jordan. "We have no one?"

Jordan chuckled under his breath. "Bentley, you are taking on projects faster than we can complete them. All of our crews are working, and we have three other projects waiting."

Aiden laughed. "I told you, Bent. We need to put this one on hold."

Bentley frowned. "No. The market is hot now. This is a great opportunity. A clean, fast in-and-out. The engineer agreed—the structures are solid. Three apartment buildings, each one needing the same thing—updating. We go in floor by floor, renovate, and move on. The values will increase, and we can make a huge profit."

"Not if we don't have the manpower." I pointed out.

He tugged at his sleeves, staring down at the plans laid out in front of him. "We've hired temporary crews before. Why can't we do it for this project?"

"The cost," Jordan stated, matter-of-factly. "This is big."

"But doable." Bentley swung his gaze in my direction. "If we had more men, doable?"

"Yes."

"Control," Jordan added. "We lose control."

Bentley tapped his fingers on the desk. "No. We do the plans, designs, and they work for us. Follow our guidelines. We need the manpower, nothing else."

Beside me, Liv, who had been quiet up until this point, spoke. "What do you want from me, Bentley? What is your vision?"

"Play up the old-world charm. The buildings are sound and the layouts flow. Great bones, but they're suffering from neglect. I want to highlight their beauty and make them come back to life." He handed her a stack of photos. "See for yourself."

"Okay," she murmured, taking the photos. She flipped through them, nodding. I knew her mind was already coming up with ideas.

She was brilliant that way. It was hard to sit here and not stare at her. Or touch her. My fingers itched to feel her soft skin again. To taste her lips.

But I knew it wasn't going to happen. Not at this moment.

Instead, I looked at the pictures Liv handed to me when she finished going through them. The three buildings sat on a cul-de-sac and had all been owned by one man. When he died, his family put them up for sale, and BAM jumped. Bentley had a vision.

Bentley always had a vision.

"Renting or condos?" I asked.

"Both. Our property management group will handle all of it," Aiden said. "Occupancy rates are down because the buildings were being neglected. People living there get first dibs on staying. We're clearing out one building, and as soon as it's done, moving people from the next one in, and again with the last building. We'll have no problem finding both renters and buyers."

"Time frame?"

"ASAP," Aiden stated unapologetically. "Find the right company, hire the crews, and get on it." He looked at Jordan. "You can hire the crews, right?"

"Yes."

"And Liv, you can design the floor plans?"

She pursed her lips. "Each one is the same layout?"

"Yes," Bentley said. "Each building is three floors, four units per floor—the same layout. Two bedrooms, self-contained, with laundry. The basements are mechanical, storage, and all the other building equipment." He leaned forward, meeting Liv's gaze. "The apartments are charming. Gumwood, chair rails, hardwood floors, cove molding. Play it up but give them all the modern conveniences."

"Join the old with the new," she murmured.

"Yes!" He smacked the table. "That's what I want."

"I can do that."

"I knew you could." He winked.

I knew it as well. She was talented.

Bentley turned to me. "Van, I know this is a bigger scope than the houses we work on, but I want you to oversee it. I need your eye for detail and expertise with carpentry. The woodwork in these places will astound you, and I want to make sure the integrity is maintained."

I was intrigued and the thought of using my woodworking skills appealing, but I had to ask. "What about the other three houses we're working on?"

He waved his hand. "You told me Jenkins was a great manager. Give him a chance, let him oversee those with you backing him up, and concentrate on these," he instructed. "Same with you, Liv. Hand over the designs to your assistant, Kim. Let's see what they've got. I'll even let you off the Miller project."

We all laughed. Liv shut her notebook. "It's almost done, Bentley. I'll make sure it's complete."

"I know you will," he said, looking pleased. "That's why the two of you are my best team."

I had to agree. We were a good team.

He smirked, crossing his leg and leaning back in his chair as he turned his attention back to me. "I know you're dying to see what these places look like, Van, and you'd love the challenge of a different type of project."

I had to laugh. Bentley knew me too well.

"If Jordan finds me the men, I'll make sure it happens. They can gut and build, Liv will design, and I'll handle the finishes and oversee the project." I regarded him steadily. "I'll need help, though. I can't do it all on my own. This is gonna cost you, Bent. This is a specialized field."

"It'll be worth every penny. You know someone, right?"

"Yeah, I do."

"Then get them. The project will net us millions." Bentley looked around the table. "So we're all on the same page?"

Jordan shut his laptop. "I'll send it out for tender and get the bodies we need." He stood. "In fact, I'll go start, if you're done with me, Bentley?"

"Thanks, Jordan. Keep me apprised."

"Yep."

He strode from the room, stopping to hold the door open for Sandy. She entered with her arms filled with files and set them on the table.

"The Niagara project. Here is all the documentation on it and the long list of guidelines for building since it's in a protected area. Once you've checked it out, Jordan can start procuring all the proper permits."

Sandy winked at me. "A little something to do in your downtime, Van. Between flipping houses, custom woodwork, overseeing crews, and a couple of hours a sleep a night, you should be able to fit this in, correct?"

I chuckled at her drollness. She was the glue of BAM. She knew everyone by name, their lives, their families, and always made a point to ask after them. She was the right hand to the partners, oversaw all the staff, worked closely with HR, and was everyone's favorite person. She never forgot a birthday, made sure all special occasions were marked, and handled a thousand and one details with the ease of a general. I knew how much the guys depended on her.

"I can forgo the sleep, I suppose. A nap at my desk should suffice."

She rolled her eyes. "That's the spirit."

Reid strolled in, his laptop tucked under his arm. His smirk was wide, his hair, as usual, looking as if he'd run his hands through it repeatedly. As he went by Sandy, he pressed a kiss to her cheek. "Thanks for the sandwich. I forgot to eat again."

She shook her head, looking at him fondly. "I told Becca I would look after you while she was visiting her dad. Just because your wife is away for a week, you don't have to slip back into your old routines," she chided him.

"I do when Bentley sends me new projects he wants handled ASAP."

Sandy peered at Bentley over the rim of her glasses. "You need to peddle it back, young man."

Her words amused everyone. Bentley had no idea how to "peddle it back." He was on fire lately with projects and deals. Knowing him the way I did, I knew it was because his wife, Emmy, was only days away from giving birth. He was overprotective and tense, so, like me, he slept very little and used work to occupy his mind.

BAM was overflowing with acquisitions and projects.

He glanced at his phone. "Soon," he mumbled.

Sandy patted his shoulder and left the room.

Reid opened his laptop. "Okay, so you want this new project all wired up?"

Bentley was frowning at something on his phone, so Aiden spoke. "Yeah, Reid. Work with Liv and Van. This place is old-school—it still has hardwired jacks in all the units. Bring it into the twenty-first century, technology-wise."

Reid looked excited. "Awesome. I'll build it, and they will come."

I chuckled.

Aiden stood. "We can discuss it between us and Liv. We'll do a site visit so we can see what we're dealing with later today, if that works for everyone."

I was excited to see the buildings. We all agreed on a time, then Aiden and Reid left, talking about various ideas.

Bentley set down his phone. "Okay. Now the Niagara project."

He smirked. "I know we have a lot going on, and this one is going to take a while. The cabin is in a protected part of the Niagara Peninsula, so we have special permits and guidelines to adhere to. I'd like to drive up and look around, see what's there, and then come up with a strategy. I don't plan on starting on it until spring. Jordan tells me the permit process is slow with the conservation people."

"It is, but if we're aware and plan accordingly, they are usually cooperative. But I suggest we have Plan B as well."

"Great, then we'll plan and make sure it is all within their guidelines. Have a backup, and we'll go from there." He picked up his phone. "What day works for you two? I want as early as possible in the week. It's about a ninety-minute drive each way, and we'll need a couple of hours I assume? I'm sticking close to home, in case..." His voice trailed off, and he cleared his throat. "For Emmy."

I smiled as I glanced at my calendar. Liv spoke.

"Whatever is good for you, Bentley. Van and I can adjust our schedules," she assured him. "First babies are often late."

He tugged on his sleeves. "So her doctor assures me. He also has told me she is in perfect health, but I prefer to be close—although it seems our daughter is in no hurry to arrive."

"Understandable," she agreed. "How about Tuesday?"

"That works. We'll leave early? Is it doable for you, Liv?"

She jotted down notes quickly. She was conscientious and admittedly forgetful at times. I recalled her confession of relying on her calendar a lot. "Yes. My mom can take Sammy to day care for me and pick her up if needed. Mom is going away to see her sister soon, so Tuesday works."

"Once the day care here is open, Sammy can come to work with you," Bentley pointed out, raising one eyebrow. "It's going to be free to the staff."

Liv lifted her shoulder. "Sammy's been at this place since she could walk, Bentley. There're lots of kids her age, and it's right by my place and close to my mom. She's going to school next year, so I don't want to take her out of her routine."

He pursed his lips.

"I'll bring her on occasion if there is a problem. It's not that I don't appreciate the offer," she stated gently. "But it's the best for her."

"I understand. Maybe your next one."

Liv didn't say anything, and I shifted in my seat, suddenly uncomfortable.

Bentley stood, letting us know the conversation was done.

"Okay, we'll pick you up at your place, and we'll head out. You good with that, Van?"

"Why don't I drive? The place has been empty for a while, and the road is bound to be overgrown. The truck can handle it better than one of your fancy cars. Plus, I can have some tools with me."

He acquiesced fast. "That works."

I stood, waiting for Liv to join me. "Okay, Tuesday it is. We'll see you at the site later?"

He shook our hands. "Yes. And thanks. As usual, you are both amazing."

We walked down the hall, Liv in front of me. I liked watching her walk—the gentle sway of her hips, and the way the light reflected off her hair. It was up again today, but I knew how soft it was when she let the waves loose. I remembered the way she felt in my arms. How she tasted. Smelled. Sounded. Her loose clothing hid her from the world, but I had felt her curves and knew what was underneath the material. I cleared my throat.

"Could I speak to you for a moment?"

She glanced back at me, her eyes worried. "Now?"

From the moment I saw her this morning, I had wanted to be alone with her. She had been on my mind since I left her place two evenings prior. Yesterday had been crazy with meetings and plans, and I had debated all evening about calling her, wondering if it would be crossing a line. I was determined to clear up some of the rules and talk to her today.

"Yes, now."

Jordan passed us in the hall. "Heading for caffeine and sustenance. Can I grab you the usual?"

"Sure. I'd appreciate it. Liv, you want something?"

She shook her head. "No, I'm good."

Jordan grinned. "Your loss. I've been smelling the Danishes baking all morning. I can't resist anymore."

He passed us, and I reached out, tugging Liv into my office. I shut the door and, without hesitation, spun her in my arms. I covered her mouth with mine, kissing her deeply. She wound her hands into my hair, gripping the strands hard and kissing me back with equal vigor. I yanked her tight, taking advantage of her willingness. I needed to kiss her as long as possible, and I hoped the café was busy. I wanted Jordan absent for a long time.

Except Liv pushed away, her eyes wide. "Van," she gasped softly. "We can't."

"Oh, we can," I disagreed. "Maybe we shouldn't, but I had to. I've had to kiss you since I left you the other night."

She traced my lips with her finger, the digit shaking as it touched my mouth. I kissed the tip and stepped back regretfully. "Are you all right?"

She nodded, looking shy. "I wanted you to kiss me too," she admitted.

"Good."

"But the office..."

I held up my hand. "I know. I get it, and I'll try to rein myself in. You simply looked too pretty not to kiss today."

She grinned at my words.

"I wanted to call you last night," I confessed. "I didn't know if I should or not. I'm not sure what the rules are between us."

She leaned on the edge of my desk, her arms crossed. "I don't know either, Van. I'm still trying to wrap my head around the concept of you."

"The concept of me?" I repeated.

"Of you. Of us."

"I like the sound of us."

"I like the sound of it too, but it's still a scary one."

"As long as you're willing to try, I'm willing to take it slow. Tell me what you need, Liv."

"Just some time."

"But I can see you? Spend some time with you and Mouse?"

"Yes."

"Can I call you?"

"Anytime."

I reached behind me and opened the door. Jordan would wonder why I had shut it. I crossed the room and stood in front of Liv. "Then we'll start there." I reached out and traced her cheekbone. "I can be patient."

She leaned into my caress, her eyes drifting shut. It took everything in me not to sweep her into my arms and kiss her again.

I heard Jordan's footsteps, and I stepped back. "Can I drive you to the site this afternoon? Maybe we can have coffee afterward?"

"Sure."

Jordan walked in, his hands full. Liv and I were standing far enough apart it looked as though we were discussing something business-related.

"I got you a coffee, Liv."

She eyed the box in his hands. "How many Danish did you get?"

He snickered. "A lot. They're still warm." He flipped open the lid. "How can you resist?"

Liv reached into the box, but her eyes were on me when she answered. "I can't, it seems."

I snagged one for myself with a grin. "Nope. Resistance is futile."

Liv bit into the pastry. "So I'm discovering."

I hid my smile.

"These are wonderful!" Liv gushed as we walked through an empty unit. "The woodwork and detail are exquisite."

I ran my hand along a chair rail. "They are."

"Some of the units are in bad shape. Can you match the trims and colors?" Bentley inquired.

"I can. It'll take some work, but I can do it." I bent down and picked up a loose piece of trim. "There's a company that can analyze the stain so it can be matched. There is another that can replicate the cuts."

"Excellent," Bentley stated.

"I'll have to figure it out place by place. If it's bad enough, it might be cheaper to tear it out and replace rather than piece it together."

"Whatever you need."

Liv was busy with her sketchbook. She was enthralled as she walked around, eyeing up the layout and planning. Maddox had joined us, and the two of them were in a discussion about costs. He was a brilliant numbers man, and I knew he, no doubt, already had mapped out budgets.

Bentley was correct. The structure was sound, the apartments a good size, but all in need of updating. He had found a hidden treasure. It needed some polishing, but once complete, it would be a goldmine. Maddox would be pleased.

"What about outside?"

Jordan spoke. "We'll sandblast and clean. New windows and doors, fresh trim, and that's all they need. Because the entire road is private, we'll spruce it up. Liv suggested cobblestone, some benches—play up the uniqueness of it."

"The parking area needs some attention."

"Already on the list."

"Then I'd say we're already in good shape."

Jordan agreed. "I'll send you the tenders to look over. Once you and Bentley approve, I'll send them out. I'm thinking two different crews—one for the inside, one for the outside. We can get it done faster, and the cost will even out since we can finish quicker. As our projects wind down, we can bring our own people to finish up."

"That works."

He turned and went over to talk to Reid who was like a kid in a candy store. The place was a time warp, and he was excited about what he could do to bring it up to his technological standards.

Bentley crossed his arms, looking pleased. "So you're playing this weekend?"

"Yeah, Friday and Saturday."

He nodded. "What time are you on?"

"Two sets Friday—nine and eleven. One Saturday at ten."

Aiden looked over at me, grinning. "A bunch of us are coming from the office on Friday."

"I appreciate the support."

"Emmy wants to come on Friday." Bentley chuckled. "If she's still awake, we'll be there. Usually, she's out by eight thirty, but she says she's having an extra-long nap. She loves coming to see you."

I smiled at his words and the tone of his voice. He was a doting husband—protective and caring—very different from the no-nonsense businessman most people knew him as.

"I've already reserved a couple of tables in the corner, away from the bar. If she can come, she'll be away from the rowdies."

Bentley slapped my shoulder. "Thanks."

Jordan and Reid joined us. "I'm looking forward to Friday," Reid said. "Becca will come with me —she gets home in the afternoon."

Maddox and Liv strolled over. "Dee and I will be there. You coming, Liv?"

She briefly met my eyes. "Yes. I'll be there on Friday."

I grinned. I always enjoyed playing, but suddenly Friday night seemed more exciting.

Liv would be there.

SIX

Van

The club was packed, the crowd ready for us. We had been playing together so long, our gigs were smooth and easy. We changed up songs and sets, but we all knew the music. Most of the songs, I wrote. But together, we made the sound come alive.

The tables I had reserved were full, plus a few others had additional people from the office scattered around the club. Liv sat next to Becca, sipping a glass of wine. She wore her hair down tonight, her outfit more tailored than usual. It showed off her full, high breasts without being too much. She was classy and beautiful.

And every time our eyes met, she smiled.

Midway through the set, I took the mic, strumming my guitar as I looked over the crowd.

"We're happy to see you all tonight. Lots of regulars. Aren't you sick of us yet?"

The whoops and hollers made us happy. We had a great following and we all enjoyed performing. That was where it ended for all of us. But it was a huge part of our lives, and we loved playing as much as they enjoyed listening. I hoped it wouldn't change for a long time.

"I've got a new song I thought I'd share." I found Liv's golden eyes in the crowd. "This one came to me late one night and wouldn't leave until I finished it. It's called 'Smile for Me.'"

As I expected, Liv looked down, her smile hidden. But I saw it, and I knew it was for me.

The room grew silent as I played and sang. It was rare I took center stage, but this song was personal for me. Inspired by Liv, the way she made me feel and how I loved her smile, it flowed out of me. I let every emotion I was feeling saturate the words, the simplicity of the song rich with emotion. I sang of the fear of love, the loneliness of life, and finding unexpected happiness in the smile of a beautiful woman. As the last notes faded, I rested my hand on the neck of my guitar, bowed my head, and waited. The place burst into applause, hands slapping tabletops, and feet stomping on the floor in appreciation. I lifted my hand in gratitude and stood.

"Thanks. We're grateful for the support. We've got a short break, then we'll be back. Be sure to tip the waitstaff—they deserve it."

I stepped from the stage, joining my friends and coworkers. Emmy leaned forward, tears in her eyes.

"You were amazing! That song—it's-it's beautiful."

"Thanks," I replied, concerned. "Are you okay?"

"Pregnancy hormones," she sniffed. "It happens all the time."

Bentley wrapped an arm around her shoulders, kissing her head with a tender expression. "Yes, it does. But it was a great song."

Cami beamed at me. "It was one of the most beautiful pieces of music I have ever heard." She hunched closer. "Who did you write it for?"

"An image in my mind," I bluffed. "An idea—a wish, if you will. I was in a good frame of mind, and it came to me."

She looked skeptical. "It was so lovely. Whoever it was for should be shouting it from the rooftops."

Aiden leaned close. "I could write you a song, Sunshine. Maybe something about your stellar skills in—"

She covered his mouth, her cheeks turning pink. "I think we'll leave the songwriting to Van."

Aiden huffed a sigh. "I offered."

"And I love you for it."

He kissed her, then picked up his beer. He threw me a wink and I laughed.

I finally got the nerve to look across the table. Liv was looking everywhere but at me. Her fingers worked the edge of the table nervously. She stood and mumbled her apologies and hurried down the hallway. I watched her go, confused. I thought she'd like the song. I lifted the bottle of water one of the waitstaff brought me and drained it. I stood.

"Excuse me."

Everyone was busy talking. I had a feeling Emmy and Bentley would be gone when I returned. She looked sleepy and uncomfortable, and he looked concerned. Becca was yawning after her long day of travel, and Reid was hovering close. I appreciated them showing up for support, but I understood. Their lives were elsewhere. Dee and Maddox would stay, and so would Aiden and Cami, and I was good with that.

But I had to find Liv.

I hurried in the direction she had gone, past the long line outside the ladies' room. There was a back patio where people sometimes went for some fresh air or privacy, and I had a feeling she had headed there.

I opened the door and stepped outside. I saw her in the shadows, standing alone in the corner, her back to me. I approached her cautiously.

"Livvy, you okay?"

She nodded, not speaking or turning around.

I laid a hand on her shoulder. "I told you I would play for you."

She spun, facing me. Tears streamed down her face.

"Hey," I questioned. "What's this?"

"How," she choked. "How did you write that? How did you know?"

"I see you, Liv. When you smile, I see your soul."

She launched herself at me. I caught her around the waist, pulling her close. Her mouth was hot, sweet, and wet. Her grip tight and frantic. She pressed her body close to mine, kissing me hard. I tugged her as close as I could, kissing her back with all the passion I felt for her.

Jesus, she was perfect.

I moved us farther into the shadows, knowing her privacy was important. When we finally surfaced for air, I buried my face in her neck.

"Your words," she whispered. "They were so beautiful."

"I wrote them for you."

She tightened her arms.

In the distance, I could hear myself being paged.

"I have to get back."

"I know."

"You'll stay?"

"Yes."

The rest of the night went smoothly. I sat with Maddox and Aiden between the sets, Liv, Cami, and Dee chatting. I slipped my hand under the table and found Liv's, squeezing her fingers. Her palm rested in mine as if it was meant to be there.

"I don't think I'll make it through the next set," Dee said with a yawn. "It was a busy week."

Maddox winked as he teased her. "That's what happens when you get old."

She elbowed him in the ribs. "Take me home, and I'll show you old."

He stood quickly. "That, my friends, is an invitation I cannot resist. Anyone need a lift? Liv, you good?"

"Yes," she assured him. "I'm going to stay."

"Okay."

Aiden stood. "We should grab a ride with you. We took an Uber since I knew I'd be drinking."

"Sure," Maddox agreed. "We'll drop you." He furrowed his brow. "You sure, Liv?"

"Yeah, a friend is meeting me. I'm good."

"All right."

They left after lots of hugs and fist bumps, leaving Liv and me at the table. I nudged her gently. "A friend?"

"You said we were friends."

I lifted her hand to mine and kissed it. "I did. We are."

"You play until twelve?"

"Yep. Then we're going somewhere alone."

She inhaled fast. "Um..."

"I only want some time, Liv. To talk and to be with you. I don't expect anything."

"Sammy is with Judy until Sunday. I'll pick her up, and we'll go to the park after breakfast."

"And?"

"We can go to the apartment—if you want."

I squeezed her hand. "I want."

Liv's apartment seemed quiet without Mouse. I wandered around, looking at the pictures she had of Sammy growing up. Many of them were photos of the two of them smiling into the camera. I recognized a lot of spots around Toronto and thought of a few places I could take them. Maybe we could make some more memories to add to the walls.

Liv disappeared into the kitchen and returned, handing me a steaming mug.

"What's this?"

"Your voice sounds a little rough. It's herbal tea with some honey to soothe it."

I sipped the sweet liquid. "Thanks."

"You're very popular."

I shrugged. "We have a good following, and we enjoy it."

"No big aspirations for stardom?"

Suddenly restless, I prowled the room. I finished my tea, setting down the mug.

"I'm content with my life, Liv. Stardom and the trappings of it hold no appeal to me."

She frowned. "I'm sorry. I feel as if I hit a sore spot there."

"Sore spot—no. A part of my life I try not to think about a lot —yes."

"I'm sorry."

"Don't be. It's in the past, but at times, it's difficult to think about." I ran a hand through my hair. "I wish I could go back and warn myself."

She reached out her hand and I took it, sitting beside her.

"I understand," she murmured.

I thought of the personal stories she had shared with me. I squared my shoulders, knowing if we were going to go forward, I would have to share my past with her as well.

"I know you do. I think you, of all people, would understand." I huffed out a lungful of air. "And if you want to know, I'll tell you."

"You would?" she asked, hesitant. "It's not too personal? I want to know you, but I don't want to push."

I tangled my hand into her hair and brushed a kiss to her head, inhaling the sweet fragrance of her shampoo. Honey and wildflowers. It was intoxicating.

"No, Livvy, it's not too personal. I don't like to talk about it, but you deserve to know."

She squeezed my hand.

I heaved a long, heavy sigh and sorted my thoughts out in my head.

"When I was in my twenties, music was my dream. Hell, as long as I can remember, it was my goal. Play music, travel the world, and have a family. I wanted it all—but when I was younger, music was the drive. My parents weren't as big on the idea, although they were supportive." I chuckled at a memory. "My dad was a carpenter. He could build anything, and I used to work with him in his shop. When I was young, I watched him create pieces of furniture, and I was fascinated. When I got older, I started helping him. He taught me everything I know. I know he hoped I would take over his business, but music was my first love."

"Did you always play blues?"

"No, when I was younger, rock and country were my favorites. I got my first guitar when I was nine. I bugged my parents for months before they finally took me to a pawn shop and bought me a secondhand guitar. I think they thought it was a phase."

"But it wasn't."

"Nope. I had three things in my life. Music, school, and working with my dad. Because of my size, the coaches at school were constantly after me to be part of the football or basketball team, but I was never interested. I liked the gym and working out, but team sports weren't for me. I would rather go for a run early in the morning, then spend the day with my guitar or in the shop with my dad."

"Somehow that doesn't surprise me."

I tapped the end of her nose playfully. "Like all fledgling musicians, I became part of a band when I was a teenager. I was in a few of them until I met Brett. We formed our own band, and it became quite successful. We were sort of a cross between rock and country. Edgy, but with soul. We practiced a lot and got a few gigs at local schools and places like that. I wrote a lot of our stuff, and we became quite well known. Eventually we got noticed by a label and signed."

"Wow. Would I know the name of your band?"

"The Back Roads."

Her eyes widened. "Oh my God."

I lifted one shoulder. "We were successful for a while."

"You were *huge*. I remember your music. I have your music!" She gazed at me in shock. "How did I not know you were part of them?"

"I was one of the guitar players. Not the front guy. Brett was the main focus most of the time. I wrote the music and played it. He loved the spotlight, and I was happy for him to have it. We all were."

I scrubbed my face as memories began to reshape and take form in my head. Memories I hated to think about, let alone share with anyone. Even Liv.

"I was young and foolish, Liv. Living my dream. Life was an endless stream of rituals. We toured constantly. Hotel rooms, tour buses, planes. Women. Alcohol. Any cliché you want to throw out there about the music industry, I probably lived it at some point."

I met her eyes. "I never did drugs, and I wasn't a man whore. I had lots of opportunities for both, but I tried to hold on to at least some of the values my parents taught me. I wasn't an angel, but I certainly wasn't as bad as some of the guys were. Even in my own band. We had to have more than one intervention at times to keep us going."

"What happened, Van?"

"I met a girl one day. Her name was Tonya. I fell pretty hard. She was different from the other girls I had met. Quieter, not as flashy. She was a journalist and had come to interview us. Usually, Brett took the lead, but she kept directing her questions at me. After the interview was done, we kept talking, and I took her out for coffee. She fascinated me, and it seemed she felt the same way."

Liv shifted, her hands restless. I lifted one to my mouth, kissing the knuckles.

"Do you want me to stop?"

"No, I feel..." She hesitated. "Jealous, okay? I feel jealous."

I leaned forward and kissed her. "Don't. How I felt about her and how I feel about you are worlds apart. I was young, stupid, and lonely. She paid attention to me. Not Brett, not Jared the drummer. Me. One of the guitar players—not even the popular one." I barked out a laugh. "She played me well."

"She hurt you?"

I stood, feeling restless. I walked around the room, absently picking up objects, setting them down, and moving again. I stood by the window, looking into the darkness of the night.

"Yes, she did. It wasn't really me she wanted. It was Brett." Agitated, I ran a hand through my hair. "I was so smitten, I never saw what was happening right under my own nose."

"Tell me."

"We moved fast—too fast. She came on tour with us. She got on well with everyone—including Brett. I thought I'd found the perfect girl. I loved her, my friends liked her, she understood the business. It seemed right." I lifted one shoulder, feeling the twinge. "But nothing was what it seemed."

I stared out the window, thoughts and images swirling through my head. "I should have known. I should have seen. But Tonya had a way of clouding my mind. Twisting things so they suited her. She said and did all the right things." I was quiet for a moment. "I was getting tired of the touring and the lifestyle. The other guys still loved it, but my dream had begun to change. I wanted a family. I have always loved kids, and I wanted to settle down and make a home and family. My dream was to write music, sell it, maybe play guitar in the studio for recordings. I had rediscovered my love of carpentry, and I entertained thoughts of opening my own place. I thought I could have it all. Music, working with my hands, a family..."

Silence filled the room as I struggled to form the words I had to share with Liv. I started when her arms wrapped around me, and she pressed herself to my back.

"You don't have to tell me, Van."

I covered her hands with mine and squeezed. Her touch helped to center me, and I let out a long breath.

"Yeah, I do."

"Whatever it is, remember it's in the past. It can't hurt you now." She pressed closer. "I'm right here."

I looked down at our hands. I was so broad, her arms could barely wrap around me, yet I felt completely wrapped up in her. Safe and protected.

No one had ever made me feel that way until now.

"Tonya knew my dreams. I thought she was on board with them. In fact, we began trying to get pregnant. I spoke with the guys about leaving. They understood but supported me. They were thrilled I wanted to keep writing for them and helping in the studio. I promised them I wasn't in a hurry, and we would take it slow. Find the perfect person to fill my spot. So I kept planning and dreaming. Trying to make a baby with Tonya. Looking to the future." I laughed, the bitter sound loud in the room. "I should have been paying more attention to the present."

"There was an accident," she murmured. "I remember reading about it."

"Yes. We were on a day off and out for a car ride. Brett and I liked to drive and talk or work on music. It had been a long tour, and it was almost over. I had been feeling unsettled and tense. Something was wrong, and I couldn't figure out what it was. I put it down to being tired and ready for the tour to be over. I thought the drive would help clear my head. A day away from the usual monotony of touring. Tonya wanted to come with us, and I was happy to have her. She had been acting oddly, and I figured she was feeling the same exhaustion."

I shut my eyes briefly, remembering the last few minutes when my life seemed normal.

"Tonya was driving. Brett was in the passenger seat, and I was in the back. We were working on a song, so I had my guitar and needed the room. I don't remember what happened. One moment we were traveling, the next there was chaos. Metal crunching, glass breaking, the car flipping. I blacked out, and when I woke, I was in the hospital."

"You were badly hurt." It wasn't a question, but a statement.

"Yeah. My left side took the brunt. I had a lot of surgeries and physio. They weren't sure I would ever regain the use of my left arm, but I did. I have a shit-ton of pins and screws in my shoulder, arm, and leg, but I survived."

My voice dropped. "Tonya was killed instantly. Brett suffered massive trauma and died before I woke up."

"Oh, Van."

"I found out she wasn't paying attention. She blew through a stop sign, and we were hit. The car we were in flipped and rolled. I saw what was left of the car later. The fact that one person lived through it was astounding. That it was me..."

She slipped in front of me, her embrace hard. "Oh, baby," she whispered. "I can't even imagine what you went through. Losing your best friend and your partner."

"My world changed in the blink of an eye, Liv. I went from the world I knew as normal to one filled with pain—both physical and emotional. And it was only beginning."

She stepped back, tugging me to the sofa. "Do you want to stop?"

"No. I need to get it out now that I've started."

"Okay." She handed me a bottle of water, and I drained it in long swallows. Still, my throat felt dry and arid.

"I was in the hospital for a long time. When I got out, I needed help. I hired a great physio person, and he worked with me daily to help me recover. I pushed myself. I had already lost so much, and I didn't want to lose my independence." I met her sympathetic gaze. "There was a lot of trauma to my body, Liv. I was pinned in the car for a long time." I cleared my throat. "I found out I couldn't have kids. All of my dreams were gone."

She inhaled sharply. "I'm so sorry."

I could only nod.

"Can you tell me what happened next?"

"Tonya was an only child, and her parents were dead. We had been together for almost a year, and all of her things were at my place, except what she had with us on the road. It was all sent to me, and I decided one day to open the boxes and sort through it all. I had been missing her and thought maybe seeing her things would help me feel closer to her again." I snorted. "It did the opposite."

She gripped my hand. "Tell me, Van."

"I found her journal. She was always scribbling in it. A throwback to her journalist days, I suppose. It never occurred to me to look at it—it was private—but when I saw it, I thought being able to see her thoughts would bring me some closure." The pain that had hit me when I read her words flowed into my chest.

"She didn't love me. She didn't want a family. She'd secretly still been using birth control. All the times she'd told me she wanted a family as much as I did were a lie. She'd been screwing Brett for months." I felt the intensity of their betrayal race through me as if it were only yesterday, and I gripped the back of the chair. "My best friend and the woman he knew I was in love with. Both of them deliberately hurting me."

"Oh, Van," Liv murmured. "What a shock for you."

"Between her journal, putting together bits of the puzzle on my own, and talking to some other people, I found out a lot of things I had been blind to. Brett wasn't happy about my plans to leave. He was working behind the scenes to cut me out of the group entirely. Tonya didn't want to be involved in a humdrum life with a carpenter. She loved the road. The life. The attention being with a celebrity gave her. She had been stealing my songs behind my back and getting them to Brett. He was recording them and planning on fighting me, saying I stole them from him so I wouldn't get any of the credit or the royalties." I rubbed my chest, feeling the depth of their deception once again. "I realized I didn't even know the woman who wrote the words I read. She was a stranger, and I had fallen for her act. Reading the shit about the two of them made me ill. The deception. The wild sex behind my back." I shook my head. "I was so stupid. So caught up in my dreams and what I thought was going to happen that I never saw it. I thought they were great friends and I had the best of both worlds." I sighed. "I was an idiot."

"You trusted people you loved. It doesn't make you an idiot." She hesitated. "Why would she write all those personal details down in a book?"

"One of her entries was about a meeting with a publisher. She was going to write an expose. I guess she wanted to keep the details fresh." I shook my head in sorrow. "Reading them was humiliating and made me ill." I flexed my hand, feeling the ache in my bones, which was a constant in my life. A reminder.

"All the lies she told me. The disappointment I would feel when she would tell me she wasn't pregnant that month. She even made me think it was my fault. I went and had testing done to make sure it wasn't me. She told me she had done the same, and her doctor said we simply needed to relax. I believed her, of course."

"There was no reason for you not to, Van. It made sense. It happens to a lot of couples, especially when they're under stress."

I barked out a laugh, the sound loud and bitter. "Stress is one word for it. She was busy setting up her new life, with plans on dumping me and my sorry un-achieving ass. She had a long list of names for me in her precious journal—none of them very flattering. I was simply a means to an end. Use me to get to Brett since he was harder to get close to. I was an easy target."

A tear ran down her cheek.

"I went from grieving to furious instantly. The trouble was, the people I was angry with were dead. I had no one to take it out on. I went through a bad few months. I drank and raged. I wrote some music that would shred your heart. I was on a downward spiral until my parents and my manager stepped in. They did an intervention and made me see I had to stop. No one else could do it—it had to be me."

I sat down, too tired to stay standing. "I went for counseling. Stopped using alcohol to hide from my feelings. I met with my ex-bandmates. They suspected what was going on between Tonya and Brett but didn't have any proof. They had no idea what Brett was up to behind the scenes. We agreed to retire as The Back Roads, and we let the lawyers work it out," I stated grimly. "The royalties show up in the bank every month, and I let them sit there."

"When did you start playing music again?"

"About six months later. I was doing my therapy, but my hand was still pretty useless. I was standing in my closet one day, and in the corner was my old guitar. The one my parents had given me that I had never let go. I picked it up and tried to play. It was awful. Worse than the first time I had tried when I was a kid. Something inside me clicked, though. I had missed it. The sounds of the guitar. The way the strings felt under my fingers—the steel biting into my skin. How the wood felt resting on my leg and the vibrations I felt when I strummed." I paused, remembering the feeling of rightness that had settled over me. "I started practicing—the same way I did as a kid. Every day, for hours on end. It took a long time, and I will never have the same stamina or fluidity I did before the accident, but I got the music back. I started writing again. Sold some songs. Then the Notes found me, and they asked me to be part of their group. I made them a deal. I would play and be part of the group, but I wasn't interested in a career or chasing the dream again. It almost destroyed me the first time."

For a moment, silence hung between us.

"Is that enough for you?" Liv asked.

"Yes, it is. None of them were interested in a career in music either. We play when we want to. They simply want to play for the love of music. I still sell songs to a lot of artists. On occasion, I go into the studio and lay down tracks for them. I hear my music on the radio. I get to play with a great bunch of guys. We play a few of my old tunes and some songs I wrote for them, but I keep all the rights myself. I will never put myself out there with another person the way I did with Brett. No one gets my music except me."

"I can understand that."

I sat beside her, lifting her hand to my mouth and pressing a kiss to her skin. "That's my story, Liv. It's not pretty, and it doesn't have a happy ending. I'm broken and I have trust issues."

"Do you trust me?"

"Yeah, I do. You make me feel differently than Tonya did, Liv. She would wind me up, and I was always on edge around her—something I didn't realize until she was gone. With you, I feel easy and content. I don't have to work all the time to prove myself."

"There is nothing to prove. I like Van. Carpenter, planner, friend, coworker, musician—" she grinned, the dimples in her cheeks appearing "—man who has a tea party with my daughter when she asks, Prince Van."

"Hey," I chuckled. "She makes a great cup of tea. And there were cookies. How am I supposed to resist?"

She kissed me, her lips full and sweet against mine.

"You're wonderful with her. She adores you."

"She is easy to adore back," I mused. I met her gaze. "Rather like her mother."

She smiled, her gaze focused down. I tilted her chin.

"I meant that."

"I know," she whispered. "I still have trouble believing it."

"I'm not the men in your past, Liv."

She grabbed my hand, kissing the rough knuckles. "I know. God, I know that."

"We've both been burned."

"Yes." She paused. "The accident—that's the reason for your discomfort?"

"Yeah, it has left me with chronic pain. I deal with it most of the time, but when the job is hard, I suffer more."

"I hate seeing you in pain."

I acknowledged her words with a tilt of my head. "I try not to overdo, but at times, I forget. I get into the groove, and it's not until I stop that I realize how much pain I'm in. I don't like relying on medication. I'm careful that way."

"Have you tried massage and reflexology?"

"Um, not really. I disliked being touched too much after the accident. Physio and therapy were enough."

"I would come with you. My friend is an awesome reflexologist. She would even show me how to do a few things to help you."

"You'd do that?" I asked, surprised.

"Yes. For you, I would."

"Then please make an appointment."

She leaned forward and brushed a kiss to my lips. "Thank you."

"You're so easy to please," I murmured.

She shrugged. "I've learned to be grateful for small things. In the end, they make life worth living."

I mulled over her words. She was right. I had a feeling she was right about a lot of things and was going to teach me.

I cleared my throat, knowing I had to address the issue. "Like I said before, I can't ever have a child of my own. I can't ever give you another child. There was too much damage."

She leaned forward, pressing a kiss to my mouth. "I have Sammy."

"You should have a whole houseful. You're an amazing mother."

She smiled. "Thank you." Picking up my hand, she played with my fingers.

"Does it make a difference?" I asked, anxious. "If you wanted more kids in the future, I understand."

She was quiet for a moment. "If you mean, does it change my mind about pursuing something with you, the answer is no."

I exhaled hard. "Okay." I linked our hands. "How I feel about you scares me at times, Liv."

"Me too."

"I still want to explore this with you."

She sighed, the sound low and shaky. "I do as well. I worry about Sammy, though. She gets attached fast."

I lifted her chin, meeting her gentle gaze.

"I'm getting attached to both of you. You need to know that. You need to know how big that is for me since I didn't think I would ever allow myself to feel something for a woman again. I agree with you—we need to take this slow." I studied her expression. "For all of us."

"Yes," she responded. "Slow is good for me."

Her voice became vulnerable, her expression pleading. "The last two people I trusted turned out not to be the people I thought they were. They let me down. They let Sammy down. Don't hurt us, Van. Please."

I pressed my mouth to hers. "I won't, baby."

SEVEN

Van

Leaving Liv the night before had been hard, but I was determined to stick to my word. I arrived at the club Saturday feeling exhilarated. She would be there again tonight, and I planned on taking her to my favorite all-night diner after we were done for a late-night/early morning breakfast, then spending some more time with her.

Talking to her the night before had been cathartic. A release of sorts. I had never told another person my past. But Liv was different. She had been hurt by people she trusted, so she understood my pain. She could identify with the wariness of trusting someone else.

Yet, we both felt the pull toward each other. The firm belief that this was different. *We* were different. Her company eased me. Spending time with her and Mouse was effortless. I wanted to get to know both of them more. And for them to get to know me.

Liv had asked me some direct questions, all of which I thought about before answering.

"Sammy is my number one priority," she said. "Always. Can you deal with that?"

"Yes. It's one of the things I admire about you, Liv. You're an amazing mother. I wouldn't expect anything less from you."

She hesitated. "The fact that she isn't yours—does it give you pause?"

I shook my head. "Love doesn't have boundaries, Liv. Simply because I'm not her biological father doesn't mean I can't love her."

"Is she part of the draw? I mean, do you need to fill that void in your life, and she fits the bill?"

I mulled over her words, trying to find the right response.

"First and foremost, neither of you are simply filling a void. The fact is, I was always attracted to you. I only hesitated because of my own issues and doubts. Discovering you had a child didn't scare me away. Seeing you with her only cemented the attraction. To me, Mouse is a bonus. I get two of you." I sucked in a deep breath. "I'm prepared for the responsibility that comes with being involved with a single mother. I'm not in this for the short term."

Her cheeks colored. "All right, then."

"What about you? Can you trust me enough to let me into your life —into both of your lives?"

"I want to try." She slid her hand into mine. "Like you, trust doesn't usually come easy for me, but with you, it feels...right."

I squeezed her fingers. "Yeah, it does. Like a puzzle piece, right?"

"Yes."

I asked her a direct question which simmered below every thought I had about a future with her.

"And the fact that I can never give you another child? You must have some concerns on that subject."

Her reply was prompt. "Sammy is more than I ever dreamed I would have."

"You're still young. You might want another child."

She lifted my hand, studying the calluses left by hard work. "Do you know Reid's story?"

"Yeah. He told me his past, or at least the gist of it. He went through a lot as a kid."

She continued. "There are hundreds, thousands of kids like him, Van. Kids who need a family—someone to love them. If at some point, I decided I wanted another child, and we were together, how would you feel about loving one of those kids?" She paused. "Or a few of them if that was how it worked out? We could make our own family by loving a child no one else did. Love without boundaries, I think you said."

My answer had been to tug her into my arms and kiss her until she was a mass of need and want under me. It had taken everything in me not to have her right then and there.

Her words gave me something I hadn't felt in years.

Hope.

Hope for a future.

Mark walked into the dressing room at the club and flung himself into a chair beside me. We were all laid-back and wore our street clothes, so the dressing room was really the place we came together to chill before the gig and discuss any changes or ideas we had.

But tonight, he looked perturbed.

"What's going on?"

He ran a hand through his hair. "We got company."

Andy chuckled beside me, tipping back his chair. "One of your groupies getting too handsy?"

Mark gripped his hair. "Vicky's in the club."

A collective groan filled the room. I rested my head on the back of my chair. "I thought she'd finally left town. What is she doing here?"

"I didn't stop to ask. As soon as I saw her, I ducked down the hall and came in here."

"Let's not jump to conclusions," I said hopefully. "Maybe it's a coincidence she's here."

"Maybe my dick will drop off if I don't stop wanking on it the way my mom told me," Mark snorted. "If she's here, it's to cause trouble."

"Only if we let her. Stay away from her. Don't engage." I looked at Andy. "Go tell Billy we want a security guy close tonight."

He nodded and left the room. I gripped the back of my head. Of all the nights for Vicky to show up, why was it tonight? I didn't want her anywhere near Liv. Vicky was poison, and she spread it as far as she could.

Andy returned and picked up his drumsticks. "We're on in five. Billy said no problem. I looked around but couldn't see her, so maybe she was here for a drink and left."

I stood, grabbing my guitar. "If she's here, ignore her. Don't give her a reason to start anything."

Mark bent down and picked up his bass. "You were the one she was focused on last. Maybe she has unfinished business?"

"There was no business. She was loony. She invented shit in her head, and it became real to her." I slid my guitar strap over my shoulder, feeling the tension building. "Saying hello was the equivalent of an affair to her. She did it to all of us."

I met the gaze of our lead singer, Alex. "She especially screwed you over."

She'd almost cost him his marriage with her lies.

He looked grim remembering everything that had occurred.

"If she approaches any of us, we stick together. Don't be alone with her. Don't give her the chance."

Alex flexed his shoulders. "Right. We stick together, lads," he stated, his British accent thick.

I held out my hand, and we did our usual group fist bump.

"Together."

Liv was at the same table, so it was easy to spot her. She had her hair swept up from her face and was dressed in leggings with some sort of glittery top. She looked casual and pretty—and entirely kissable. On the way to the stage, I stopped at the table and leaned down, indicating the burly security guard beside me.

"This is Brent. Stick close tonight, okay?"

"Is everything all right?"

"I'll explain later, but promise me."

"Okay."

Resisting the urge to kiss her, I squeezed her shoulder and

climbed onstage. My gaze swept the crowd, recognizing a lot of the patrons, but there was no sign of Vicky.

Maybe Mark had been mistaken.

Maybe Andy was right—she was here but left.

Alex met my eyes with a nod. I know he'd been looking as well.

"Ready?" he mouthed.

I tilted my head and he counted us down. I let the music take over and forgot about Vicky.

The crowd was enthusiastic and engaging tonight. We changed it up from the previous evening, adding a few different numbers. I stayed in the background until the end of the first set, then stepped forward and performed two songs. My gaze locked with Liv's as I played "Smile for Me." Her eyes glowed in the dim light, her smile bright and easy to see. It was there, just as I asked, for me, and I basked in its warmth.

After the applause, we took a break, and I sat beside Liv. Tonight, she was open and affectionate. I kissed her cheek, and we sat close, our fingers entwined. I tried not to laugh when a steaming mug appeared in front of me instead of my usual water.

"Your woman asked me to bring this," Sherry informed me with a wink. "She had me make it special for you."

I picked up the mug, letting the soothing herbal tea and honey coat my throat. I turned to press a kiss to Liv's head in thanks when I saw her.

Tall, blond, and dangerous. Vicky leaned against the bar, her usual shot glass of tequila by her elbow. She stared at me balefully, her expression bitter and twisted.

My body froze. Her gaze moved from me to Liv, and a sneer crossed her face. She picked up her tequila, tossed it back, threw some money on the bar, and stomped away. She pushed her way through the crowd and disappeared out of the door.

"Van?" Liv asked. "Are you okay?"

"Yeah, I'm fine."

"You worried me earlier."

I dropped a kiss to her head, relaxing now that Vicky had stormed out. "Sorry. Problem with an overzealous fan."

"Does it happen a lot?"

"No. But we wanted to take precautions."

"Okay. You still seem tense."

I lowered my head. "Maybe you can find a way to make me less tense later, Liv?"

She touched her lips to mine. Too lightly and too briefly.

"Maybe."

I grinned.

We finished our set to loud applause. All of us had seen Vicky storm out, so we were relaxed and jovial for the remainder of the night. We headed to the dressing room, grabbed our stuff and talked about the next gig we had in a few weeks. If we wanted, we could play weekly, probably nightly, around town and in various other cities, but we all agreed it wasn't what we preferred. We had a list of places we liked, and we rotated. Our fans followed us and we enjoyed the sets, but it was a hobby, not our lives. The guys all knew my history and the fact that if they wanted more, I had no issues stepping back. But surprisingly, we were all like-minded when it came to our group. We had a couple of self-produced CDs which sold well, but we refused to take it to the next level. I had experienced it already, and none of my band members wanted that level of crazy. We all only wanted to make music.

"Come join me for a drink and meet Liv," I suggested.

"Finally got the balls to ask her out there, mate?" Alex chuckled.

"What are you on about?"

They all laughed.

"You have no idea how often you talked about her, do you?" Mark asked. "Liv this, Liv that, she is brilliant...blah, blah, blah."

"I didn't."

"Bloody right, you did," Alex crowed. "And it was obvious she liked you. I'd see her in the back of the bar, nursing a drink, watching us. Watching you with this-*this look* on her face. It was amusing since you never saw her."

I shook my head. *How had I not noticed her?*

Andy clapped me on the shoulder. "Don't feel bad. She kept herself hidden. I have a better vantage point from the kit, and I let the others know. We enjoyed watching your fan ogle you. You're always so lost in the music, you never notice anything."

Mark grinned widely. "He's right. Your ass could be on fire, and we'd have to put it out when you're playing."

Still fooling around, we headed toward the front. The amusement died in my throat when I saw who was at the table with Liv.

Vicky.

She was talking, gesturing wildly, her eyes narrowed as she leaned close to Liv, no doubt spewing her venom.

I could only imagine what horrid lies Vicky was telling her.

"Fuck," I swore.

"Goddamn bitch is at it again," Alex muttered.

We all hurried forward.

Liv looked up as we hit the table, the four of us converging on it as one. Her expression was neutral, her voice calm as she spoke.

"Hey, guys."

I leaned on the table, my fists digging into the scarred wood, trying to rein in my temper. "What are you doing here, Vicky? You know you're not welcome."

She tossed her hair, the bleached blond strands stiff under the lights. "It's a free country."

I scowled. "Not where we're concerned. You know the rules. You broke them. That means we're getting the restraining order we warned you about."

Her cheeks were flushed. I could see from the haze in her eyes she'd been drinking a lot, which made her even more dangerous and me more tense.

"You wouldn't."

Andy crossed his arms. "Watch us, you loon. We've tried to play nice."

She flashed him what I was sure she thought was a sexy smile. It was more of a sneer. "I remember you didn't like to play nice. Rough was the way you liked it."

He shoved off the table, cursing and getting ready to lunge. Mark stepped behind him, placing an arm across his chest. "Easy, don't give her ammunition."

"Get her out of my sight."

Liv watched the entire exchange in silence. She turned to Vicky, her voice cool. "Thanks for the warning, but I can make up my own mind when it comes to who I have a relationship with. Frankly, I have no interest in anything else you have to say since it's probably all bullshit. Maybe you should do yourself a favor and leave. The way security is eyeing you up, it might be best if you leave now before he comes over here." She paused and slid her hand across the table, covering mine. "Or before one of these gentlemen helps to escort you from the building."

"*Gentlemen*," Vicky scoffed. "That's not what I'd call them."

"In case I haven't made it clear, I don't care what you call them, and I have no interest in listening."

Vicky's eyes narrowed. "You're making a mistake."

"Then the mistake is mine." Liv stood. "I'm not in the mood for a drink now, Van. Can we go home?"

I stood straight, pulling Liv close. "Yep."

Mark pushed Andy toward Alex. "Take him home." He waved me off as Brent stepped forward. "Take your lady and go, Van. Brent and I are going to have a little talk with Vicky."

"Mark..." I warned. Talking with Vicky was dangerous. She twisted your words and created entire conversations that never occurred.

"It's fine. Brent has my back, right?"

Brent crossed his arms. "I've got great ears, and my memory is as sharp as a tack."

I met Mark's steady gaze. He was determined, and I knew I couldn't stop him.

"Call me."

He nodded. "I will."

I tugged Liv behind me and left the club. I didn't look back.

We sat across from each other in the diner, cups of coffee in our hands. Neither of us was hungry. I drained my cup and signaled for a refill, knowing sleep was going to be elusive tonight.

"Can you tell me?" Liv asked.

"There isn't a lot to tell."

"She certainly had a lot to say. None of it good." Liv grimaced. "In fact, some of it was downright disgusting."

I ran a hand through my hair and sighed. "I can only imagine. Whatever she said was lies, Liv. I swear to you."

She looked serious. "I already figured that out. I don't see you into group-sharing-wild-orgy sex."

"Jesus, no." I rubbed my eyes. "Is that what she's saying now?"

"That, plus she had affairs with all of you."

I hunched over the table, tapping it with my finger. "I never slept with her. Ever. There was no affair, no relationship. Nothing."

"With anyone?"

"Early on, she and Andy had a fling. It ended fast, and afterward, things went downhill. The woman is deranged." My head fell back against the booth. "I'm sorry you got dragged into this."

"How did you meet her?"

"She was a waitress at the first club we played at together. We became regulars, and she was always there. She seemed great. Friendly, supportive, always bringing us beverages and making sure we were okay. She was easy to talk with, and we all liked her. I mean, we liked all the staff, but she always went the extra mile."

"Then?"

"She and Andy got together. She became strange. Obsessive. He broke it off, and suddenly it got weird. She'd say things to us individually, as if she was trying to pick us off one by one. Turn us against each other. We started hearing rumors about things she was telling people in the club. She went after Mark, then made Alex's life a living hell. Went to his wife and said they were having an affair. His pregnant, emotional, vulnerable wife. He went crazy. His wife was having a hard time and actually believed Vicky's lies. It took a lot of work to smooth it over."

"Oh, wow. She's a headcase."

"She spiraled out of control," I continued. "She was drinking a lot. She quit her job but only because the manager was going to fire her after we went to him and told him what was going on. She disappeared, but every so often would appear with some ludicrous story or lie. She showed up at my house one night, telling me she knew I was secretly interested. I kicked her out, but it made no difference. She told people we were having an affair."

"But you weren't."

I met her gaze. "Never, Liv. I thought she was our friend. Nothing more."

"Okay." She nodded. "I believe you."

"She showed up one night and caused a scene at the club. We met with her and our lawyer as a group. We gave her a choice. Shut up, and leave us alone, or we'd get a restraining order against her, which would have made her life difficult since she waited tables at a bunch of different clubs we played at." I huffed out a long breath of air. "That was four months ago. She seemed contrite and apologized. Disappeared. We heard she'd stopped drinking, was getting counseling, and left town. I didn't think we'd ever see her again."

"Why do you think she showed up tonight?"

"I have no idea, but I hope it's the last we see of her. I'll talk to Mark later and see what he thinks."

"Why would he insist on talking to her?"

"He's a professional mediator. He knows how to listen and what to say to defuse tense situations. If he thinks it's a problem, we'll talk to our lawyer about the restraining order."

She observed me for a moment. "Sometimes restraining orders mean nothing to someone who is determined."

I frowned. "Do you have experience with this sort of thing? Did Sammy's dad pull something?"

"No, not him. My mother had to get a restraining order against my father. It meant nothing to him, and he kept hassling her. He was arrested, and it finally stopped, but only because he left town."

I scrubbed my face. "I'm sorry. This is bringing up bad memories for you."

She shrugged. "No memory of my father is good."

"You shouldn't have to deal with this sort of situation." I picked up her hand, stroking the thin skin of her wrist. "You have enough to deal with."

"Let's hope it's the only time I have to see her."

I was amazed at how calm she was. I didn't want to add stress to her life, and it was making me uncomfortable.

"It will be," I said firmly. "It's us she is obsessed with—you happened to be in the right place at the wrong time. She won't bother you."

The entire evening was ruined by Vicky's appearance. The plans I had for the night with Liv were put aside. After we left the diner, I took her home, walking her to her door. Our kisses were still deep and passionate, filled with longing and want, but they went nowhere past the door. It wasn't the right time. We both knew it.

I didn't get much sleep. Mark texted me and said he had been very clear with Vicky. None of us were interested in anything she had to say. He told her to stay away from us and to move on with her life. He told me Brent had escorted her out and put her in a cab. He said as a precaution he had sent our lawyer an email, asking about the restraining order we had discussed.

I think I may have gotten through to her. I hope we don't need it, his last text read.

I hoped so as well. If anyone could get through to Vicky, it would be Mark. Still, I worried.

Unable to sleep, I worked on my latest project—Sammy's bookcase. It had taken a while to design and cut all the wood. Once it was sanded smooth and pieced together came the task of painting it— and adding the beloved glitter. She had informed me there could never be enough glitter.

"I love the sparkles, Mr. Van! They make me happy."

I was determined this bookcase would elate her. She didn't know I was building it—as Liv had stated, she thought we were drawing for fun. I planned on surprising her with it.

But the damn glitter.

As I discovered, no matter how careful I was, the stuff went everywhere. By the time I finished applying it, I was certain, if I sneezed, glitter would come from my nose. I stood back, staring at the bookcase. The light caught the glitter, sending cascades of reflections all over the walls. It was horrendous.

Sammy was going to love it.

I glanced at my watch. I knew Liv was taking her to the park, and I wanted to see them both today. Maybe I could take them to lunch once Sammy had her fill of the park. Spend some time with them. I showered, dressed and drove to the park, then walked the path that led me to the playground. I saw Sammy hanging upside down on the monkey bars, laughing and playing with a friend. I watched her for a moment, her carefree spirit making me smile. She saw me and did a flip, so she landed on her feet, making a beeline for me. I crouched down and met her enthusiastic expression.

"Mr. Van!"

"Hey, Mouse. Having fun?"

She nodded fast, her curls bouncing. "Yeah!" Then she frowned, leaning forward. "Mr. Van, why do you have sparkles in your hair?"

I stifled my groan. I had washed my hair twice, but I couldn't get all the damn glitter out.

Sammy's eyes grew round. "Did you lose a tooth? Did the tooth fairy come and leave you money? I always know when she's been there because there are sparkles on my pillow."

I ran a hand through my hair. "Something like that."

She beamed, her eyes wide. "You have to tell Mommy. She'll be so surprised. She says the tooth fairy never comes to her anymore since she is too old."

I chuckled and glanced toward the bench where I figured Liv was sitting. I froze. She wasn't alone.

Vicky sat next to her.

Rage tore through me. It was bad enough she had made my life miserable. Tried to destroy my relationship with my friends. Ruin their lives with her lies. But to cross the line and show up here and confront Liv? Especially when it had been made clear to her to back off? With Sammy so close?

Jesus, the last thing I wanted was for her to get near Sammy. God only knew what she would do or say. She would frighten the shit out of the child, regardless.

Not fucking happening.

I stood and glanced down at Sammy. "Go back and play. I have to do something," I said through tight lips.

She frowned. "What's the matter, Mr. Van? Why are you mad?"

I struggled to hold on to my temper. "I'm not, but I need to talk to your mom."

Sammy pointed behind her. "She's right there. She's talking to that lady."

"Did you talk to the lady?"

She shook her head. "No."

I sighed in relief. "Okay, Mouse. I'll be over in a minute, okay? I'll push you on the swings again."

She turned and scampered away.

I stalked forward, angry and intent on getting Vicky as far away from them both as possible. Fury poured off my body. My fists were clenched tight to my sides. I struggled to stay calm as I approached. I didn't want to frighten Liv, or God forbid, Sammy.

I failed.

Sammy yelled my name, waving frantically from her upside-down position trying to get my attention. I waved back but kept walking, undeterred.

Vicky looked up, her face paling at the sight of me. Liv met my gaze, shaking her head, warning me not to come closer.

Fuck that.

Leaning down, I wrapped my hand around Vicky's arm, pulling her to her feet.

"We need to talk."

She began to protest.

"Now."

"Van," Liv began, "it's not what it looks like—"

"I'll talk to you in a minute," I interrupted her. "Vicky and I have some important things to discuss."

"No, wait—" Liv protested.

Vicky shot Liv a glance. "It's fine. Thanks for listening."

I pulled her down the path, around the corner. I could still see Liv and Sammy, but we were out of earshot. Liv watched us go with a frown on her face.

"I warned you," I hissed. "I am done being nice. I want you to get out of my life. All our lives and not come back."

She began to speak, but I continued my rant. "How fucking dare you come here and harass Liv? What did we ever do to you that gives you the right to mess with our lives? Haven't you already caused enough damage?" My voice was rising even though I was struggling to maintain my composure. "You are not getting near that child. Or

Liv." I stepped closer, almost snarling in my anger. "Back. The. Fuck. Off."

She shook off my grip and stepped back. Her next words shocked me.

"I know, Van. I get it."

I grimaced. "What?"

She blew out a deep sigh. "I *am* sorry. I overheard Liv last night say she was coming to this park today, so I came here to apologize to her. I only came back to town to get a few things and head back up North." She passed a hand over her eyes. "I made a mistake last night and fell back into my bad habits. I haven't had a drink since I left town, but something hit me yesterday, and I started drinking again. All the hate and anger I thought I had worked through hit me, and I acted out. Fell into my old behavior and said some nasty things. Mark talked to me last night, and his words were so spot-on." She sighed ruefully as she rubbed her arm. "I need to apologize to all of you. But I also need to leave Toronto and all the memories behind. I'm never coming back."

Her words seemed genuine. Her gaze was tired but sincere as she met my eyes.

"I don't understand."

"I was horrid to all of you. I caused a lot of problems for you, and I was a terrible person. I've been getting counseling, going to meetings, trying to get my life back on track. I decided to come back and pick up the last of my things. As soon as I got to town, I knew it was a mistake. I should have listened to my sponsor and my friends. I wasn't ready. I became *that* person again." Her voice wavered. "I'm sorry."

My anger drained away, but I was skeptical.

She saw my doubt. "You don't have to believe me. I understand. I did and said some awful things. I'm not proud of myself, and I'm shocked how fast I slipped back into that role yesterday."

"Why?"

"I was already sliding back. I knew you guys were playing, and I decided to come see you. I meant to approach you all and apologize. Instead, I started wallowing and throwing back shots in the afternoon. When I came to the bar, I saw the way you looked at Liv. I've never seen you look that way at anyone—especially me. It made me jealous."

"We were never anything but friends, Vicky. If we were even that."

"I know. But in my head, we were. I wanted to be the one to someone. To you—to any one of you," she admitted. "I'm messed up. It's too involved to hash out, Van. I called my sponsor this morning, and we talked for a long time. I'm heading back this afternoon and I won't be returning. Once my head is clear, I'll write you all my apologies." She lifted her shoulders. "I don't think I am strong enough to face you all in person again—at least not for a very long time. I have a lot of issues to work through."

"I think it's for the best."

She glanced over her shoulder. "Liv was kinder than she had to be. I appreciated her listening to me, especially after the way I spoke last night."

"She is a good person." I narrowed my eyes in warning, still unsure if I believed her. "Leave Sammy alone."

"I won't go near either of them again."

"Okay."

"You are very protective of them."

"I care about them."

She studied me. "She's the kind of person you deserve, Van. I hope things work out for you. For what it is worth, I am sorry. You won't have to worry about me anymore."

I pursed my lips, then huffed. "Go back up North, Vicky. Fix your life. You leave us alone, we'll leave you alone."

She turned and walked away without another word. I watched her walk past Liv, only offering a small wave as she hurried by. I sucked in some much-needed lungfuls of air, calmer than I had been, but I needed to clear my head before I spoke to Liv.

I approached the bench and sat beside Liv. She was stiff and silent. We watched Sammy for a few moments, then I leaned forward, clasping my hands between my knees.

"That was unexpected," I muttered.

"It certainly was."

Her voice was unemotional. I glanced over at her. She was sitting ramrod straight, her gaze on Sammy.

"She won't bother you anymore, Liv. She promised—"

She turned her head, her eyes cool. "Was that necessary?"

"I'm sorry?"

"Dragging the poor woman away, embarrassing her, and making her leave?"

I gaped at her. "What?"

"Granted, I wasn't happy to see her, but I agreed to listen. She was apologizing, and I believe she was sincere."

"I didn't know that at the time."

"No, and you didn't bother to ask. You didn't give me the chance to explain."

I turned to her, our knees pressing. "She's a freaking headcase, Liv. All I saw was her talking to you. Once again, I assumed, spreading her lies. She was too close to you. Far too close to Sammy. I had to get her away from both of you."

"Shouldn't that be my decision?"

Once again, I gaped at her.

"I saw Vicky coming. She asked me if she could sit and talk to me. Apologize. I could have said no, but I agreed. She never went near Sammy, and if she had tried, I would have stopped her. She had been sitting here for ten minutes before you showed up, and she was getting ready to leave when you dragged her away. Frankly, your reaction startled me. It was a little over the top."

"Over the top," I repeated.

"Yes."

"You have no idea what you're talking about."

Her eyes narrowed. "Is that right?"

94

"Yes."

"I don't need you to protect me, Van. Who I choose to talk or not talk to is my decision."

"Not in this case," I almost snarled.

She stood, anger pouring off of her. "In *every* case. I'm a smart, capable woman. I can judge someone without your help. I could see she was different and she simply wanted to talk. You didn't bother to look. You jumped to the conclusion that I wasn't thinking clearly. That I couldn't possibly know what I was doing. I've already had two men in my life who dictated what I could or could not do. Say or not say. I'm not about to take on a third. I think I may have misjudged you."

I was on my feet instantly. "No, you haven't. I'm the guy you thought I was twenty minutes ago. I couldn't stand her being close to you—spouting her venom. I couldn't allow it."

Her gaze became frosty. "You couldn't *allow* it?"

I realized I had used the wrong word.

"I didn't mean it the way it sounded. I meant I couldn't risk it."

"No one tells me what to do anymore. I put up with that long enough. You don't get to *allow* me anything." Liv ran a hand through her hair, her gesture filled with frustration. "We rushed into this, and I need to stop it before it goes any further."

"What are you saying?" I asked, my heart sinking in my chest.

She lifted her eyes to mine. "I was right to begin with. We should be friends, Van. Only friends."

"Don't say that. It was the wrong word, Liv. I used the wrong word."

She shook her head. "My life was governed by wrong words for years. I won't do it anymore." She met my pleading gaze. "I'm sorry, Van. I can't."

She turned and hurried away, calling for Sammy. I watched them walk away, stunned. More than once, Sammy turned her head, peered at me over her shoulder, and gestured to her mother, but Liv kept hold of her hand and soon they disappeared from my sight.

I sat down on the bench, reviewing the last screwed-up twenty minutes in my head. I had come here hoping to spend the day with them. I hadn't expected Vicky. I hadn't planned on Liv seeing my temper. I hadn't expected her reaction.

I hung my head. I had been worried Vicky would somehow chase Liv away. Make her fearful of me.

I had managed to do it all on my own.

EIGHT

Van

"Vince, what is going on with you?" My mother tapped her fingers, staring at me from across the table. "And don't tell me nothing, because I'll know you're lying."

Despite my mood, I felt a grin tug on my lips. My mother was one of the few people who called me Vince. And certainly the only person who spoke to me as if I were still a kid.

After the fiasco with Liv, I had gone to see my parents. They lived close, and I didn't want to be alone. I spent a few hours with my dad in his shop, helping him with a project and talking to him about the massive undertaking Bentley was involved in with his latest project. My dad was excited when I asked him to be part of the team I was creating to do all the intricate woodwork the units would require.

"I'll ask a few of my buddies to pitch in," he offered, a gleam of excitement in his eyes. "They'd love to be part of such a huge project."

I clapped him on the shoulder as Mom called dinner was ready. "I was counting on it."

I was mostly quiet during dinner and didn't eat as much as usual, which led to my mother's inquiry.

My dad chuckled and sipped his coffee. "She's right, Van. You might as well tell her. She'll follow you home, still talking, otherwise."

I leaned my elbow on the table with a frustrated sigh. "I screwed up something today. Big-time."

"Work or personal?"

I met my mother's direct gaze. "Personal. But it involves work as well."

She regarded me wisely. "You finally did something about your feelings for Liv?"

I leaned back in my chair with a huff. "Seriously, how did you know?"

She rolled her eyes. "I'm your mother. I know you better than you know yourself. You've liked this woman from the moment you met her. Whenever you spoke about her, your tone was different. You were different."

"Thanks for telling me."

She patted my cheek. "You had to figure it out for yourself. Now tell me what you did."

She listened as I told her, pursing her lips when I mentioned Vicky. She let me get it all out before she spoke.

"First off," she began, "you were right to be cautious when it comes to that woman. I remember everything she did. Second, while I understand your first concern was Liv and Sammy, it's obvious Liv has some past trauma that your behavior triggered."

"I only wanted to get Vicky away from Liv." I ran a hand through my hair. "I spoke to Mark, and he said he thought Vicky was sincere. He said their conversation was pretty frank last night. I didn't know it at the time, and I certainly didn't mean to frighten Liv."

Mom patted my hand in sympathy. "I know. You need to let her calm down, then speak to her. It sounds as if she went through more than you know about, and she needs to work it through in her head. I'm sure once she calms down and you talk, things will get back on track."

"I hope so."

"You really like this woman."

"She's amazing. And Sammy is beyond adorable."

"I want to meet them."

I had to chuckle—I knew she'd want to get to know them. "Let's not get ahead of ourselves. I need to talk to Liv and get her to forgive me."

"Give her some time, Vince. Don't force her. I get the feeling she has had that happen far too often in her life."

I nodded in silent agreement. I hated thinking what Liv had gone through. I loathed the fact that my behavior triggered bad memories for her. I wanted to be a positive force in her life, not one that brought her more worries or fear.

I drained my coffee. "I'll be as patient as I can be."

Mom fixed me a look. "Can you?"

I shrugged.

For Liv, I would try. I might not succeed, but I would try.

Monday, I was unsure how to handle Liv at work. I had spent the rest of Sunday evening working on the bookcase to stay busy and stop myself from going to Liv's place and refusing to leave until she talked to me, knowing it would only make things worse. My mom was correct, and I needed to give Liv some space and time, but I was resolved to at least attempt to apologize and get her to listen to me.

I had added several layers of varnish to the bookcase, making sure to seal in the glitter so it would last Sammy a long time. Regardless of what happened with Liv, I had promised Mouse I would make it for her, and I refused to break my promise.

I heard Liv's voice down the hall, and I knew we would be seeing each other at the meeting. Plus, we had plans with Bentley to drive to the cabin the next day, so we would be forced to be in close proximity then. I couldn't apologize with him around, but I hoped she would give me a chance at some point today to speak my mind.

Finally, about three, she came to my office, her hands filled with files. She hesitated at the door when she saw Jordan wasn't at his desk, but I waved her in. I was on the phone, and I took advantage of the one-sided conversation to study her.

She looked as tired as I felt, and although I was sorry she was exhausted, I hoped it meant she was regretting her decision yesterday. That she would listen to me. I finished my call and hung up.

"Liv," I said quietly.

"Van," she responded. "I have some sketches of the new project. Bentley asked me to let you have them and see if the moldings are the way you envisioned."

"You got it done already?" I asked, holding out my hand for the folder. I glanced through the drawings. "These are amazing."

She nodded, not meeting my eyes. "I couldn't sleep, so I worked last night."

I put the folder on my desk. "Liv," I prompted.

She looked up, her gaze anxious. I could see the slight tremor in her hands, and it took everything in me not to reach across the desk and wrap my hands around hers.

"I want to apologize again for yesterday. I didn't mean to frighten you or make you think I questioned your decision-making capabilities. I respect you too much to ever do that. You have proven to me time and again how intelligent you are." I huffed. "Vicky caused so much trouble for my friends, and when I saw her beside you, all I could think was she was going to mess up the best thing I've had in my life in a very long time. I was horrified thinking what lies she would be telling you, and what she might say around Sammy. Her words are pure venom. Or at least, they used to be, which is why I acted the way I did. I know I should have controlled my temper better, and I'm sorry."

I leaned forward, my elbows on the desk. "Please don't throw away something with so much promise because I acted like a jerk. The history I have with her overrode everything else. My first instinct was to protect you and Sammy. I didn't mean for you to think I was questioning your parenting skills or your thought processes. I knew how she worked, and I reacted." I held her gaze. "If I felt you and Sammy were in any danger—however slight or misconceived on my part—I would step in, because it's how I work. And why I reacted the way I did."

"I know," she stated quietly.

My eyebrows shot up. "You do?"

"Yes. I thought about it a lot. I spoke to my mom and told her. She informed me I overreacted as well, and I wasn't giving you the benefit of the doubt. She said I was reacting to the behavior of men in my past, not you."

"Liv." I breathed her name. "Tell me you forgive me, and we can move on. I hate this feeling of being separate from you." My fingers flexed on the desk. "I want to hold you. I need to kiss you."

She sighed. "I do forgive you. I apologize as well."

Before I could react, she held up her hand. "But I need to think this over, Van. Maybe I'm not ready for a relationship."

"We'll take it slow. I already told you that. Whatever pace you need—please don't shut me out."

She smiled sadly. "The problem is, I don't think there is a slow with you. Now that we've flipped that switch, it's as if I'm full steam ahead when I'm around you. You're like a flame I want to hold, but I know I'm going to get burned."

I shook my head, my voice low and serious. "You won't. I need you to tell me your story—all of it. Tell me why you're so skittish and let me help you figure us out. We're good together. All three of us." I took a chance and grabbed her hand, holding it tight. "God, Liv, one day and I missed you and Sammy. All I wanted was to come talk to you and make it right. That has to count for something."

She looked down at our hands. "It does."

I withdrew my touch, sensing her hesitation. "But it's not enough?"

She stood. "I need a little time, Van. Just a little time. Can you give me that?"

Her voice was pleading, her eyes conflicted. But they weren't angry. She needed time, and I could give her that.

"If you say I'm forgiven, I can give you some space."

"You are forgiven, but yesterday did frighten me, and I need to think."

I hated the thought I had frightened her. But I knew she had to figure this out without my pushing her.

I heard Jordan's voice in the hall, approaching the office. I stood, holding the file she had brought me. "Thank you."

She walked toward the door.

"Liv," I called.

She turned.

"I'll give you time, but I can't promise I'll be patient. You're too special. You and Mouse. I want you to know that."

She hurried away, but I saw her smile.

I sat down, feeling torn. Things weren't as dark as they seemed yesterday, but was it enough?

Liv

When Van pulled up on Tuesday morning, I was surprised to see him alone. He stepped out of the truck, rounding the front. He was wearing jeans, and his denim shirt was stretched across his broad chest and shoulders, pulling slightly at the seams.

"Change of plans," he announced. "Bentley called just before I got here. They're on their way to the hospital."

"Oh."

"He asked if next week was okay."

I went through my schedule in my head. "Yeah. My mom is still in town to help with the day care drop-off, so it should be good."

He opened the door for me, offering his hand to help me up. I tamped down the feeling of disappointment he hadn't lifted me in again. He was following my request for time, after all.

He eased himself behind the wheel, checked his mirrors, then swung the truck around.

"Van, the office is the other way."

He looked mischievous. "No one is expecting us, Liv. We're playing hooky, and I'm taking you for coffee."

"Coffee," I repeated.

"Yep. *Coffee*. Two people drinking caffeine, getting to know each other."

I felt a grin tug at my lips. He made it sound so simple and innocent. Yet, knowing him, I knew it was neither.

He chuckled and patted my leg. "C'mon, Liv. It's coffee. What could possibly happen?"

I had no response.

At the restaurant, I followed him to a booth. He waited as I slid in, then took a seat opposite me. He filled the bench, his massive shoulders looking even bigger in the enclosed space. I noticed a cut on his wrist as he handed me a menu. His wound looked raw and sore. Without thinking, I grabbed his hand. "What happened?"

He shrugged, staring at my fingers as they traced the cut. "Saw slipped—the edge caught me."

"It should be covered."

"Oh. I thought it needed to air."

Clucking my tongue, I dug through my purse, pulling out a small first aid kit. He watched, amused, as I cleaned his wrist with an alcohol wipe, then dabbed some antiseptic ointment on it, and covered it with a bandage.

"You have an entire clinic in your bag, Livvy?" he asked, his eyes crinkling with amusement.

I shook my head. "Part of the job, both as a designer and a mother. Someone is always getting cuts or scrapes."

"I'll remember that in the future when I'm bleeding." He flexed his hand, then reached across the table and squeezed my fingers. "Thanks."

"Keep it covered and clean. I'll check it tomorrow."

He bent his head to study the menu. "I look forward to it."

His hand stayed where it was, covering mine, and for some

reason, I let it. When the huge breakfast he ordered arrived, he gave my fingers a final squeeze. My fingers felt cold without his warmth.

He frowned at the bagel and fruit I had ordered.

"That's not breakfast, Livvy. That's a snack."

I chuckled. "I had coffee and cereal earlier with Sammy."

He rolled his eyes. "With the energy you put out in a day, you need more protein." He sliced off a wedge of his omelet and slid it onto my plate. He added a couple strips of bacon, then satisfied, went back to eating.

"I can't eat your breakfast."

"It's yours now. You never eat enough. I need you healthy and strong."

I picked up the bacon and nibbled at it, shutting my eyes as the flavor filled my mouth. "I love bacon," I admitted.

"Then why didn't you get some?"

I shifted, feeling uncomfortable. "I watch what I eat. My weight has always been a sore spot for me."

He stopped chewing, laying down his utensils. He swallowed, then hunched over the table, his eyes boring into mine. "Your weight —you—are perfect. I appreciate you want to be healthy, but there is nothing wrong with you. I love how you look. How you feel. Everything about you. Understood? Whatever, whoever, put such a crazy notion in your head—they were wrong. You are beautiful. Exactly the way you are. Got it?"

I blinked. Swallowed. Stared at him. His gaze was intense and steady, his words firm. Finally, I whispered, "Got it."

"Good." He raised his hand, beckoning the waitress. "Another order of bacon, please. And may I have more coffee?"

She winked. "Sure, hun. Need to fuel that furnace of yours, eh?"

He picked up his fork with a grin, throwing me a wink.

"Oh, it's fueled. I'm just waiting for the spark. I'm all set to explode."

I tried not to laugh.

I failed.

Sunday morning, I shifted on the park bench, waving at Sammy as she hung upside down. I covered my mouth, trying to hide the continuous yawns that kept escaping.

I wasn't sleeping well. I kept busy during the days, but once Sammy had gone to bed and I was alone, my thoughts were filled with Van. If I was being honest, he crept into my head during the day as well, but it was easier to push those thoughts aside when I had something else to concentrate on.

He stuck to his promise, giving me space and not pushing me. Aside from our coffee date on Tuesday, we hadn't been alone. But it didn't mean he wasn't trying.

Every day, he brought me coffee and a treat from the café. They waited on my desk each morning. Twice, a small bunch of flowers had appeared. A pretty new day planner showed up in the middle of my desk, with penciled-in V's filling in upcoming weekends and evenings. I was touched he remembered my need to jot down notes to jog my memory. And his gift made me smile.

Regardless of where he was working from during the day, he called me every afternoon at two. He asked the same questions.

"How's your day going, Livvy?"

"How's Mouse?"

"Anything you need?"

And he always finished the call the same way.

"I loved hearing your voice, and I miss you. I'll call you tonight if that's okay."

"Yes," I would reply.

"Okay. You know where I am if you need me."

Indeed, I did. I felt his presence everywhere. It was as if my body was tuned to his. I knew when he was in his office. I felt his absence when he left the building. I longed for two o'clock every day, and my nights were no longer complete without his call.

The evening calls were different. Personal. He talked about his life in the band. Shared amusing stories of life on the road. Talked about his parents. Asked me countless questions about growing up and Sammy when she was a baby. It was as if he wanted to know as much about us as possible. I told him things I had never told anyone, and he listened.

One night, he called earlier than normal. Sammy was still awake, and I put him on speaker. They talked for over thirty minutes. I realized it was the first time I had ever heard her talk to someone for that long aside from my mother or me.

She was more than attached already.

And I was beginning to think I was as well.

I passed a weary hand over my face, feeling confused.

How had Van Morrison slipped so deeply under my skin without me even realizing it?

Then, as if I had conjured him up, he was there. Standing beside the park bench, a tray of steaming coffees in one hand and a brown bag in the other.

I blinked at him in surprise.

He looked nervous and worried.

"I wanted to come and say hi. I thought we could have coffee together while you watched Mouse." He hesitated. "If that's okay?"

The words were out before I could think. "Yeah. More than okay."

His smile was brilliant. He sat beside me, handing me a cup. Then he dug into the bag and handed me one of his favorite lemon Danishes. Sammy spotted him and, with a whoop of delight, ran toward us. Van set down the food and met her partway, bending low to catch her. I felt a lump build in my throat. He was as happy to see her as she was to see him. He brought her to the bench and sat her on his knee, listening to her rapid conversation as she tried to fill him in on her life since she last saw him.

"Whoa, take a breath, Sammy," I chuckled.

"But, Mommy, I have to tell Mr. Van about the spelling bee! I won second place!"

He ruffled her hair. "Good job, Mouse."

She grimaced. "The last word was too hard. But Mommy says I learned something new." She peeked into the bag. "Is one of these for me?"

He chuckled and handed her another lemon Danish, then opened a small container of milk. He pulled out the last Danish, and together, they munched. There was a running commentary between bites, and I was content to sip my coffee and watch them together. Van's immense form filled the park bench, and Sammy looked so small on his knee. He kept one arm wrapped around her in a protective gesture, and my heart warmed at the sight. He listened intently, although his gaze drifted to me often. When she finished her snack, she jumped up, demanding he watch her as she went back to playing.

He produced a wet-nap from his pocket. "You know the drill, Mouse. Hands up."

Giggling, she held out her fingers, and he gently wiped the sticky icing from them. He tapped the end of her nose. "You go play, and I'll watch as I talk to Mommy, okay?"

She flung her arms around his neck, squeezing him. "I'm so glad you're here! I missed you!" She scampered off.

He sat back, finally opening his own coffee and sipping. He was quiet for a few moments, then stretched his arms casually along the back of the bench.

"You look tired," he observed. "You feeling okay, Livvy?"

"I'm good, Van. No need to worry about me."

"But I do." I felt his fingers tangle in my hair, rubbing the strands. "I miss you," he murmured. "Both of you."

My breath caught, but I wasn't sure what to say.

"Any chance you might miss me?" he asked, his voice tense. "I know it's only been a week, but it feels like longer to me."

I glanced at his profile. He was watching Sammy, his jaw tight, the strain around his eyes evident. The need to ease his pain stirred within me.

"Yeah," I sighed. "We both do."

He exhaled long and hard. "That's good to hear."

"I'm not ready yet, Van."

He leaned forward, his elbows braced on his knees. "I know. I told you I would wait."

Sammy called to him and he stood. "I'm not giving up, Liv."

Then before I could say anything, he leaned down and pressed a kiss to my forehead. "And I'm not going anywhere. You let me know when you're ready to move forward."

Then he hurried toward Sammy and played with her. My heart swelled watching them together—the gentle giant and my daughter.

I thought about my fears. Although he had overreacted with Vicky, his anger hadn't been directed at me. It was born out of worry and fear of what she would say or do, not something I had done. He had apologized, more than once, and shown me nothing but patience and care every day.

And I did miss him. I missed everything about him. Especially his touch and the way he looked at me.

I ran a hand over my head, weary and confused. Was I ready to move forward? Could I trust him? Could I trust myself?

The low rumble of his laughter caught my attention. He was on the ground, Sammy lifted high on his feet as he supported her with his hands. She was laughing with him, her trust in him absolute.

Their antics made me chuckle.

Van made me happy.

Were we more attached than I realized, as I had thought earlier?

I thought perhaps I had my answer.

Van

Tuesday morning, the sky was overcast and gray. It matched my mood. I hadn't slept much lately, and the early call I'd had made me tense. I wasn't sure how Liv was going to react. I wasn't sure how I was going to handle the day. I had kept my promise as best I could. But the daily phone calls to Liv were all I had, and she hadn't asked me to stop. I sensed a growing closeness happening between us, and I hoped I wasn't wrong.

I pulled up to the curb and climbed out of the truck. Liv was waiting, looking over my shoulder toward the cab.

"I thought you were picking up Bentley?" she asked, confused. "More Braxton Hicks with Emmy?"

"He called me about five a.m. Her water broke and she started having contractions—the real kind—and they're on their way to the hospital."

"Oh!"

"I asked him if he wanted us to handle it today, and he said he'd be grateful. He didn't want more time to pass, and he wasn't sure when he'd be able to make the time over the next while. I told him it wasn't a problem." I eyed her speculatively. "Is it a problem, Liv? Should I call Bentley and tell him we need to reschedule?"

She straightened her shoulders. "No, it's fine. Mom is taking Sammy after day care, and they're having a sleepover, so my day is free. If we put it off, there could be an issue since my mom is going to Florida to see her sister next week, and I would have to make other arrangements for Sammy."

"Well then, I guess it's just us."

"Right."

She shifted on her feet, obviously feeling as uncomfortable as I was at the moment. I didn't want to do anything that would jeopardize the subtle changes in our relationship.

I opened the door, offering her my hand. "Let's go, Liv. I need coffee and a breakfast sandwich for the road."

She began to scramble up into the cab when I noticed the bandage around her ankle. I stilled her actions. "What happened?"

She grimaced self-consciously. "I slipped off the bottom rung of the ladder yesterday. It's nothing."

Without asking, I slid my arm around her waist and lifted her into the truck. I didn't want her to hurt herself trying to climb in with a bad ankle. I grabbed the seat belt and buckled her in. I didn't fail to notice the way her hands gripped my biceps, or the way they lingered on my body.

"Okay?" I asked, my voice gruff even to my own ears.

Her hands dropped to her lap. "Oh, um, yes. Thanks."

I stepped back, even though everything in me wanted to lift her face and kiss her. Even though all I wanted to do was to pull her into my arms and hold her until she told me she was wrong and didn't need any time. That we could move on together.

But I didn't know if she was ready, and I didn't want to push. She was still on guard and might always be. I had probably blown my chance with her because of my temper. It didn't come out very often, but when it did, it wasn't pretty.

I crossed the front of the truck and climbed into the driver's seat, holding in my sigh.

It was going to be a long day.

We finally found the overgrown road leading to the secluded cabin. I carefully maneuvered the truck up the steep, beaten track that once passed as a driveway. The ruts and broken limbs made the hill bumpy and treacherous. It was badly planned, filled with twists and turns, making it difficult to navigate. Even in low gear, the truck slid on the overgrowth, and the low-hanging branches slapped against the sides of the cab. Liv held on to the handle with a death grip. She was already pale, and I could see this part of the drive was making her nervous. Without taking my hands off the wheel, I spoke.

"It's okay, Liv. It's solid, just neglected. Nothing is going to happen to you when you're with me. I've got you."

From the corner of my eye, I saw her deep exhale.

"I know," she whispered.

I wished she believed those words.

We hit the top of the hill, and each of us was grateful. I pulled close to the cabin and slammed the truck into park. Liv turned slightly in her seat.

"How bad is it going to be going down?"

"It's going to be fine. The truck is more than capable of getting us down safely."

She peeked out of the window. "Even if it's raining?"

I opened the door and crossed to her side of the truck. I lifted her down and carefully set her on the uneven ground. "Even if it's raining." I paused and held out my hand. "It's slippery. I think you should hold on to me."

I kept my face impassive as she threaded her fingers through mine. Simply the feel of her small hand tucked into mine made my heart beat faster. She stepped closer, and her foot caught on the wet undergrowth, causing her to stumble. She lurched forward, barreling into my chest, and instantly, I wrapped my arm around her waist, steadying her. For a moment, I felt her in the safety of my embrace. Warm. Small. Perfect.

Then she stepped back, her eyes downcast as she mumbled an apology.

"Not a problem, Liv," I assured her, shutting the door, disappointment making my voice low. "Watch your step, though. It's hazardous underfoot." I shortened my stride to stay beside her. The ground was treacherous beneath our feet, and though she had accepted my hand, I wasn't sure she would allow me to carry her. We rounded the corner, and both of us stopped and stared.

"Oh, wow," Liv breathed as we walked toward the front of the property.

Below us, the Niagara River wound its way through a maze of curves and angles. Huge expanses of trees lined the banks. Sunlight peeked through the clouds, the muted light glinting off the water, a vast span of blue and green swirling with the waves that rolled and broke on the surface. Boats made their way down the channel. A few cottages dotted the landscape, but they were so far away, it was as if you were set high above the world, looking down. The scenery was spectacular.

"A million-dollar view," I mused.

"It's breathtaking."

I glanced down at her. The diffused light caught her hair, casting a glow around her face. Her golden eyes were wide and awed.

"Yes," I agreed. "It's breathtaking."

She glanced up, her eyes meeting mine. They widened, the emotions she fought to hide from me blatant. The want she denied. The need. The fear. I saw it all. I wanted to fix it all. Calm her fears, take away the want and fulfill every need she had. I pivoted on my heel, turning toward her. I opened my mouth to speak, but she backed away, breaking our gaze. She turned and limped away.

"We should check out the cabin."

I followed her, tapping down my impatience. She was running again.

This time, however, she could only go so far.

I noticed the way her hand shook as she fumbled with the keys. The heavy door creaked in protest as it swung inward. Without thinking, I went ahead of her, unsure as to what condition the cabin would be inside. I didn't want her falling in a hole or coming face-to-face with a raccoon who had made a nest inside the abandoned cabin.

"Wait here," I stated firmly. I held my flashlight high, pleased to see everything intact. I crossed the room and pushed back the heavy material covering the windows, allowing the light to fill the room. I turned around, my gaze sweeping the space. Liv shut the door, moving forward, her eyes scanning, taking in the same things I was seeing.

"Great bones," I murmured.

"Yes."

"Want to explore?"

Her excitement was evident. "Yes!"

For the next while, we were simply coworkers. We went through the cabin, each of us looking from a different angle yet on the same page. It was a simple layout. A large main room with a kitchen/eat-in area to one side. Two good-sized bedrooms and a shared bath. I was pleased to see the structure was solid, well-built, and sturdy. It was in desperate need of repairs and refurbishing, but I had every confidence Liv would make it spectacular. I already had ideas on improvements. Leaving Liv to think, I scoped the outside, noting the large space around the cabin. I had a feeling Liv would want to do some expansion, and there was plenty of room. I drew in long, calming lungfuls of the fresh air, studying the rapidly darkening sky, all evidence of sunlight now gone. In the distance, I could hear the rumble of thunder, and I knew the rain Liv worried about was going to happen soon.

Returning to the interior, I noticed there was some furniture in the cabin, and I lifted one of the heavy dustcovers, surprised to see a chaise lounge in deep blue leather hidden underneath. I tossed the cover on the floor and sat, watching Liv. She had her sketch pad out, her hand flying over the page as she walked around. Even given the frustration I was feeling, I enjoyed watching her work—creating something new from the old.

She paused in front of the dirty windows. "Could these be removed?"

"Yeah. I was thinking of sliding glass doors to make the most of the view."

She spoke eagerly. "Yes. A huge flagstone patio with a fire pit."

"What vibe are you going with? Does Bentley want modern or traditional?"

She flashed me a grin. "He gets both. Traditional with all the modern requirements hidden. I want to add to the rustic feel. Reclaimed wood floors. A cool texture to the walls. Skylights to add more sun. A huge hearth over the fireplace."

"I was thinking about adding logs to the outside."

"Yes! A log cabin in the woods. It's the right setting."

"Tell me your plans."

"We gut it. Blow out the front and make it the focal point." She indicated the left side. "Can you expand that wall? Make a sunroom off the kitchen for a dining area?"

I knew it.

"I think so. We'll need planning approval, but as long as we're sympathetic to the land, we should get it."

"We can upgrade everything and make it a retreat."

"What about the bedrooms?"

"They're a good size. Maybe we can add to the perimeter of the whole place?"

"It's all on a slab, so it can be done. We can get Jordan to check the building codes. There's enough space, so I think it can easily be accomplished. What about outside? You want to add to that?"

She tilted her head in thought. "A patio and fire pit, maybe a gazebo closer to the edge of the property?" She set down her sketchbook. "I want to go and see what kind of slope or edge there is to deal with."

I stood, following her. Outside, the wind had picked up, and Liv eyed the sky with trepidation. "We need to hurry so we can get out of here."

I walked beside her again, carefully finding my way toward the front of the property. Close to the edge, I stopped, peering over the steep embankment. "This will have to be addressed. Huge risk factor of falling," I observed, kicking at what was left of a safety rail.

"What could we do?"

"Some rock work and a reinforced steel wall."

"Would it detract from the view?"

"No, we'd incorporate it the right way. Make it aesthetically pleasing, but safe." I indicated a flat spot behind us to the left. "You could do your gazebo there. Awesome view."

She nodded, walking toward the spot. She turned in circles, looking around the property. "Not a place for kids."

"Not long term. More an adult getaway sanctuary. A place to recharge. Although, you could add a small pool and a play area to the right, far away from this ledge. It would be a nice way to cool off for everyone in the summer and appeal to a family for short-term stays if Bent decides to use this place as a rental property."

"And the driveway?"

I laughed. "If we're going to do some redesigning of the cabin, we can redesign the driveway. Make it an easier journey up. It'll be the most expensive part, by the time we have the plans completed, get permission, and remove some trees. We'll have to plant more to replace them, but it can be done, I'm sure. I'll get Jordan on it with an engineer."

She sighed. "I love it."

"What if we went up?" I asked. "Add a loft—a retreat for the adults. One large room with a private bath. The stairs could go up the back wall off the living area."

"Oh," she breathed. "That would be amazing. Huge windows so you wake up to the view every day."

"We'll have to check code and the structure, but I think from what I've seen, it could work."

"I can imagine waking up here every day," she said dreamily. "It would be spectacular."

I resisted telling her waking up beside her *would be* fucking spectacular. Instead, I cleared my throat.

"I hope Bentley is prepared for the expense."

She crossed her arms, her expression wistful. "I hope so too. He already had an offer to buy it as is, but he wanted to keep and develop it." She eyed the cabin. "It's hidden, but the potential is huge."

I studied her. "I agree. So much potential. It would be a shame to let something so amazing slip through our fingers."

I wasn't only talking about the cabin. She met my gaze, her eyes widening as she took in my stare. She knew I was referring to more than the wooden structure behind us.

"A smart person once told me that with time and effort, what was broken can be mended," I stated. "If a person is willing to put in the time, you can create something beautiful—and lasting."

Her mouth opened, but no words came out. A large crack of thunder made us jump. The skies suddenly opened, and the rain beat down hard, soaking us in seconds. Another clap of thunder made me move fast. I lunged, scooping her up and running for the cabin. She clung to my biceps, not fighting me, a fact I was grateful for.

In the cabin, I set her on her feet, shutting the door behind me. Streams of water hit the floor, and I pushed the wet hair off my forehead.

"I think we're stuck for a while."

She sighed. "I think you're right."

"Stay here." I hurried to the back of the cabin and rushed out to my truck, grabbing my workout bag. Once back inside, I dug around and handed Liv one of the towels I always carried with me. "At least this will help a little."

"Thanks," she mumbled.

I toweled off my hair as I peered out the window. The wind was picking up, the trees bending under the force. The rain was teeming, the holes in the roof now evident as the drips began hitting the floor. I pushed the lounger I had been sitting on earlier to a spot which was hole-free.

"At least we can sit," I said, glancing up, not expecting the image that met my eyes.

Frozen, I stared across the dilapidated cabin. Liv had pulled off the oversized shirt she was wearing, leaving her in a tank top. It clung to her like a second skin, showing every curve she kept hidden. She was unconsciously sexy, her creamy shoulders glistening, and her nipples stiff and straining against the thin material covering them.

My cock hardened.

When she lifted her eyes to mine, our gazes locked. She tugged at the material uselessly, pulling at it with frantic fingers to loosen it from her wet, slick skin. It hid nothing from my view. Her expression was tormented. She twisted her hands repeatedly. I knew I should turn around. Say something.

But I only stared.

VAN

Her cheeks flushed, her breathing becoming deep and labored. She tugged at her braid, the wet strands heavy and streaming over her shoulder.

"You should loosen your hair, so it can dry," I uttered, my voice hoarse.

She hesitated, and another word slipped from my mouth, the sound almost guttural.

"Please."

Our eyes locked as she lifted her arms, her hands shaking. She plucked at the clip, the strands falling in a long mass of waves down her back. She shivered, her body shuddering in a lingering, slow roll.

From trepidation or desire, I didn't know.

I couldn't tear my gaze off her.

The thunder rolled, lightning crackling outside with an intensity I felt deep within my bones.

I wanted her with every fiber of my being. I wanted to calm her anxiety, stroke her desire, and claim her.

Make her mine.

Right now.

NINE

Van

The last words I unwittingly spoke out loud echoed in the stillness of the cabin around us.

Liv gasped.

I stepped forward.

She stepped back.

Our gazes remained locked as I shrugged out of my hoodie, dropping it to the floor.

"Liv," I pleaded, desire dripping from the one word. The distance between us was killing me.

"I can't," she whispered.

"You can. Please."

She held up her hand, warning me not to move. "It can't happen, Van. We can't let it."

"We can. I want you, Liv. I want you so much, I'm aching for you. Stop fighting it. Stop fighting us."

"I-I can't chance it."

I edged closer. "It's not a gamble, Liv."

"What if...what if we don't work?"

I risked reaching out and touching her cheek. "We already do, Liv. But you have to take the next step."

"Which is?"

"Forgive me. *Trust me.* Trust this thing between us. Let me show you how good we are. How good we can be."

She shuddered, her body trembling. Her head shook with denial, and I dropped my hand, stepping back. I sensed her fear, and I never wanted to elicit that emotion from her.

"You are forgiven," she said. "Completely forgiven."

But she couldn't move on. I heard the unspoken words as loudly as if she'd said them. Pain lanced through my chest.

"I'm sorry," I said, regret filling my voice. "I won't bother you again." I forced a smile to my face. "Still friends, Liv. Always friends." I lifted one shoulder. "That will never change. I promise."

I crossed the room, bending to pick up my hoodie, forcing down my disappointment and sadness. "We need to sit this storm out, and then we'll head back."

Liv's voice was filled with agony. "Van."

I looked up, not prepared for what happened next. Liv launched herself across the room, stumbling with her weak ankle, and I met her halfway. I caught her as she slammed into me, clasped her around the waist, and yanked her tight to my chest. Our mouths met in a series of blistering, passionate kisses. Desire hummed in my veins, the sensation of her body flush against mine sending me into a frenzy. I tugged on her shirt, pulling the material away from her damp skin, kissing every inch as it was unveiled. Her full breasts filled my hands, and I sucked on the hard nubs, easing away the cold and making her whimper. She moaned my name, the sound vibrating in her throat. It was my undoing. I needed to feel all of her skin against mine. In seconds, I tore the thin material of her tank, the fabric no match for my fists. Liv's fingers fumbled and pulled, yanking away the material of my shirt that separated our skin, pushing it off my shoulders. Her full, soft breasts pressed into the hard planes of my chest and made me groan.

"Fuck, baby, I want you." I licked and sucked at the fragrant skin on her neck. "Tell me I can have you. Right now."

She tugged on my belt, releasing the leather, then pushed on the denim, the cold air of the cabin hitting my naked skin. I kicked out of my jeans, then I lifted her with one arm, the other busy pushing away her leggings and sneakers. I slid my hands over her rounded ass, cupping the firm cheeks. "Say it," I insisted.

"Yes, Van, I want you. *Now.*"

In a few steps, she was under me on the lounger. I felt the cold of her body warming underneath mine, could feel the way her desire blossomed. She tugged at my hair, her restless hands all over my back and arms, pulling me closer, moaning my name.

"This is more than now, Liv. You need to know that," I groaned against the delicate skin of her neck. "This follows us beyond here."

"I know." She kissed me, her mouth urgent.

"Tell me you want this," I demanded. "Or tell me to stop now."

"I want you, Van. All of you," she replied. "Feel how much I want you."

I slid my hand to her center, groaning at the heat and wetness.

"You're so soft, Liv. So wet."

"I'm always wet when I think about you this way, Van."

Jesus.

"How often do you think of me?" I asked, pushing her open wider, caressing her more.

She pressed her lips to my ear. "Every time I see you. The way you move. How sexy you are. I imagine you inside me every single day."

I grew harder, her words making me crazy. "You don't have to imagine it anymore."

She bucked against my hand. Circling her clit, I strummed gently as she threw back her head, gasping my name. I slid one digit into her heat, then another, groaning at the tightness. She was going to strangle my cock.

I was desperate to feel it.

Our mouths fused together as I worked her with my hand. Her tongue was nectar in my mouth, her breath hot and sweet. I fisted her hair, controlling her movements, controlling her, my need to have her building and growing.

She wrapped her hand around my cock, stroking me. Her thumb

ran over my crown, circling slowly, spreading the wetness. Pleasure made me shudder, and I pulled my mouth from hers. She lifted her hand to her lips, her tongue darting out, licking her thumb.

"I want to taste more of you." She sat up on her elbows. "I want to know how you feel in my mouth."

My heavy breathing became erratic. The image of her with her lips around my cock made my head swim. I shook my head, knowing I wouldn't last long. I was too far gone right now. "Soon, baby. Right now, I need to be inside you."

She eased back, a vision against the leather. Her hair was a mess, her cheeks flushed, and her lips swollen from my mouth. Her chest rose and fell in deep gasps of air. She stroked my thighs with her gentle hands. "Then take me. Make me yours."

Her simple words were all I needed. "Protection," I gasped. "My wallet. I want you to feel safe."

She cupped my cheek. "I *am* safe with you. I know that."

I met her gaze. "It's been a long time for me, Liv. Over a year. I'm clean."

"Then let me feel you."

I pushed her farther up the lounger and nestled between her legs. The blunt head of my cock nudged at her entrance, and she lifted her hips to bring me closer. I wrapped her leg around my hips and slid inside of her inch by inch. Our gazes were locked, filled with passion and the discovery of each other as I sank into her. She groaned, the sound low and needy in her chest. I breathed her name. I stilled when our bodies were flush, savoring the heat and feel of her.

"Jesus, Liv. You feel fantastic."

She arched her back in agreement. "Please, Van," she begged. "I need you."

"Hold tight, baby. I need you too."

I took and she gave. I demanded and she surrendered. I begged and she responded. I drowned in her and she engulfed me. We moved and rocked. Fucked and loved. The lounger creaked in protest and I didn't give a care if we ended up on the floor. I couldn't stop.

Liv surrounded me, her cries music to my ears, her body a temple I wanted to worship in for the rest of my life. Her skin was supple and smooth, her hair a mass of fragrant waves around us. Her body was rounded and full, rich and malleable under my hands. Despite the differences in our bodies, we meshed perfectly, her curves fitting to my muscles as if sculpted for me alone. The feel of her hands on my body was heaven. I had never felt touches so gentle and warm. They made me ache with a tenderness that overwhelmed me. Caught me off guard yet felt as if I had come home.

The feel of her, *of us*, was more than I ever imagined it could ever be.

Despite the cool air surrounding us, we were on fire. Sweat poured down my back, my breathing uneven and hard. I slid my hands under Liv, lifting her so our chests melded, and she was encased in my arms. She wrapped her legs around my hips, letting me sink even deeper into her. I gripped her hips, thrusting hard, the lounger scraping along the floor in time with our movements. She wound her hands into my hair, her head falling back as she cried out in pleasure at the new angle.

The world shrank down to one small bubble. Liv. Me. Together. Her pussy. My cock. Me inside her—her body moving with mine. Our slick skin touching in perfect unison, the sounds of our lovemaking filling the cabin. Our grunts and groans. Muted gasps of pleasure. Long sighs of need. The heat and passion that built and soared until it hit the pinnacle for us both.

She gasped out my name, her fingers digging into my shoulders as her orgasm tore through her. My balls tightened, and my release swept over me. I stilled, emptying deep within her, her name a long, low groan on my lips.

The lounger held firm.

My embrace became a vise, and I held her as close as I could. I lowered us to the lounger and collapsed on her chest, my breathing uneven, my body sated, a blissful numbness overtaking my mind.

I eased beside her, tugging her back into my arms. The feeling of her body, the slightness of her form compared to mine, registered through my dulled senses.

"Are you okay, Liv? Was I too rough?"

She pressed a kiss to my chest. "You were perfect."

I chuckled. "I think you're the perfect one, baby." I rested my chin on her hair, the silken strands tickling my nose. "What changed your mind?"

"You," she said simply. "Everything you did last week. The calls, the words. Your patience."

"I missed you so much last week. It drove me crazy not being able to be close to you. I didn't know how I was going to cope if you said you were done for good," I admitted.

"I don't think that could happen, Van. I was tired of saying no to myself," she admitted. "To you. It was so hard to see you go on Sunday. Then today, I saw the hurt my words caused you, yet you responded with patience and tenderness. I knew I needed to try. I knew you were worth the risk."

"You won't regret it."

She pressed a kiss to the roughness of my chin. "I know."

The storm raged on outside. The cabin, leaky roof and all, proved to be a warm haven for us. We sat on the lounger, Liv wrapped in my arms, talking about anything and everything.

"Sammy would like it here," she murmured.

"Wouldn't you be worried about the drop-off?"

"No. She's as scared of heights as I am. If I showed it to her and explained, she would stay away. She's cautious like me." She hummed, her breath warm on my skin.

I pressed a kiss to her head. "She is a great kid."

"If there were a play area, she'd stick to that, and she'd play with her dolls or read. She's very good at reading and she loves it."

"Like you?"

"Yes."

"I've been working on her bookshelf. It will be ready soon."

She traced my chin with her fingers. Her eyes glowed in the muted light. "She'll love it."

"I hope so."

"I know so."

I settled her back on my chest. "I know you're up and down ladders. How do you handle the scared of heights thing?" I asked, curious.

"I only go so high. My staff know I get nervous. They do the cutting and edging, and I roll when I'm helping them paint." She lifted her foot and flexed it slowly. "I rarely have accidents, though. I think I was distracted yesterday and slipped. I have enough staff, I don't need to, but I enjoy painting, so every so often, I pitch in."

"You're amazing."

She glanced up. "I think you're the amazing one."

Passion simmered in the air around us. I ran my knuckles over her cheek. "I didn't plan on making love to you today in a broken-down cabin with a leaky roof."

A smile played on her lips. "Good thing. I'm not sure Bentley would have been on board with your plan. He would have objected loudly when you put your idea into action."

I laughed. "Probably." I became serious. "You deserve silk sheets, champagne, and a fancy hotel room. Not an old lounger, dust, and rubble."

"But the lounger and dust have you."

"*You* have me."

She surprised me by sitting up and straddling me. Her wet pussy pressed against my growing cock. Her voice was husky. "Do I have you, Van?"

I bucked into her heat. "Fuck yes, Liv. You have me."

"*Can* I have you?"

"Yes."

She leaned forward, kissing me, her tongue languid and

exploring. Her lips trailed down my chest, her teeth biting teasingly at my nipples, making me hiss. She sank down on my cock, slowing taking me in.

I gripped her hips. "Ride me, baby."

A slow, sexy smirk pulled at her lips. "Oh, I intend to, Van. It's your turn to hold on tight. It's gonna be a bumpy ride."

The rain finally let up, and regretfully, we rose from the lounger. Few words were spoken as we searched for our clothing. Liv grimaced at her shirt, shivering as she pulled the still-damp material over her head. Her tank was a torn scrap of fabric on the floor. She lifted it, meeting my pleased expression with a raised eyebrow that looked sexy on her. I dug into my bag and handed her a long-sleeved plaid flannel shirt of mine.

"It'll be too big, but it's dry and warm."

"What about you?"

I held up an extra Henley. "I'm good."

I chuckled at the size of my shirt on her. With a grin, I helped her roll up the sleeves. "I like you in my clothes. It's my second favorite look on you."

"What's your favorite?"

I kissed the end of her nose. "No clothes and your skin pressed to mine."

Two bright spots of color appeared on her cheeks, and she dropped her eyes. I slipped a finger under her chin. "What did I tell you about hiding your smile? Let me see it."

It lit the gloomy room. I loved seeing it, and I loved the fact that I was the one who made it happen.

Her stomach growled, making me laugh. "Come on, Liv. Let's lock up, navigate the driveway, and I'll take you to eat."

"Is it safe?"

"Yes. I promised you it was."

"By getting something to eat, you mean stop at a drive-through, right?"

"No," I frowned. "I mean I'll take you out for a meal. I saw a cool-looking pub in the town we passed. We can try it out."

"I can't go out like this," Liv protested. "I'm a mess!"

"No, you're not. You're gorgeous."

She snorted. "I'm hardly gorgeous when I try, Van. I'm certainly not when I've been caught in a storm, fucked repeatedly for hours and have no way to get cleaned up."

"Stop it."

"What?"

I crowded her to the wall, kissing her hard. "First off, I didn't simply fuck you. It was way more than that, and you know it. Stop belittling yourself. I hate it. Do you have any idea how beautiful you are to me? How incredibly sexy and perfect you are?"

"I am?"

I dropped my head to her neck. "Jesus, woman, how can you not know?"

"I-I've never...no one has ever..."

I pulled back, meeting her gaze with a fierce one of my own. "I am." I lifted her, punching my hips forward. "Do I need to prove it to you again? Because I will. You're not leaving this cabin until you believe me."

"You already had me. Many times."

"Not often enough apparently. For either of us."

"But my hair's a mess, and my clothes are wrinkled."

I bent low, my voice firm. "Your hair is a mess from my hands. Because it's soft and rich and I love touching it as I make love to you. Your clothes are wrinkled because I took them off you to see your beautiful body. What you see as a mess, I see as my job well done."

Her eyes widened, her head falling back. A small purple bruise stood out on the base of her neck. I lowered my face, running my tongue along the edges of the blemish. I traced the mark, a sense of smugness filling my chest.

126

"I marked you," I murmured.

"You did?"

"Mmm-hmm," I mumbled, licking up her neck to her ear. "If I marked you, that means only one thing. You belong to me. *My* beautiful, sexy woman." I bit down on her lobe. "All mine."

She groaned, and I smirked against her skin. "I think my woman needs me to prove how beautiful and sexy she is." I ground my pelvis against her.

"Yes, Van, show me," she pleaded. "Make me yours."

I laughed against her mouth. "Oh, Liv, you already are."

We found the pub and hurried to the door as fast as Liv could hobble. It was deserted due to the time of the day and the weather. After a quick glance at the menu, we ordered a late lunch and mugs of steaming coffee. I added a shot of Bailey's to Liv's but kept mine plain. The heat would help chase away the last of the remaining chill.

Liv glanced up from her phone. "Aiden says Emmy is still in labor but doing fine." She smiled. "Better, apparently, than Bentley is doing."

I swallowed a long sip of coffee with a chuckle. "Not surprising. He is rather protective. He'd hate seeing her in any sort of pain."

"Like you," she observed, wrapping her hands around her mug.

I studied her over the rim of my mug. She looked different. More relaxed. There was color in her cheeks, and her eyes were gentle as they regarded me.

"Like me," I repeated. "Which bothers you."

"No," she insisted. "I like how you make me feel, Van. I reacted to a memory the other day, not you," she admitted and pushed her hair over her shoulder. "Every so often, my past creeps up on me, and I need to remember not to let it control my life."

"Can you tell me, Liv?"

"My father," she stated simply.

I nodded. I had figured that much already.

"He was a control freak. He ordered my mother around as if she were an employee. Everything had to be perfect. In its place. She had to look perfect. The house. Me. Nothing was ever good enough, though. He was never pleased, and he liked to express his displeasure." She huffed a long breath. "I was a kid. A chubby, shy kid. I was far from perfect. He didn't like that. He was critical and mean. Put me down all the time. How I looked. Spoke. Acted. The clothes I wore, my hair. Everything."

I frowned. Her voice dropped, her gaze fixed on the table.

"He questioned every decision my mother ever made. He made me so frightened, I stopped talking. He told me everything I said was wrong, so I stopped trying."

"Liv, baby..." I murmured, reaching for her hand to stop the constant movement of her fingers. She stared at our hands, clutching my fingers like a lifeline.

"I don't know what caused it, but one day he was starting in on me, and my mother snapped. She told him off in no uncertain terms. There was a huge screaming match, and he stormed out. She didn't hesitate. She packed a bag, and we left. She kept saying it was one thing to criticize her, but she was done with his treatment of me. We went to my uncle's place, and he helped us. She filed for divorce right away and I never saw him again." She met my gaze. "It took me a long time to talk again, to be able to speak for myself. Chris tried to take my voice away too, and I almost allowed it. I can't let it happen again."

"And it won't. I love your strength and independence. I will never try to take that away from you. I overreacted to Vicky as well. It was a lapse, not a normal kind of behavior for me." I squeezed her hand. "You know me better than that. I promise."

She leaned over the table. "I know I do. You aren't like either of them."

"No, I'm not." I regarded her in wonder. "I'm surprised you're willing to even try, given your history, to be honest."

She lifted one shoulder. "My father was controlling and mean. His words were meant to hurt, and he knew how to use them. Chris was controlling but more cunning. The way he spoke and the things he said were insidious. They got in my head and festered and ate away at me, making me feel worthless. That was how he controlled me until he decided he no longer wanted me. And Evan, well, he was simply selfish. Three men all of whom liked to use people. You aren't a user."

"I try not to be."

She waited until our food was delivered before she spoke again.

"I've had enough experience with them to know." She picked up her fork. "And you are not one," she added vehemently, stabbing her salad.

"Okay, Livvy. Don't take it out on the poor lettuce."

She grimaced. "Sorry."

Unable to resist, I leaned over the table, clasped the back of her neck and kissed her. "Don't be sorry for feeling so strongly about me. I'm good with it."

I sat back, grinning at the flush spread across her cheeks. I took a big bite of my burger, chewing it slowly. She ate quietly for a moment, then met my gaze.

"My mom leaves in a couple of days for Florida. I'd like you to meet her, if it isn't too fast. Would you...would you like to come to dinner tomorrow?"

I dragged some fries through the ketchup on my plate. "Not too soon, and yes. I would love to." I paused before taking another bite. "She has Mouse all night, though, right?"

"Yes."

"So I get you until tomorrow morning."

"Oh, ah..."

"Is that an issue?"

"No, if that's what you want. I didn't want to presume."

I chewed and swallowed before replying. "Presume away. It's what I want. I am nowhere close to being finished with you today."

Her cheeks grew even darker, but she met my eyes, her golden pupils glowing in the light. "Maybe I should have ordered something other than a salad."

I cut my burger in half and slid it onto her plate. "Start with this. You're gonna need it."

130

TEN

Van

I stepped outside, the air cool and clear from the rainstorms that had swept the area yesterday. It was barely after five a.m.—the sun still a long way from being visible, but it might as well have been beaming down on my face, given the mood I was in.

Euphoric would be an understatement.

I left Liv slumbering in her bed, her sleepy goodbye kiss still lingering on my mouth, her double-sized bed that was too small for me. The only way I fit was angled across the mattress, and even then, my feet hung off. Liv slept draped over my chest, her silky, sweet-smelling hair spread out on my skin. I was as stiff as fuck, exhausted from lack of sleep, my shoulders ached from the odd position I had forced myself to lie in all night—and I couldn't stop smiling.

We had spent the evening talking. Laughing. Confessing. Making love. I finally let her sleep around three and left even earlier than we agreed to make sure Mouse and her mother didn't catch me leaving. It was too soon to try to have to explain to either of them.

I climbed in my truck, the sight of a parking ticket on my dash not even enough to dampen my mood. I had remembered I should go and move my truck but hadn't wanted to disturb Liv, so the fine was worth it. I liked how it felt to have her sleep on me. She was warm, smelled good, and, every time I nudged her awake, was more than receptive to my advances. In fact, she woke me once, her talented mouth teasing my nipples as she stroked my hard shaft.

"You were poking me," she explained with a wink.

I dragged her up my torso, settling her on my thighs, my cock at her entrance. "I'll show you poking."

She was astounding.

I glanced in the rearview mirror, her building fading from sight. I already missed her, which meant only one thing.

I was a goner and already totally pussy-whipped.

Surprisingly, I was good with that.

I heard her voice in the hall during the day. I saw her by Sandy's desk, chatting excitedly about the birth of Bentley's daughter, Addison. She glanced up as I passed, our gazes locking and a thousand silent words passing between us. The slight flush on her cheeks made me grin, and I winked but kept walking. If I stopped, I knew I wouldn't be able to resist touching her, and Sandy was too perceptive not to notice the change in our relationship.

Around four, Liv knocked on my door, hesitating. I leaned back in my chair, smiling.

"Hey, Liv. Come in."

She glanced toward Jordan's desk, and I rolled my eyes.

"He's in with Aiden."

"Okay." She entered and sat across from me, looking unsure. "Um, having a good day?"

Amusement burst from my throat. "Yeah, you could say that." I hunched closer over the desk. "You could say you had a lot to do with my good day."

"Oh. Ah, good. That's good."

"What about you, *Livvy*? You having a good day?"

"It could be better."

I frowned. "What's wrong? What do you need?"

"I'd like to kiss you, but I know that's inappropriate here."

Her words were unexpected since she was adamant our relationship remain private.

"I'd like to kiss you too."

She nodded, tapping her chin and glancing around. "Do you have a pencil I could borrow? I seem to be fresh out."

"Ah, yeah, we keep them in the cabinet behind the door over there." I pointed to it, confused by the sudden change in conversation.

She pushed the door to the hallway closed. "This cabinet?"

"Yes."

She opened the door and peeked in. "I don't see them." She glanced over her shoulder. "Maybe you can find them."

I crossed the room and looked over her shoulder. "Right there, Liv. There's a whole box on the top shelf."

She rose up on her toes, tilted her head back, and leaned into me, her eyes dancing. "Right where?"

I started to laugh, realizing how slow I was being to her broad hints. I wrapped my arm around her waist, dropping my face to hers. "Right here, Liv."

I planned to kiss her fast. A swift meeting of our mouths to stop the craving to feel her. Except, once our lips touched, fast went out the window. I slid my tongue into her mouth, gliding with hers, both of us groaning with relief and desire. I cupped her face, angling her neck and kissing her deeper. Harder. She gripped the back of my neck, returning my passion fully. Every rational thought evaporated, and all I could think of was taking her right there. Against my door. Burying myself inside her and hearing her moan my name.

Then I heard Jordan's voice humming as he walked down the hall. He often hummed as he walked, a fact that I was grateful for since it gave me a chance to move. I tore myself away, hurrying back to my desk. I was glad for the thick wooden surface hiding my throbbing erection. Jordan pushed open the door as I sat down and reiterated, "There's a whole box of pencils on the top shelf, Liv."

"Oh, found them!"

Jordan stopped. "Sorry, Liv. Didn't see you there. I thought maybe Van was catching a nap at his desk and pushed the door shut so not to be disturbed."

She laughed, lifting one shoulder. "Hardly surprising. Such a slacker."

"Hey," I snarled playfully. "Some respect. If I'm going to nap, I flake out in the chair—never behind my desk."

Jordan chuckled, dropping his armful of files on his desk. "Of course. My bad."

I gazed at Liv, wondering if Jordan saw what I did. Her bright eyes and full lips that screamed, "I was just kissed," or if he noticed anything at all.

"Anything else you need, Liv, or is stealing my last box of pencils enough for today?"

"Nope. This is good. I have to get to work. I'm having dinner with my mom at six sharp, so I need to be out of here at a decent time."

I tried not to chuckle at her covert message. "Sounds good. Enjoy your evening."

She waved and hurried off. Jordan flipped open a file, scanning the contents, while I reached for the next week's schedule I'd been working on when Liv came in. For a few moments, the only sounds in the office were the scratching of pens and turning of pages.

Then Jordan cleared his throat. "Van…"

I glanced his way. "Yeah?"

He never looked up, his eyes fixed on the file in front of him. "Call it experience or friendly advice, but if you're gonna kiss your girl in the office, make sure to wipe the lip gloss off your mouth before pretending it never happened." A chuckle burst from his mouth. "Pink isn't really your color."

I swiped at my lips, cursing when I saw the pink streak on my hand. "I, ah, we—"

He held up his hand, meeting my eyes. "Your business. I think the two of you work great. I also appreciate the need for privacy, so this stays between us. But next time you're gonna kiss her, I suggest shutting the door completely. Watching you tear across the office to your desk was amusing."

"You saw that?"

"You aren't exactly easy to ignore—or the lightest person on your feet. Good cover, though. Pencils." He stared to chuckle again, picking up his file. "Too bad she took a box of Sharpies."

I began to laugh.

Apparently neither of us were good at cover-ups.

"Thanks, Jordan," I muttered, grateful for his friendship, humor, and understanding.

He grinned and went back to work.

"A coffee and a snack wouldn't go unnoticed," he said.

I stood.

"On it."

Liv's mom was an older version of her. In fact, watching the three of them across the table was like seeing the same person at three stages of their life. They shared the same body type, hair color, mannerisms, and smiles. And although the shape of their eyes was the same, the main difference between them was the color. Liv's mom had hazel-colored eyes, Liv had the gorgeous golden-brown, and Mouse's eyes were a deep chocolate. I had to assume both Liv and Mouse had inherited their father's eye color. I enjoyed watching them together. It was easy to see their closeness.

Liv's mom, Eleanor, or Elly, as she insisted I call her, was intelligent, direct, and blunt. I liked her. She refused the hand I held out to shake, instead enveloping me in the kind of hug only a mom could bestow. I had a feeling she and my mom were going to get along well.

Dinner was a loud affair, Mouse excited to have a captive audience at her disposal. She was lively and chatty, often making me laugh with her drollness. She watched me eat, her eyes wide with amazement.

"Are you sure you're not a giant, Mr. Van? You eat like one."

Liv groaned and Elly chuckled.

"Nope. But your mom's cooking is awesome and a big treat."

Mouse stared at her plate, mystified. "Treat? It's meatloaf." She poked at the meat, pursing her lips. "A treat is a chocolate bar."

I laughed and helped myself to more of the meatloaf from the platter on the table. "Not for me, Mouse. I live alone, so meatloaf is a huge treat."

Her eyes grew even bigger. "You should eat here all the time, then. Mom makes stuff like this every night." She sighed. "My best friend Sharon's mom doesn't cook. They order in every night." She whined. "It's so cool."

Liv grimaced. "And unhealthy. Not to mention expensive."

I leaned toward Sammy. "You know what, Mouse? I bet if I asked Sharon, she'd think having a mom who cooks is better than ordering out all the time. I know I do."

"Really?"

I wiped my mouth. "Yep. Cooking is a talent. One of your mom's many talents." I winked at Liv. "I'd be happy to eat here anytime."

She stared at her plate, then broke off a piece of meatloaf with her fork. "Yeah, Mom is pretty cool. And I like meatloaf."

I locked my eyes on Liv. "Yeah, she is."

Elly watched us, clearly amused. After dinner, she kept Mouse busy giving her a bath, while Liv came downstairs and helped me carry up the bookcase I'd made for Mouse. We got it into her room, and I stood back, brushing my hands on my pants.

"Damn glitter. Even sealed, it attaches itself to me."

Liv agreed. "It goes everywhere. I live in a state of perpetual glitter." She ran her hand over the bookcase, inspecting it. I plugged in the lighting I had added, making the glitter sparkle.

"This is beyond anything she ever dreamed of, Van. She's going to go crazy." She stepped back and placed her hand on my chest. Her eyes were tender and glowing as she spoke. "I can't thank you enough for making it for her."

I covered her hand with mine. "I wanted to. She's an awesome kid. I like her, Liv. I like her a lot."

"I know."

"I like her mother too." I snaked my arm around her waist, pulling her close. "I really like her mother."

She rose up on her toes, brushing her lips over mine. "She likes you." She wrapped her arms around my neck and pulled herself tight to me in a warm hug. Her breath on my neck made me shiver. She felt so right nestled in my arms, fitting to me perfectly. "She likes you so much."

I held her close, acutely aware of two things. How much closer I wanted her, and the fact that her mom and Mouse were ten feet away and would appear at any moment, so I couldn't. But I held her tight, enjoying the sensation of her body pressed to mine. From down the hall, I heard Elly telling Mouse to go to her room.

Liv eased back, running her fingers across my jaw. "Are you ready for the squeals?"

"Bring them on."

Liv chuckled. "You have no idea."

I rolled my eyes. Sammy was a little girl. How bad could it be?

Mouse tripped in, her long nightgown trailing on the floor behind her. Her hair was damp, already curling into ringlets around her face. She beamed at us, then stopped, her gaze riveted to the bookshelf beside me. Her dark eyes widened to the point of hilarity, and she clasped her hands in front of her in delight but remained silent.

"Is it what you wanted, Mouse?"

I thought Liv was being funny when she warned me. But I swear, the sound that came from Sammy's mouth could shatter glass. A shriek pierced the air, and she lunged toward me. Bending, I caught her, still reeling from the sound she'd made. She was laughing, pointing, talking, and somehow, still squeezing my neck at the same time. Even her voice was a higher pitch.

"Mr. Van! Look at the turrets and the lights!"

"Mommy, the glitter! All the glitter!"

She turned her head, calling loudly for Elly. *"Grammie! Come see my bookcase! Mr. Van made it for me like our drawing!"*

She turned to face me, her face anxious. "Is it really for me?"

"Of course it is, Mouse. It's all yours. I made it for you."

A thousand little kisses were plastered on my face before she kicked away, sliding down my torso and rushing over to her bookcase, running her hands over the turrets and shelves, excited and showing Liv everything she had asked me for.

"Can we put my books on it now, Mommy?"

Liv looked at me, almost pleading. I cleared my throat. "It needs to dry one more night, okay, Mouse? You can load it up tomorrow."

"Okay," she acquiesced easily. "May I leave it on for a bit to look at, Mommy, once you read me a story?"

Liv ran a hand over Sammy's head affectionately. "Yeah, baby, we can do that. I think Mr. Van added the lights exactly for that reason. But you have to sleep soon. You'll need to be well rested to fill it up tomorrow, right?"

Mouse touched the glitter on the turrets with adoration. She looked at me, her eyes shining in the light. When she spoke, her voice was as serious as I had ever heard Mouse.

"This is the best present I ever got, Mr. Van. Thank you for making it for me." She darted forward, wrapping her arms around my legs. "You're my favorite aside from Grammie and Mommy."

I had to swallow a thickness that rose in my throat.

Shit, this kid was gonna kill me.

"You're my favorite too, Mouse."

Elly leaned against the doorframe watching us, her arms crossed. "I think Mr. Van needs another piece of cake and some coffee while Mommy reads your book, don't you, Sammy?"

Sammy nodded hard.

"Say goodnight to Mr. Van," Liv said.

Sammy held up her arms, and I lifted her, letting her wrap her arms around my neck.

"Goodnight, Mr. Van. Thank you for my bookshelf. I love it."

"You're welcome, Mouse."

She pressed her lips to my cheek, her quiet voice a whisper in my ear.

"I love you too, Mr. Van."

She slid down to the floor and took Liv's hand, leaving me reeling once again, for a very different reason.

"That's quite the bookcase," Elly stated, peering at me over the rim of her mug.

"It's wood and glue. That's what I do." I shrugged. "She's a great kid, and I enjoy making things."

"You're having quite the effect on my daughter and granddaughter."

Thinking of Sammy's whispered words, I had to shake my head. "They're having an effect on me too."

"I see that." She tilted her head, studying me. "They are *both*"— she stressed the word carefully—"vulnerable in their own way."

I swallowed some coffee before replying. "I am aware of that. I'm not playing games here, Elly. I'm aware of Liv's past and how easy it is to break a child's heart. I have no plan for hurting either of them."

She was quiet for a moment. "Liv's father was a selfish, arrogant man. I never saw his cruel nature until it was too late. I was young, pregnant, and alone other than him. I stayed in a relationship that was toxic. It took me a long time to find the courage to leave. I took Liv and left when I realized he was going to do the same things to her as he did to me. Belittle and knock her down until she didn't even know herself anymore."

"That took guts."

"I should have done it sooner. I don't think I was ever prouder of

Liv as when she walked away from Chris. It was a difficult time for her, but it was the right decision. She was far braver than I was. I never liked him. He was even worse than my ex."

"Insidious, Liv called him."

"Yes. He was awful. I'm grateful he wanted nothing to do with Sammy. I shudder to think of his influence on her."

"Liv has done an amazing job with her."

She studied me briefly. "I've gotten good at reading people, Van. I like you. I like how Liv looks when you're around."

Unable to resist, I teased her. "How does she look, Elly?"

A smile played around her lips. "If I were someone other than her mother, I would say sexually fulfilled. But since I am her mother, let's just say happy. Happier than I have ever seen her. I want her to stay that way."

I laughed, feeling a punch of pride at the fact that Liv was sexually satisfied. God knew I wanted to satisfy her—as often as possible.

"So do I."

"Good. Now enough of me intimidating you. I want to interrogate you. I want to know about your parents, your job, where you live, and your tax bracket." She winked. "And how you managed to get me in to see Phil for my migraines. He is a wonder!"

"Interrogate away."

I drained my coffee and glanced at my watch. "Are they always this long?"

Elly grinned and stood. "Follow me."

We went down the hall, stopping at Mouse's door. Elly peeked in with a knowing smile.

"I thought so."

I peered over her shoulder. The room was dim, the only light coming from the bookcase. Liv was stretched out beside Mouse on the bed. Sammy was curled into her mother. A book was open beside them, and they were both asleep.

"She often falls asleep reading to Sammy," Elly mused. "I'll wake her."

"No," I protested, my heart doing strange things in my chest as I watched them slumber. "I know Liv is tired. Let her sleep. Maybe we can cover them up?"

Elly peered up at me with a frown. "And what will you do?"

"Drive you home and head to my place."

"I think Liv wanted to spend some time with you this evening."

I glanced back toward the bed. I had wanted to spend some alone time with Liv, too, but they both looked so peaceful, and I had thought earlier Liv looked tired. She needed the rest.

"We'll spend some time together this weekend."

She pursed her lips. "I was thinking I would take Sammy overnight for a sleepover before I left to go see my sister. Maybe Friday night would work."

I gently squeezed her shoulder. "Sounds like a plan."

She winked. "There's a blanket on the sofa."

I hurried down the hall and grabbed it, returning to the room and carefully placing it over their sleeping forms. I gazed down at them, thinking what a pretty pair they were—mother and child.

My girls.

My heart skipped a beat in my chest.

My girls. I liked that.

Mine to look after. Mine to care for. Mine to...*love?*

Sammy's little voice whispered in my head. *"I love you too, Mr. Van."*

The words sank in. I swallowed.

Love.

Was that possible?

Glancing at them one last time before I left, I realized the answer.

Yes, it was entirely possible.

I was in love with both of them.

ELEVEN

Van

The next morning, Bentley closed the file he was studying and looked up, smiling. "This is great work." He tapped the folder. "I love all the ideas for the cabin. It will be spectacular."

I chuckled at his enthusiasm, wondering how much of it had to do with the plans and how much had to do with the high due to the birth of his daughter. I had never seen Bentley so animated. He practically beamed—an odd occurrence for him. His usual stern expression was relaxed, and he was fast to pull out his phone and show off pictures of Addison to anyone who expressed any interest. Or even if they didn't. He was a very proud dad.

"Thanks." I offered. "Liv's talent brought it all to life."

Liv scoffed beside me. "Van had as much to do with it as I did. He had some brilliant ideas. I simply put them to paper."

Bentley lifted his shoulders. "You're a great team, and you only get better every time you work on a project. I'm truly in awe of what you've come up with. You've surpassed my expectations."

"And my budget," Maddox added dryly. "But I agree. If these plans are approved, this will be spectacular, and the profit will be through the roof, even with the added costs."

Jordan flipped through some papers. "I've got all the paperwork you need to sign, Bentley. Once the plans are complete and drawn up, I'll submit to the council. It's going to take time and patience to get it all approved. I expect some pushback on a few issues, but I know Liv and Van have backup plans."

"Yeah, we do," I agreed. "But we adhered to all the guidelines and rules, even if a few were pushed a bit. We'll figure it all out."

Bentley leaned back, steepling his fingers under his chin. "Great." He swung his gaze back to Jordan. "Now the remodel on the buildings."

"Right." Jordan opened a thick file. "I went through a lot of bids. Some I rejected outright. Way too high, or so low I knew we'd regret it. I narrowed the choices to the top two. One we've worked with before, the other a newer company. Good reputation, seems to be a well-run organization, and they are willing to work within our guidelines." He grimaced. "In fact, they seemed eager to do so."

Bentley frowned. "Something bothering you, Jordan?"

Jordan was quiet as he mulled over his thoughts. It was something I liked about him. He never rushed with an important decision, and he always thought every angle through completely.

"I met with the owners of both companies. Able Construction was slightly higher in the bids, but we've used them before and they were good. Not great, but good. This new company, WIN Construction, opened an office here two years ago. Their first place was out west, and all the reports I received had nothing but good things to say..." His voice trailed off, and he rubbed a finger across his chin.

"But?" Bentley prompted.

Jordan shrugged. "But, nothing. I met with the owner, John, and his foreman, Nolan. This is their specialty—providing crews. In and out—all the work, none of the end responsibility. They said all the right things and put it in writing to back it up. If I'm being honest, I think perhaps it was simply a personal thing on my end. I didn't really like either of them, especially the foreman, much. I got the feeling he was going to be difficult to keep in line. But again, I could be wrong." He lifted one shoulder. "Not that it should matter. I can work with them, and I did like some of their ideas."

"What didn't you like about the foreman?" I asked. Jordan was insightful and smart. If there was something off about this guy, I trusted Jordan.

He thought about my question. "That's the thing. I have no idea. Maybe his arrogance or his over-the-top bluntness. Or maybe," he added, "it was my mood that day. The bottom line is, his crew is the right size, the guarantees for deadlines are backed up with penalties John has written himself, the references are good, so there is no reason not to use them." He smirked. "We won't be going out for beers after work, but I have you for that anyway, Van. You'll be the one dealing with Nolan way more than I will be. You too, Liv."

I chuckled.

"Nolan knew your work, Liv. He mentioned the magazine spread you were featured in a few months ago."

"Arrogant, but he has good taste," I teased.

Liv rolled her eyes.

Maddox spoke. "The numbers are solid. Actually better than Able, the way they outlined the various aspects. I checked the references too. All came back positive."

"Are you sure you can work with him, Jordan?"

"Yeah. As I said, it may have been my mood that day. I want the best for this building, and I think they might be it. The other projects they have done have certainly been successful."

Bentley nodded. "Okay, I guess we'll meet with him and finalize a deal." He stood. "Once that's done, you, Jordan, and Liv can have a meeting and start the final planning stages."

"Sounds good."

"You are going to be very busy for the next while," Bentley stated.

"Try to hold back from adding to that, okay?" I asked with a laugh.

He chuckled. "I think a certain little miss is going to keep me busy for a while, so you're safe."

"Good."

We moved to our own offices, Jordan stopping first to grab a thermos of coffee from the main break room. His addiction to caffeine was scary—far worse than mine. When I had teased him about it, he only grinned.

"Even my doctor gave up. I have cut back over the years, but it is really my only vice. My wife used to tease me about it all the time." He sat back, contemplative. *"It was one of the things I missed about her the most when she passed. The last thing she did every night was set up the coffeemaker, so it was ready when I got up. She made the best damn coffee I ever tasted."* A sad look passed over his face. *"Mornings were the hardest part of the day for me for the longest time. She wasn't beside me when I woke up, and there was no coffee to share with her."*

It was rare Jordan got personal.

"I'm sorry," I offered.

He nodded. "I learned to live again. Took a long time—but thanks to my kids and grandkids, I kept going and life was okay. Not the way it was, but okay." He glanced around. *"This place helped. The people. The routine. And Sandy's coffee. Next to Anna's, it's the best."* A glimmer of a smile crossed his face. *"Next to Anna, she's the best."*

I left that remark alone. I had wondered more than once if Jordan felt something for Sandy. His gaze followed her around, his attention mainly on her in meetings. He was always the first to offer her a hand, or to help if she needed it. When her husband died, he had been a great friend to her, but I had a sense his feelings had grown and changed. How she felt, I had no idea, since she was as intensely private as Jordan. And I knew better than to ask him. When he was ready, he would talk to me. We respected and knew each other enough to know when the time was right to confide in one another.

I hadn't even sat down when Liv came into the office. She was smiling, her hands empty.

"No decoy?" I asked with a chuckle.

"Figured there was no point."

I nodded in agreement. I had told her what Jordan said and assured her he would be discreet. She knew and trusted him to know he would keep his word, although she was insistent we still keep our relationship private.

She approached my desk and sat down. She looked rested today and relaxed. She leaned forward, her hair slipping over her shoulders. I resisted the urge to hunch closer and wrap her hair in my hands and kiss her. Hard. Instead, I winked.

"Hey, beautiful."

Her smile lit her face. While I hated the fact that being called beautiful was something new to her, I loved the idea of how much it pleased her. How much I pleased her.

"Hey yourself," she replied.

"Sleep well?"

"Very. I woke up about five, still in Sammy's bed. I'm sorry about falling asleep."

"Not an issue. I enjoyed my time with Elly."

She rolled her eyes and laughed. "I'm sure 'enjoyed' is a strong word. No doubt she interrogated you endlessly."

I lifted one shoulder. "Once I promised to have copies of the last four years' tax forms and bank statements to her by tomorrow, she eased up."

Liv gaped and I chuckled.

"She was fine, Liv. She asked some questions. I answered. I had her tell me some funny stories of you growing up, so I have some ammunition, and we're all good."

She joined in my amusement, then sighed. "Well, you must have charmed her too. She likes you."

"How can you tell?"

"She called me before the meeting to tell me she and her best friend Phyllis have decided to take their granddaughters to Great Wolf Lodge"—her eyes widened dramatically—"for the weekend."

The meaning of her words sunk in. "You mean I get you *all* weekend?"

"If you want me."

I leaned closer. "Let me be clear. I want you. I want you at my place all weekend."

"Your place?"

My gaze skittered to the door. The hall was empty—the crews out working, Jordan still getting coffee and no doubt talking to Sandy. I rose over the desk and wrapped my hand around Liv's neck, pulling her close. Her scent drifted around me—soft, warm, and inviting. Our eyes locked.

"I want you in my house. Sitting on my sofa. Eating at my table. In my bed."

She whimpered, the sound low and needy. I slid my hand into her hair, fisting the silky curls.

"I plan on fucking you everywhere in my house. It's gonna take a while, but we'll start this weekend."

Her cheeks flushed.

"I want to wake up after you're gone and smell you on my sheets. Taste you in the air. Use the mug you touched, knowing your lips pressed on the rim so it feels as if I'm kissing you even when you're not there."

"Kiss me now," she pleaded.

My mouth covered hers, our tongues sliding together. Coffee, sweet, and Liv. She gripped my neck, her nails scratching lightly on the skin. I fisted her hair, keeping her close. I heard the humming in the hall, and regretfully eased back, dropping three fast kisses to her mouth, then one to the tip of her nose before sitting down.

"I have an off-site meeting on Friday afternoon. Pack your bag and come to me as soon as you leave work. The code to the door is 8645. I'll send you the address." I paused. "Liv, take an Uber or a cab. I'll pay for it. Understand?"

She nodded in agreement and stood. She ran her hands over her hair and straightened her shirt. Her eyes were glazed, her lips wet.

"Don't bother packing too much. I don't plan on letting you out of the house, and you're not going to need many clothes," I added.

She inhaled sharply and spun on her heel, hurrying to her office. I liked watching the sway of her hips as she moved away. I heard Jordan call out a greeting, and before he came into the office, I wiped my mouth, knowing Liv's gloss was there.

I wasn't going to give him the satisfaction again.

Liv

I stepped out of the Uber and stood looking at Van's house. He only lived a short distance from me—on the other side of the park Sammy and I went to all the time, but the area was vastly different. Mine was filled with condo towers and busy traffic. His house sat on a relatively quiet street. The houses were Victorian and solid, most of them three stories, built of brick with big windows. The yard was small, but with land at a premium in Toronto, any yard was a bonus. He had a wide porch, with a big swing to one side. Light glowed behind the closed shutters.

I swallowed and took a calming breath, gripping the handle of my knapsack tightly. Why was I so nervous? It was *Van*.

I swallowed again.

Because it was Van.

The man I had liked privately for so long. Who amazed me. Inspired me. The man who went from coworker and friend, to lover and protector in a short space of time, and the man I was certain I was losing my heart to.

I knew once I fell for him, there would be no turning back, and life would never be the same.

I huffed out a long exhale of air, looking down at the bag in my hand. I hadn't spent a weekend with a man in a very long time. I followed Van's instructions, but I did a little shopping this afternoon in between some appointments. I was sure he was going to approve of what I bought.

The front door opened, and Van stepped out onto his porch. His massive shoulders filled his doorway. Dressed in a Henley with the sleeves pushed up his forearms and jeans, he was incredibly sexy. There was a dish towel thrown over his shoulder, and his feet were bare. The porch light caught the glints of silver in his hair. He frowned in worry as he stepped forward.

"Livvy? You okay, baby?"

His term of endearment melted away my nerves.

It was *Van*, for God's sake.

"Just admiring your house."

His wide grin lit his face, and he held out his hand. "There's more to see inside. Come with me and I'll show you."

I hurried forward, suddenly wanting to close the distance between us. He met me at the stairs, his hand still extended. I slipped my palm into his and let him tug me up the steps. He pulled me close, pressing a kiss to my mouth.

"I've been waiting, Liv. I was getting worried. When I saw you outside, I thought you changed your mind."

"Sorry," I breathed against his lips. "I was sort of lost in my thoughts."

I felt his smile. "I'll let you make it up to me." He dropped a kiss to the end of my nose. "Now let me get you inside so I can kiss you properly."

"Okay."

He led me inside, taking my jacket and bag. As soon as the door shut, he swept me into his arms, his mouth covering mine. His kiss was long and passionate. It said "Hello, and I missed you. I'm glad you're here." The way his arms held me close made me feel safe and welcome.

I wanted to be greeted that way every day.

By him.

He pulled back, dropping one last kiss to my mouth. "I've been waiting all day to do that."

I touched his lips with my finger. "I hope it was worth it."

He captured the end of my finger, swirling his tongue on the digit. "Completely." He wrapped his arms around me, tucking me close. "I'm glad you're here, Livvy."

I sighed in contentment, nestling into his solid chest. "Me too."

He drew back and picked up my bag. He indicated the rooms ahead. "Dinner will be ready soon. I'll go put this in my bedroom. I have wine open on the counter, so help yourself. Look around and make yourself at home."

I found the wine and poured myself a glass, sipping the heady red wine appreciatively. I looked around in admiration. The house was so...Van. The creamy-colored walls were set off with gorgeous mahogany woodwork. The hardwood floors were smooth and polished under my feet. The kitchen was sleek and modern. The large living/dining room felt homey with comfortable furniture in navy and gray. The huge mantel had obviously been carefully restored and updated with a gas fireplace. I could imagine being curled up in one of the deep chairs while the fireplace warmed the room and snow fell outside.

Oddly enough, I could picture Sammy coloring on the rug, and Van napping on the sofa as I read, all three of us content to be close on a lazy day. I shook my head to clear those thoughts. I was getting ahead of myself. Still, I glanced back as I walked toward the kitchen, the image firmly planted in my mind.

Van looked up from the oven as I slid onto a barstool at the high counter. "Hey. How was your afternoon?"

I perched my elbow on the counter, leaning my chin on my hand. "Tiring, but good. We handed over the keys to Mrs. Miller, so the job is done."

He chuckled and slid a plate of antipasto in front of me. "Why do you think I had the wine ready?"

I popped an olive into my mouth, humming at the salty flavor.

"How was she?"

"Fine. She loved almost everything. I think it helped that Bentley, Aiden, and Maddox were there. The three of them are pretty intimidating as a group. Anything she picked at, one of them had an answer for, which shut her up fast. Especially when Maddox started on the fact that we went over budget because of her demands."

Van smirked and swallowed the cheese he'd been munching. "Maddox's budget and the one the client sees are two different things. We were well under the real one. Bentley was impressed with how well we did."

I picked up a piece of Asiago cheese, enjoying the sharp taste. "Yes, he told me. He also promised never to do this again. Once was enough. If I wanted to deal with clients harping at me all day, I would have stayed at my other job."

Van picked up a thin slice of baguette, adding some cheese and another olive and held it up for me. He leaned on the counter, watching me eat it.

"I'm glad you left that job, Liv. You're right where you should be."

"At BAM, you mean?"

The timer on the oven pinged, and he grabbed the oven mitts.

"At BAM, yes. With me at BAM," he added with a wink. "Especially with me."

I had to smile.

TWELVE

Liv

"That was the best lasagna I've ever eaten."

Van dipped his head in acknowledgment as he picked up his wine. "It's one of my favorites. Plus, I can make a huge pan and eat well for a week."

"You, ah, do have a healthy appetite."

He threw back his head in laughter. "That's being polite. My mom always says I ate them out of house and home as a teenager. To be honest, it hasn't changed much. I burn it off fast and I always seem to be hungry."

I couldn't help but eye him in appreciation. His body was amazing. Strong, thick, and powerful. His muscles rippled as he moved, and I loved watching him. He was very sexy.

He met my gaze, one eyebrow lifting in amusement. "See something you like, Livvy?"

I tried not to be embarrassed at staring, but I failed. Van caught my hand and lifted it to his mouth. He pressed a long kiss to my knuckles and laid my hand on his chest.

"Stare away, baby. Whatever you see when you look at me is yours."

"Mine?" I squeaked.

"All yours. If my body gives you pleasure, stare away. I like knowing I please you."

The words were out before I could stop them. "Oh, you please, all right."

He leaned closer, draping his arm across the back of my chair, tugging me close. "I aim to please you a lot tonight, Liv. You up for that?"

I rested my hand on his thigh, meeting his open, honest gaze. His dark eyes were lit from within with a warmth and sincerity I found appealing. His candor was refreshing. He didn't play games or say things he didn't mean. He wanted me, and he wanted me to know that. I slid my hand farther up his leg, running my fingers over the growing bulge.

"Certainly feels like you are," I murmured, tracing the ridge of him under the denim.

He groaned low in his chest. "Unless you want to be dessert, I suggest you stop and let me get coffee and the cupcakes I picked up for you."

My hand stilled. "Cupcakes?" I hesitated. "What kind of cupcakes?"

He chuckled, lifted my hand from his leg and brushed his mouth over my knuckles. "Cockblocked by baked goods." He kissed me, his teasing tone letting me know he wasn't upset. "White with vanilla frosting from Joan's Bakery. I've seen how territorial you get over those at the office. Didn't take me long to figure out those were your favorite."

I slid my hand back to his leg, squeezing his cock lightly. "So is this."

He leaned close, brushing his lips over mine. "Guess what, Liv? You get to have your cake and eat it too. You get both tonight. In fact, I got a dozen cupcakes. You get both all weekend."

I met his intense gaze with one of my own. "Good."

Together we cleaned up the kitchen and loaded the dishwasher. Van's kitchen was well-equipped and organized—much the same as the rest of his house. I gazed around the open concept of the main floor.

"You have such a great place. I love the layout."

"I did a lot of work to it when I moved in. Like so many older houses, it was a bunch of little rooms. I knocked down some walls and opened it up."

"It's lovely."

He braced his arms on the counter, looking around the room. "I like it. It's got three big bedrooms, a dry basement, and the holy grail of all wish lists for homeowners in Toronto."

My brow furrowed. "Which is?"

He chuckled. "A backyard and a garage. There's a spot to park my truck and a place to sit in the summer. Both of which are hard to get here."

He flicked on a light and opened the patio door. I stepped onto the deck, looking around, curious. Small, but well laid-out, the backyard had a deck with a built-in gazebo that offered privacy and shade from both the sun and neighbors. A small footpath led to the garage. A tall fence surrounded the yard. There was even a garden—tiny but flourishing. "What a great space."

He stepped beside me. "Yeah. I planned on adding a hot tub in the corner here, but I seem to be too busy at work to get around to it." He indicated the garden. "My mom helped me plant that. She loves gardening. Good thing, or it would be overgrown pretty fast. I never have time to work on it these days either."

"Bentley does keep us busy."

"Yeah, he does."

"Are you worried about this new company we have to work with?" I asked. "Do you know anything about them?"

He shrugged. "Not really. I checked them out, and the rep is solid. If Jordan is okay with them, it's fine. It's really a simple job for them. Demo and rebuild to our plans. As long as they follow orders, it's good. I don't have to like them, just work with them. And they'll only be there for the first part of the project. As other projects finish, I'll bring in our own people, then you can work your magic."

"I guess we'll meet them on Tuesday." Jordan had scheduled a meeting for us all to meet in the morning. It would be a planning session, and all the details would be hammered out. Once it happened, the project would begin.

Van nodded, rolling his shoulders, a small grimace crossing his face. He had done the same motion a few times during dinner. "Yep." Before I could speak again, he wound his arm around my waist. "No more work talk. The only thing I want to concentrate on this weekend is you."

"I like the sound of that."

"Then let's start with cupcakes and go from there."

"Okay."

"You missed a bit."

"Pardon?"

Van smirked and tapped the edge of my mouth. "Icing. You missed a bit of icing."

"Oh." I licked at the edge of my mouth. "Can't have that."

He laughed. The cupcakes were delicious. Light and fluffy, with mounds of rich buttercream piled on top. Van was amused as I instructed him the proper way of eating them.

"You break them in half and turn the top over," I explained, *demonstrating. "It's a cupcake sandwich. You get icing in every bite!"*

Still, due to the large amount of the sweet frosting, I got it on my face. It never failed. Van shook his head, edging closer, lowering his face to mine. "You still missed," he breathed. "I'll have to get it for you."

His tongue touched the corner of my mouth, sweeping along the edge of my lips. He slid his hand up my neck, pulling me close as he dipped inside. We kissed—long, unhurried kisses that tasted of sweet vanilla and promises of what would happen later.

Until he flinched and eased back, another grimace crossing his face.

"Sorry," he muttered.

"Van, what is it? You keep grimacing."

With a deep sigh, he sat back, rubbing his shoulder. "I was helping tear down a kitchen this morning. I had two crew members call in sick, so I had to step in and lend a hand. The sink and counter fought back." He rolled his neck. "They won." At my worried gaze, he waved off my concern. "It will settle, Liv. I took some pills. It takes longer sometimes than others."

I studied him and stood. I hurried to the bathroom and grabbed the bottle of lotion I had seen earlier. When I returned to the living room, I sat in one of the large chairs and tossed a cushion on the floor. I opened my legs and indicated the cushion. "Take off your shirt and sit here."

"Um..."

"Don't argue, Van. Just do it."

His eyebrows rose slowly. "Okay, Ms. Bossy." He stood and tugged his Henley over his head in the effortless way only guys could do. It was sexy and slow, but I hated seeing the glimmer of pain cross his face at the action. He lowered himself to the floor, squeezing between my legs. I could feel his tension as he eased back, wrapping his arms around my calves.

For the first time, I fully saw his scars. I had felt them before and even glimpsed them, but this was the first time I had actually seen them up close. Deep and long, they ran down his shoulder and back, a crisscross of pain he carried with him at all times. Gently, I ran my fingers over the grooves. He stiffened at my touch.

"Does it hurt?" I asked.

"No," he replied. "Your touch never hurts." He drew in a long breath. "They're ugly, though."

I leaned down and feathered kisses along the marred skin. I traced each line with my mouth, making sure to touch every one. He shuddered in long spasms that raced down his spine.

I pressed my mouth to his ear. "Nothing about you is ugly, Van.

Your scars are a part of you—a part of your past that makes you who you are."

"Who am I?" he asked, his voice so low, I had to strain to hear him.

"Mine," I replied. "You're mine."

He turned his head fast, capturing my mouth and kissing me hard. He buried his hand in my hair, holding my face close as he ravished my mouth. When we broke apart, my breathing was erratic, and his eyes were intense and wild. "I am yours, Liv. Completely."

I could only nod.

"And you're mine."

"Yes," I acknowledged.

"Let me take you upstairs."

"Once I get rid of your pain."

"Liv…"

"Please?" I asked. "Let me do this."

He captured my hand and kissed it. "Okay, baby. Go ahead and try."

Van

I'd had massages in the past. Therapeutic, deep tissue, hot stone, every kind there was, in order to try to alleviate some of the discomfort at times. A few proved somewhat effective; some were a total waste of time.

Liv put them all to shame. Her touch was different. Her surprisingly strong fingers found knots and spasms and worked to ease them. She stroked and soothed. Pulled and released. Dug in and opened pathways that took away some of the pain. The whole time she worked, she hummed, the sound low and pleasant.

"I like that." I informed her. "You have a great tone."

She laughed quietly. "Sammy likes it when I sing to her."

"Me too."

She dropped a kiss to my neck. "Good."

I let my head fall forward, totally relaxed as she worked. Normally, no matter how hard I tried, I couldn't relax under the hands of a masseuse. But Liv was different. Her touch was different. I was able to allow myself to only feel. I basked in her touch. In her words that kept echoing in my head.

"Nothing about you is ugly, Van. Your scars are a part of you—a part of your past that makes you who you are."

"Mine. You're mine."

I was hers. There was no doubt in my mind. I belonged to her, and she to me. The same with Sammy. She had crept into my heart as well, and I needed them both in my life.

Liv tilted my head, her fingers digging into the juncture of my neck. It was a constant stress point for me, and I groaned as she found the nerve that always seemed to be inflamed.

"Too much?" she asked.

"No," I replied. "Keep going."

"I need closer," she murmured and shifted, draping her leg around my chest. I wrapped my arms around her calf and lowered my head. As she worked, the pain morphed into relief, the constant ache dissipating. My body felt loose, at ease for the first time in a long while. My shoulders sagged as the pressure released, my arms going slack, unable to hold her anymore.

"Can you lie down on the couch? On your stomach please."

I knew I should protest. Tell her she'd done enough. But her touch was addictive, and I wanted more of it, so I did as she asked. She settled on my thighs, working my lower back.

She continued to work and hum. The world seemed to recede, quiet settling into my brain. I felt adrift and at ease. I shut my eyes, unable to keep them open anymore.

Slowly, free from pain and surrounded by my Liv, I slipped into sleep.

I woke up, my eyes slowly focusing. The room was dim and quiet. In front of me, sitting on the floor, was Liv, her Kindle light faint in the dark. Her head was resting against the sofa cushion, her legs drawn up to her chest. Reflections of flames from the fireplace flickered on her face as she read, seemingly absorbed in her book.

Briefly, I was confused. The last thing I remembered was Liv working on my back with her magical fingers. I realized I had fallen asleep, leaving Liv on her own.

Great.

"Liv," I groaned out her name.

Her head turned, a gentle expression on her face. "Hey."

I scrubbed a hand over my face. "I am so sorry."

She frowned, confused. "Why are you sorry?"

I sat up and stretched. I noted the usual twinge that always followed my movement was absent. I peered down at her. "For falling asleep on you. Some romantic evening you've had."

She lifted a shoulder, dismissing my words. She snapped her Kindle closed. "Frankly, Van, it's been one of the nicest evenings I've had in a long time."

"You prefer my company when I'm unconscious?"

She laughed. "I'm thrilled I was able to give you enough relief from your pain so you were able to sleep a little."

"Leaving you bored and alone."

"Nope. Leaving me pleased and with time on my hands—a rare occurrence for me. I helped myself to another glass of wine, turned on your fireplace, and read. I can't remember the last time I was able to do that for more than five minutes. Usually by the time I get Sammy settled, get ready for the next day, finish whatever work is waiting, and go to bed, I'm too tired to read. And it's one of my favorite things to do."

"Why didn't you at least sit on a chair? Why are you on the floor?"

Her smile was shy. "I liked sitting beside you and reading. Being close. But I would love to curl up in one of those chairs one day and enjoy this lovely room."

Bending low, I captured her mouth with mine. I kissed her sweetly—long and slow. It was a kiss of thanks, for what she did for me, her words, and for being her.

"You can be here anytime you want. I would love to see you in one of those chairs, relaxing."

"How is your neck?"

I kissed her again. "It feels great."

"Really?"

"Liv, I have never fallen asleep during a massage. Usually, I can hardly wait to get off the table. Your hands are magic." I rolled my shoulders, my muscles loose and flexible. "Seriously, magic."

She chuckled, her eyes dancing in the firelight. "Do you remember what you said the other day—at the cabin?"

I ran my hand over her head. "I said a lot of things, Livvy. Which one in particular?"

"You said making me look messy meant you did your job well. So you feeling better means I did my job well too."

I cupped her chin, stroking her bottom lip with my thumb. "Very well. I have to figure out a way to say thank you. Maybe show you how great I feel right now."

"Oh," she breathed.

I lowered my face to hers, ghosting my lips over hers. "Would you like that, Liv? Show you the fruits of your labors?"

She rose up on her knees, pressing her mouth to mine. She flicked her tongue on my bottom lip, and our mouths melded, her tongue stroking along mine. With a low groan, I bent, picking her up, and standing. She wrapped her legs around my waist, our lips never separating as I carried her upstairs. I laid her on my bed, hovering over her. Our eyes locked and held.

"I've been wanting to have you in my bed for a long time now, Liv."

She played with the ends of my hair, her expression gentle. "You have me now, Van."

She made me feel so many things all at once. Passion, desire, and longing. The need to be as close to her as I could get. Claim her as my own. Yet, right now, there was another emotion weaving its way through my heart.

The sheer wonder of all she was. Warm, giving, patient, and sweet. And looking at me with the same growing passion I was feeling.

I slid my hand under her shirt, tugging it over her head. The action spread her hair around her head, the golden color a bright contrast to the dark sheets. She lifted her hips, pulling away her leggings. Pretty pink lingerie met my gaze. I traced the lace along the edge of the bra and trailed my finger down to her hips, fingering the tiny bows. "These are nice."

"I bought them today—for you."

"Hmm," I hummed, pulling on one bow, then another. "Very pretty." The scraps of lace and silk fell away. "Nothing is as pretty as your pussy, though." I ran my finger along the edge of her, smiling as her breathing hitched and her legs opened for me. I dipped my finger inside, feeling the heat and wetness waiting for me.

"I love how ready you are, baby."

"I want you," she whispered. "I've been thinking about you all day, Van. Please."

"I want to take my time." I met her pleading gaze. "You're going to come on my hand first. My mouth next. Then I'll use my cock."

She grew wetter with my words.

"You like that, Liv? Hearing how often I'm going to make you come?"

She whimpered, arching her back to get closer to my fingers. I slid one inside, then added another, pushing into her slowly. She cried out, fisting the sheets.

"More," she begged.

I pressed her clit with my thumb, rubbing circles around the bundle of nerves. I captured her nipple in my mouth, sucking and licking, alternating sides. Her hips moved in time with my hand, and she clutched my hair, calling out my name as she shattered. I slowed down, drawing out her orgasm, and before she had finished, I buried my face between her legs, licking and teasing at her sensitive flesh, tasting her climax and driving her toward the next one. She gasped, begging me, God, and anyone else who would listen, for mercy.

I showed her none.

I worked her with my mouth and fingers. As she pleaded, I slipped one finger down to her ass, pressing against the puckered knot, sliding in, and adding another pleasure point. Her entire body seized, and she flailed, screaming out her release.

I drove myself inside her. Deep and hard. Bracing my hands on the headboard I rode her, our bodies slamming together with an intensity so ferocious, the bed creaked and shook. Liv's heels dug into my ass, pulling me in tight. She gripped at my shoulders, her nails piercing my sweat-soaked skin. I crashed my mouth to hers, lost in the vortex of passion we had created. Ripples of pleasure racked my body. My balls tightened and my cock swelled, the heat and feel of her too much.

I roared my release, pumping deep into her body. She stiffened, her arms clutching me close as she moaned my name. I wrapped my arms around her and rolled, dragging her up onto my chest. For long moments, there was nothing but the sound of our hard breathing and the feel of her on top of me.

She lifted her head, her sleepy eyes content and warm.

"That was something."

I chuckled. "Good something? Bad something?"

"Very good. Very, very good."

"Then once again, my job is done."

She grinned. "I bet it is. I'm sure I look thoroughly fucked." She wiggled a little. "I certainly feel it."

I captured her face in my hands. "You are amazing."

She sighed and snuggled down onto my chest. She felt so right pressed against me. "We're amazing together."

I pressed a kiss to her head. "Yeah, we are." I stroked the hair that tumbled down her back.

"Go to sleep, Liv."

I chuckled at the soft snores.

She was already out.

THIRTEEN

Van

Liv was a warm weight on my chest all night. She slept with her face buried into the crook of my neck, her breath little puffs of air on my skin. Completely draped over me, she brushed her toes over my calves, reminding me of the difference in our size. Her small stature belied the inner strength she possessed. I loved her independence, but even more, I loved when she allowed herself to be vulnerable with me. I knew it was a side of herself she showed to few people.

The sky began to brighten, darkness giving away to diffused light when she woke, her body shifting. She lifted her head, sleepy and beautiful, already smiling.

"Hi," she rasped, her voice thick with sleep.

Keeping one arm around her, I ran my finger down her cheek. "Hey, Livvy."

She snuggled closer, burying her face beside mine on the pillow. Her voice was muffled when she spoke. "I fell asleep on you."

"Yes, you did. I liked you sleeping on me."

"Did I, um, drool?"

I chuckled. "It was the best part."

She slapped my shoulder. "Stop it. Did I really?"

I kissed her forehead. "No."

"Okay."

She moved and I tightened my grip. "What are you doing?"

"You must be uncomfortable."

I refused to let her move. "Nope."

"Van, let me go."

"Never," I growled playfully.

"You're impossible."

Her silky skin slid against my chest. Despite our size difference, she was aligned perfectly with my body, her curves fitting to mine effortlessly. I trailed my hand down her back, cupping the swell of her ass. My dick was on board with the way she felt molded into me, and he enlarged in anticipation. Liv lifted one eyebrow, a sexy smirk crossing her face.

"Someone else is up."

I groaned as she slid her hand between us, her fingers teasing the head of my cock. I grew harder, desire overtaking the teasing from minutes ago. Liv pressed against my chest, and I released my grip on her. She pushed up, settling on my hips, the warmth of her core covering my cock. I bucked up, my need beginning to overtake all my other senses. I gripped her hips as she slid along my thighs.

"You want me, Van?"

"Yeah, baby."

"Like this?" she teased, lifting one leg, letting my cock slide against her wetness.

"Fuck, yes. Give me more."

She shifted, taking the head of me inside her. I hissed at the sensation.

"More, Van? Tell me," she demanded. "Tell me exactly what you want."

I loved the bossy tone. The way she teased me. How my dick felt wrapped inside her. How much deeper it wanted to go.

I met her gaze. The golden color shone in the dim light, her passion glinting and growing.

"I want to be deep inside that tight pussy of yours," I informed her in a low voice. "I want you to ride me and come all over my cock."

Bracing herself, she slid down another couple of inches, holding herself over me. I pressed my head into the pillow, my back arching in anticipation of what was to come next.

"Jesus, Liv. I love how you feel around my cock. You are so fucking tight." I groaned. "I've never felt anything like it."

She bent low, her mouth hovering over mine. She uttered the dirtiest words I swore I had ever heard.

"Then use that huge cock of yours and loosen me up, Van."

She sat up, engulfing me. I shouted in eagerness as she began to move. She rocked slowly, bending back and gripping my thighs. I let her set the pace, her sounds of bliss spurring me toward my release.

She began to move faster, her breath coming out in quick spurts. The grip she had on my thighs tightened. Her back arched, her hair sweeping against my skin. She moaned my name, her pussy contracting around me. With a roar, I sat up, pushing her onto her back and lifting her leg over my shoulder. Mindlessly, I drove into her, not able to be close enough, deep enough, to satisfy me. She clawed at my back, crying out and spasming around me. The feel of her—her tight center, the way her body was wrapped around mine, the smoothness of her skin sliding along me, and her sounds tipped me over the edge and I came. Hard. Deep. Cursing and shouting her name, lost in the vortex of ecstasy racing through my body.

I gathered her into my arms and collapsed back onto the mattress.

"*Holy fuck*, Liv. What you do to me."

She hummed. "Yeah, I get that."

"I lose control with you. I can't even begin to describe what happens once we start with each other." I kissed the crown of her head. "I have never experienced that with anyone else. Ever."

She peeked up, her expression filled with doubt. "Really?"

I slid a finger under her chin. "Really. Making love to you is unlike anything I have ever done before now."

"Is that what we do? Make love?"

Frowning, I rolled over, so she was under me. I pushed the tangled hair away from her face. "Every. Time. Rough, fast, slow, sweet. Every time I'm with you, Liv."

"It's not just fucking, then?"

"There is definitely fucking, but even then, I'm loving you, Liv.

Always." I sucked in a much-needed breath. "Because I'm falling in love with you, and I'm showing you with my body. I need you to know that. Above all else, this means everything to me."

Her eyes—her beautiful, unique eyes—grew round. Her expression changed from worried and doubtful to happy. Joyful, in fact.

"Me too, Van. I feel so much for you and it should scare me because it's so sudden, but it doesn't. It feels so right. We feel so right."

I traced her mouth with my finger. "It's not sudden, Liv. I think we've been falling in love the whole time we've known each other. It's simply taken us a while to get to this point."

She kissed the end of my finger. "I think you're right." She played with the ends of my hair, her touch gentle. "You make me feel so special. I feel safe when I'm with you."

"You are safe. I will never let anything happen to you. You or Mouse. You both mean too much to me."

"I love the way you are with my daughter. She adores you."

"The feeling is mutual. There is nothing I wouldn't do for either of you."

"Do you know how rare you are?" she asked, her voice filled with wonder. "So many men would never be able to love another man's child."

"She is a part of you, Liv. In fact, to me, she is only yours. I see all your goodness in her. Your spirit—your loving heart. She's as easy to love as her mother."

She wrapped her arms around me, pulling me down to her chest. She sighed, the sound long and shaky.

"Thank you," she whispered.

I kissed her shoulder.

"I've got you, Livvy. Both of you."

The weekend went by too quickly. Before I knew it, we were picking up Sammy at Elly's place Sunday afternoon.

Mouse was excited to see both of us and clung to my hand when I lifted her into the back seat.

"You aren't going home right now, are you, Mr. Van?"

I tapped her on the nose. "I am, Mouse, but guess what?"

"What?"

"You and your mom are coming with me. I need to hear all about your weekend with Grammie, and I'm going to barbeque dinner for my two favorite girls."

Her eyes grew round. "Are we having hot dogs? I love hot dogs."

I chuckled, listening to her excitement and Liv's groan. "Hot dogs for sure. But you have to eat all your veggies, okay?"

She pursed her lips. "Are you gonna make your ranch sauce? Because I'll eat them all with that."

I laughed and kissed her head. She was far too cute and clever.

"Yep. The ranch is already chilling."

"Okay!"

I shut the door and turned to Liv. "All buckled in, Livvy?"

"Dinner?" she asked quietly. I hadn't asked her about dinner, but I hoped she was okay with my plans.

I leaned forward on the pretext of checking her seat belt. I brushed my lips over her cheek. "I'm not ready to give you up yet. You okay with that?"

Color spread across her cheeks, but her grin was teasing. "Well, as long as there's ranch..."

I shut the door, laughing again. They were both going to kill me— in the very best way.

Mouse's reaction to my house was nothing short of exuberant. She dashed from room to room, offering a nonstop dialogue on some improvements. Namely, more pink and some glitter.

Everywhere.

Her favorite room was the space I had always planned as an office but never really got around to completing, so it sat empty except for a few boxes. It overlooked the backyard, and the huge maple tree that stood by the house. The bay window offered a great vantage point, and Sammy climbed up onto the hard, wooden seat, informing me she would like a cushion there next time, so she could play in the window.

"Sammy," Liv admonished her. "Where are your manners? You can't demand things like that. You don't know if Van will invite us back again."

Sammy looked at her mother as if she was crazy. "He will, Mommy. He likes us a lot. I know this. I saw him kiss you earlier. You told me that's what adults do when they like someone," she protested. "And if he made me a bookshelf, I bet he can make a cushion."

Liv stiffened as I laughed at Sammy's logic and Liv's reaction to the kissing statement.

"Well, I can't Mouse. But I bet if I asked my mom, she could make you one. She loves to sew things."

She jumped off the window seat. "Can you phone her and ask?"

"Samantha Rourke!" Liv gasped.

I wrapped my arms around Liv's waist and tugged her back. "I met your mom," I murmured into her ear. "Only fair you meet mine."

She glanced up. "I wish you wouldn't encourage this behavior. This isn't like her at all."

I knew Sammy was watching us. Purposely, I leaned down and kissed Liv. Full on the mouth—a lingering, sweet kiss. Lifting my head, I met Sammy's pleased gaze. "I do like your mom, Mouse. I like you too. In fact, I think I'm going to be around a lot—what do you think about that?"

She didn't look surprised, instead, settling down on the wood seat and crossing her arms. "I'm good."

"Okay, let's call my mom about the cushion."

The call turned into a visit. My mom showed up a short time later, arms filled with material and her inquiring mother face firmly in place.

I introduced them, watching my mom's reaction closely.

"Mom, this is Liv and Sammy. Liv, this is my mom."

"Mrs. Morrison, it's so nice to meet you." Liv held out her hand.

My mom brushed it off, pulling her in for a hug. "Nonsense. It's Lila." She lowered herself to Sammy. "I've heard a lot about you, Sammy."

Sammy grinned at her. "Mr. Van calls me Mouse. Are you really his mom? He's so big! How did you carry him when he was my age?"

My mom laughed and took her hand. "He wasn't always so big. I'll show you pictures later." She winked. "And he still isn't too big for me to handle."

Sammy giggled. I watched fondly as my mom peppered Liv and Sammy with questions, discovering more about them in thirty minutes than I had found out in a year. Sammy had an equal number of questions for her. By the end of her visit, my mom loved Sammy. She loved Liv. It was as if she had known them for years, not hours. And not only had Sammy firmly ensconced herself in my mom's heart, we had another willing and eager babysitter.

"I'll take her anytime!" she exclaimed. "You two need alone time. I need Nanna time."

Sammy's eyes were huge. "Nanna? Can I call you Nanna?"

My mom didn't hesitate. "Nanna Lila. Yes."

I had held back my groan since Liv seemed fine with it. She had smiled and laughed at Sammy's enthusiasm. Mom also insisted she needed to meet Elly as soon as possible.

"Mom would enjoy meeting you too," Liv replied.

"Good. As soon as she's back from Florida, we'll have you all for dinner."

I didn't bother to object. There was no point, and besides, I was happy they were going to meet. Anything that kept Liv and Mouse close was good.

There was much discussion about the window cushion. I went downstairs once the words pink and sparkly were mentioned. I had a feeling it wasn't going to apply only to the cushion. My man card was in serious jeopardy of being revoked once Sammy and my mom got their hands on the spare room.

Still, I was okay with it. If Sammy was in the room, it meant Liv was here with me.

Win-win.

Tuesday morning, I frowned at my phone and the text that arrived.

> **Running late. Sammy is sick and waiting for backup.**

I responded right away.

> **It's fine. Take care of Mouse, and if you can't make it, you can meet with them another time. I hope she's okay.**

Her reply came back a few moments later.

> **A bit of the stomach flu, I think. Going around day care. My neighbor is going to sit with her while I come to the meeting, then will work from home this afternoon. Please apologize for me for being late. Be there asap.**

I shook my head. She was always so conscientious.

All is fine. Take your time.

Jordan came in, carrying two cups of coffee. He set one on my desk. "I spoke to Sandy. She's sending the guys down. I told her not to bother escorting them." He frowned. "Danishes aren't ready. I'll go grab some later."

I smirked. "Not ready, or you didn't want to be forced to share them with the people from WIN?"

He winked. "You know me too well."

I ran a hand over my face. "I haven't even looked at the file. Yesterday was crazy."

I had gone to the building with my dad, checking and measuring the various kinds of molding. Afterward, we had met with the company about matching the stain and the cuts. I had spent the afternoon putting out fires at one of the other places I was trying to finish up so I could concentrate on this huge project for Bentley. I had ended the day by meeting with my crews and turning over some other projects to my most trusted foremen. I would be available if needed, but as Bentley said, it was time to test their wings. The way he was going, we would all be busy for months to come. I had also spoken with the band, and we all agreed to take a break from any more gigs for a while until my schedule lightened up. I had barely had time to text Liv and hadn't seen her at all yesterday. Hearing Mouse was sick wasn't a great start to the day.

He waved his hand. "All under control. Today is simply to sit down, meet face-to-face. Then tomorrow we'll meet on site and go through everything step-by-step." He smirked. "After that, I'm done. I'll turn it over to you, and you can run the show."

"Liv is going to be late. Sammy is sick, and she's waiting on someone to look after her so she can get here."

"Kids," he deadpanned. "They bugger up plans all the time."

Before I could respond, there was a knock at the door. Two men stood, waiting for an invitation to come in. I stood at the same time

Jordan did. The older man walked in, tall and confident. His hair was silver, and his eyes pale blue and shrewd. He offered his hand.

"John Peters, owner of WIN."

I accepted his handshake. "Vince Morrison."

"I've heard a lot about you. All good, of course. I'm looking forward to seeing if your reputation holds true."

I inclined my head, letting his words pass. It felt like a challenge, and I refused to rise to the bait. I wasn't concerned with my reputation or his opinion. He was obviously all business, and it was fine with me—I could be the same way.

The other man stood back, his hands clasped behind his back. His dark-blond hair was slicked back, and his brown eyes were cool, but strangely familiar. He wasn't as big or as broad as me, but his stance was tall. His lips were pinched in a frown, and judging from the lines on his forehead, I guessed it was an expression he wore a lot.

John turned to him. "Nolan, come meet our clients."

Nolan stepped forward, his greeting short. "Gentlemen. Good to meet you." He glanced at Jordan. "Kids do bugger up the works."

Jordan frowned. "It was a joke."

Nolan lifted a shoulder. "Of course."

I had a feeling he didn't mean it. He didn't seem like a warm and fuzzy kind of guy.

He focused his gaze my way. "We'll be working closely together, Vince. I look forward to it. This is a great project."

There was something about him that bothered me immediately. I tried to shrug it off, wondering if knowing Jordan didn't personally like either of them was affecting my own opinion. I had to give them the benefit of the doubt.

"My mother calls me Vince. I go by Van around work."

He inclined his head. "Van."

I shook his hand. "Good to meet you as well. Grab a seat, and we'll get started." I indicated the small table we used for meetings. I had cleaned it off in preparation.

"Is your designer not joining us?" Nolan asked.

"She's running late. She'll be here shortly."

Nolan's mouth twisted in impatience. "I see."

The need to defend Liv was strong. "An emergency came up," I stated. "She's on her way."

He sat, looking displeased. "Personal business should be kept out of work hours."

Jordan scowled. "Life doesn't always work that way."

Nolan lifted his shoulders dismissively. "I suppose not for everyone. I make my job priority one."

I turned to my desk and grabbed some files to hide my anger. This guy was a piece of work. Arrogant and opinionated, the way Jordan had stated. Nevertheless, I only had to use his crew, not go for beers with him. I had worked with other subcontractors in the past that I didn't like personally. As long as the work was good, I could handle it.

John clapped him on the shoulder. "Relax, Nolan. Not everyone is as job-driven as you."

I sat down and picked up my cup, changing the subject. "Can we get you guys anything? Great café in the building. Or we have water and juice in the fridge."

They both declined.

Jordan and I opened the files, and we started discussing business. Personally, I knew we would never get along well. But professionally, I had to admit, Jordan was right again. They knew what they were talking about, and they wanted the project to go well. They both had ideas I liked, and my reticence eased as they spoke.

Hurried footsteps down the hall made me look toward the door. Liv rushed in, her arms full. Her hair was in its usual braid, a thick golden cord hanging over her shoulder. She looked frazzled and upset. I knew how seriously she took her job and would hate the fact that she'd arrived late. I stood, hoping to catch her eye and silently assure her all was well.

But she froze partway into the room. Her creamy complexion became pale. So pale, I was immediately concerned. She looked as if she was going into shock. Her eyes widened, her gaze focused on the man sitting at the table to my right. Her mouth opened, but no sound came out.

"Liv? You okay?" Jordan asked, concern lacing his voice.

Still, she was mute.

I began to move toward her, when Nolan spoke.

"No greeting for an old friend, Olivia?"

His words stopped me. I turned toward him with a frown.

He knew her? Had they worked together before? He never mentioned it. When she heard the name Nolan, she hadn't reacted at all.

What the hell?

Nolan remained seated and sighed impatiently. "Let's try this again. You were always a little slow at times." He cleared his throat. "Hello, Olivia. Long time."

I bristled at his words, my hands curling into fists. Before I could speak, Liv found her voice.

"What are you doing here?" she gasped through tight lips.

"I work for John now. I have for almost two years." He tilted his head. "I've been looking forward to this meeting. Seeing you again. I thought we could catch up."

If it was possible, she became paler. Every instinct in me told me to go to her. Shield her from what was happening—whatever it was. But I knew I couldn't.

Jordan spoke. "Liv, come sit down."

She moved, almost collapsing into the chair. I sat down, noticing the way her body trembled, and my anxiety grew. I wanted to reach across the table and hold her. Let her know she was safe. Mentally, I begged her to look at me, but her gaze remained focused across the table on the man who sat there.

John seemed confused but calm. Nolan leaned back in his chair looking smug, and my dislike deepened.

Liv drew in a deep breath. "Why are you here, Chris?"

Chris?

Now I was completely confused.

"For a job. And I go by Nolan now."

John laughed. "There were already three other Chris's in the company when I hired him. We started using last names, and it stuck." John clapped his shoulder. "He's my right hand. You'll be working together. It won't be a problem, will it, Olivia? Nolan says you go way back. He's been looking forward to seeing you."

It hit me.

Chris Nolan.

Liv's ex.

The bastard who'd mistreated her, then threw her and Sammy aside without regard.

Sammy's father. In the same room as Liv and me.

Holy fuck.

FOURTEEN

Van

I had never witnessed a person with as much strength as Liv until that moment. In the blink of an eye, she pulled herself together. Although she was still horribly pale, her voice was steady, and she was calm.

I was incredibly proud of her.

Reaching into her bag, she pulled out her laptop and a file. "Well, let's get down to business, shall we?" she asked, her voice cool.

Chris, or *Nolan*, smirked again. I wanted to wipe the expression off his face with my fist, but I refrained. If Liv could handle sitting at the same table as he was and could act professionally, so could I.

"How is life treating you, Olivia? How is—" he paused as if searching for a word "—your, ah, daughter?" He snapped his fingers. "Samantha, right?"

Liv's pen jerked, a jagged line appearing across the paper. Her voice was tight. "Everything is great, *Nolan*." She emphasized his name. "I prefer to keep my private life outside the office, if you don't mind."

"Unless it interferes with your work," Nolan pointed out.

Before she could respond, Jordan stepped in. "Liv is an exemplary employee. Here at BAM, family is important, and we understand things happen. Looking after your child always comes first."

Nolan's eyebrows rose slowly, silently stating his thoughts on Jordan's words.

John lifted his shoulder. "My company is my family, but I understand. I hope everything gets solved for you, Olivia."

Liv cleared her throat and acknowledged him with a tilt of her head. "Shall we get started?"

She finally met my gaze. Despite her bravado, I saw her turmoil. The anxiety she was trying to hide swirled in her eyes. There was a slight tremble to her hand. Her shoulders were stiff, her posture tense. Ignoring everything and everyone else, I spoke, my words directed only toward her.

"You take the lead, Liv. I'll follow."

She knew what I was saying. Whatever she needed, I was there for her. Her shoulders sagged a little—enough for me to know she understood me. I was there for her. Whatever she needed.

"Okay."

John and Nolan left. The meeting had gone surprisingly well after the bombs that were dropped when Liv arrived. When talking business, they were on point and seemed to have no problems with any of our requirements. I made sure to keep things short and to the point, and when the meeting was done, stood to let them know it was over.

"We'll see you on site tomorrow."

Once they were gone, Jordan turned to Liv.

"If I understood what just happened, I can cancel this right now. I'll go to Bentley and explain. But once we start, I can't break the contract."

She shook her head. "I appreciate it, Jordan, but it's not necessary."

He frowned, exchanging a glance with me. "That was Sammy's father, yes?"

Liv nodded.

"Can you work with him?" he asked. "Liv, I'm not blind. I saw the effect he had on you."

"I was shocked. I had no idea Chris was back in town. I hadn't heard about him in years." She sighed. "One thing I do know about him is that he had the highest standards when it came to business. The same insistence on perfection he had in his personal life was always applied to his work. He'll make sure the work is done properly. That's why Bentley went with WIN." She paused for a moment. "I'll figure out a way to make this work, Jordan."

She drew in a long breath. "You'll have more to do with him than I will. Both of them."

"Can you handle this?" I asked quietly.

She met my gaze. "I have no choice."

Jordan stood. "I'm going to let the two of you talk. I'll be back shortly."

He left, shutting the door behind him. In seconds, I had Liv in my arms, holding her close.

"Baby, are you all right?"

Her voice was muffled against my chest. "I can't believe he's here."

I pulled back, tilting up her chin. "I'll tell Jordan to cancel it. All of it. I'll tell Bentley it's on me—that I can't work with them."

She looked determined. "No, I don't want you to do that."

"This isn't about me being overprotective, Liv. This is about that asshole being around you. Harassing you. I don't want to risk it."

She smiled wanly. "And that's not being overprotective?"

Before I could speak, she cupped my cheek. "I've worked with clients before I haven't liked. I can handle this."

"But you don't have to," I insisted. "This is different. It's personal."

She sighed and stepped back from my embrace. "And what lesson would it teach my daughter, Van? To run when things are tough? To walk away is easier than to stay and be strong?"

"Sammy doesn't need to know about this lesson," I growled. "I'm worried about her too. What if that asshole makes trouble?"

"He didn't want us before, he doesn't want us now. He is here to show me he's still the 'man' and in control. Frankly, I don't care."

"You'll have to deal with him for a while—it's not an overnight job."

"So will you." She pointed out. "Way more than I will. Can *you* handle it?"

"As long as he behaves. If he steps out of line, I can't promise anything."

She regarded me anxiously. "Van, Chris is the kind of person who uses what he knows against people. If he thinks something upsets you, he'll find a way to do it, if only to piss you off." She paused, searching for words. "If he knows we're together, a couple, he'll use it. He'll say things to upset you. Make snide remarks about me. Talk about our past. You have to promise to ignore him. Whatever he says, whatever he does. It'll only be to get a reaction from you."

"So you want to keep us completely under wraps? Even more so than now?"

"Yes."

I had to agree with her. I had already witnessed the way he spoke down to Liv. If he knew we were together, he would make a point of running his mouth. Then I would have no choice but to introduce him to my fist. Jordan might turn the other cheek, but physical violence might not go over well with Bentley or John.

I huffed out an angry curse. "Okay. I'll watch myself. But I'm going to stick close when he's around. He'd better not have anything planned. I don't want him anywhere near Sammy either."

She tugged on her braid, rubbing the ends between her fingers anxiously. "I know. I have no idea what his plan is, and I don't care. He isn't here for me or Sammy. I know that for a fact—he's never expressed the slightest interest in her, other than to be clear he didn't want her and signing away his rights. I'll make sure not to talk about her or bring her to the jobsite. No doubt the draw of doing a project with BAM is what they were interested in, and I'm sure it's simply an added bonus for Nolan to be able to mess with me a little." She sighed and tossed her braid over her shoulder. "I don't think his boss has a clue, and I doubt he'll jeopardize his career and do anything stupid. I'll do what I have to. I don't answer to them, I answer to you. To BAM. He has no power over me business-wise, and I won't let him have power over me personally."

I yanked her back into my arms. "You're so damn strong, Livvy. You amaze me."

She looked up, her eyes luminous in the bright light. "I think knowing you'll be close helps me be strong, Van."

"I will. And anytime you need me, I'm there, do you understand?"

For a moment, she buried her face into my chest, and I held her. I meant what I said. She amazed me. She could have agreed, and in ten minutes I would have had Aiden and Bentley strike down the deal, and she never would have had to see them again. But she refused, and to me, it showed exactly how strong of a person Olivia Rourke was. I was proud of her.

She heaved a long breath and stepped back.

"Okay?" I asked quietly, running my finger down her cheek.

"Okay," she said. "We'll do this and make the buildings spectacular. Nothing else matters."

"Right." I nodded in agreement.

But I had a backup plan, and I was going to use it if needed.

Two weeks passed with no drama, and Liv and I relaxed a little. As much as I disliked it, I shared the onsite trailer with Nolan. Neither of us was interested in being friends, but I forced myself to at least be polite. There was a small office on each end of the trailer with a common room in between. I learned a lot about Nolan simply by listening and observing. He was a control freak, and as Liv had stated, a perfectionist. I often found my office door shut since it apparently bothered him to see my disorganized chaos. When he mentioned it, I simply grunted.

"I have more important things to do than dust my desk, Nolan," I muttered.

I didn't like having him around, but other than being an arrogant jerk with a lot of opinions, Nolan did exactly what he was supposed to do. As a precaution, either Jordan or I happened to be close when Liv showed up at the site. He was rarely alone with her, and I was always nearby. I didn't like the way he spoke to her or his snide remarks, but I managed to hold my tongue and ignore him. I was careful to treat Liv as a fellow coworker, never reacting to anything he said or did on a personal level, although more than once I had witnessed his remarks business-wise.

Liv knew what she was doing, and she didn't need some jerk telling her the best process for treating a wall or picking the right lighting. She could run circles around him any day, and I enjoyed listening to her tell him off by showing off her knowledge and outwitting him.

His crew arrived, and I met them all personally. I liked knowing the people who would be working on a project with me. After only a couple of days, I saw two things very clearly. The crew was hard-working, knew their stuff, and gave one hundred percent.

Second, Nolan was a terrible boss and treated the all-male crew as if they were beneath him. Whereas I worked alongside my men and women, he was the kind of foreman I despised. He sat in the trailer, barked out orders, never said thank you, and worked his men hard. The only time I saw him act decently was when John showed up on site, which I found interesting.

I had questioned the fact that Nolan had no women in his crew, and his reply said everything about him.

"Thank God I've avoided that so far," he snorted. "In my opinion, no women should be in construction. They aren't built for it."

"My female crew are outstanding," I replied. "I've never had an issue with gender. As long as their work is good, I'm all for it."

He regarded me with a slight sneer. "Better you than me." He walked away.

"Asshole," I muttered under my breath.

Beside me, one of his crew snickered, and I looked over, embarrassed at being heard.

"Sorry, that was uncalled for."

"Nope." Simon shook his head, putting his hard hat in place. "Spot-on," he replied, clapping me on the back as he walked past me. "Spot-on."

I stared at his retreating form. I liked Simon. He worked hard, never complained, and was a great leader for the other crew. I had already thought of poaching him once this project was done. I could certainly offer him a much better working environment.

I planned on looking into it as soon as this was complete.

Elly arrived home midweek, and I drove Liv to pick her up at the airport with Mouse in the back seat, excited to see her Grammie.

"What did she say—about Nolan's appearance?" I asked Liv, keeping my voice low, even though I knew Sammy was engrossed in the Disney DVD I had put in for her. She was singing along, her feet bouncing in time with the music.

"I haven't told her."

"Liv," I replied, shocked. "She should know. She would *want* to know."

She glanced behind her, smiling at Sammy and handing her a bag of goldfish to snack on.

"I will, Van," she assured me. "But I didn't want to do it over the phone and upset her."

"Okay. I'll take Mouse for a drive, and you can talk."

"No, it's fine. We're having girls' night on Friday, and once Sammy goes to bed, I'll fill her in."

"Friday?" I frowned. "I wanted you girls on Friday."

She patted my arm. "You have to share us again, Van. You've had us all to yourself for almost two weeks."

"Not true," I disagreed. "My mom has been around a lot. She hogs both of you. Now Dad is getting in on the action too."

I had taken them to lunch at my parents'. Dad adored Liv, and Sammy had charmed him in about two minutes flat. He had taken her to his workshop, insisted she call him Poppa Joe, and later during lunch informed me we had to design a headboard to go with Sammy's bookshelf.

"She had a perfectly good headboard," Liv protested.

"It doesn't really match," I pointed out, noticing Mouse was about to fall off her chair in excitement.

"Yeah, Mommy. There's no glitter."

"God forbid," Liv muttered.

"Yeah," I repeated. "We need to fix that."

My dad agreed. "I'm on it."

Mouse's squeal was loud.

Liv laughed quietly, bringing me back to the moment. "Not that much, Van. It's only one night. I need the time with my mom."

"I know," I admitted grudgingly. "I'm teasing. Sort of," I added under my breath.

Liv shook her head in amusement.

"Are you sure you want to wait until then to tell her?"

"It's tomorrow. Nothing is going to change between tonight and tomorrow. I'll let her get settled, and I'll talk to her. Promise."

"Okay." I slid my hand over hers. "But only the one night, right?"

She faced the window, but I saw her smile. "Yes. I'll make it up with dinner on Saturday."

"Lunch," I insisted. "I'll take you all to lunch. Mouse and I can have some time at the park."

Sammy clapped her hands and I chuckled.

"See? Win-win."

We arrived at the airport, and Elly was waiting outside.

"Wait until Grammie hears we're going to the park!" Sammy crowed.

"Yeah." I grinned. "It'll be the highlight of her day."

All Liv could do was laugh.

Elly looked happy and rested. I was all the happier to see her when she informed us she was taking Mouse home with her.

"I've missed my girl too much—I need some Grammie time."

"We're having a girls' night tomorrow," Liv reminded her.

"That's at your place. Tonight, I get Sammy. She has clothes at my place. I'll keep her tomorrow, and we'll meet at your apartment when you get off work. I'm sure Van would keep you company for a while tonight, won't you, Van?"

I met her eyes in the mirror and winked.

"For a while," I agreed.

"Good, it's settled."

We dropped her off, and I waited in the truck while Liv went upstairs and made sure they were okay. She slid back into the cab and turned to me.

"Well, it appears we have a free evening."

I grinned, sliding my hand up her arm and wrapping it around her neck, tugging her close.

"Whatever will we do with ourselves?"

Her breath washed over my face as she pressed her lips to the edge of mine. "I'm sure we'll come up with something."

"Something is up, all right," I chuckled against her mouth.

"Take me home, Van."

I kissed her hard. "You got it."

I was tired the next morning—in the very best of ways. Knowing I wouldn't have much time with Liv this weekend, I had kept her up most of the night. I had her on the sofa, in the hall, and the kitchen, then again in her too-small-for-me bed, the frame creaking in protest.

I left her early, going home to shower and change. Her kiss goodbye had been sweet and lingering. She was on my mind all day.

I was on site most of the day, dealing with some issues and overseeing that we were on schedule.

I went to grab coffee and overheard a conversation between Simon and Nolan.

"I said no. We're behind, and I need it made up today."

"I only need a couple of hours later, Nolan. My kid is sick, and my wife needs me to pick up the younger one. I'll be back fast."

"Make other arrangements. I said no."

He walked away and I stood, observing Simon. His shoulders dropped, and he shook his head. He saw me and lifted his shoulder in resignation and walked away. Nolan never glanced back or noticed me standing there.

I walked to the coffee shop, seething. What a jerk. Simon worked hard, and in the couple of weeks I had observed him, rarely took a break, asked for nothing, and gave Nolan his all. A couple of hours to pick up his child shouldn't be an issue. I knew I couldn't say anything which frustrated me. Jordan had made it very clear when I informed him of my dislike for the way Nolan treated his staff.

"His staff, Van. Remember that. He is there to make sure the job is done. Your job is to make sure he follows through the way you want the project done. Not how he treats his workers." He warned me. "Don't make this personal."

He was right. Simon wasn't my employee, but as I waited for my coffee, an idea came to me that might work.

I spent some time measuring for the new woodwork, then headed to find Nolan. As usual, he was in the trailer—a place I avoided as much as I could. This afternoon, he wasn't even bothering to pretend to be working. His feet were kicked up on his desk, a folder open on his lap. He looked startled when I walked in, and I had the feeling if I had done so quietly, I would have caught him asleep. As it was, I gritted my teeth, trying to be polite as I paused at his office door.

"Nolan."

"Van. What can I do for you?"

"Everything going okay?"

"For sure. We're on track, even a little ahead."

Bastard, my inner voice sneered. *Liar*.

"Could you spare someone? I need something picked up, but Liv and Jordan will be here shortly, and I want to be part of the meeting. It'll only take an hour. Two, tops. I'll provide the transportation."

"Sure," he agreed magnanimously. "Grab one of the guys."

"Thanks."

I turned and left before he could state which guy and hurried to find Simon. I slid my truck keys into his hand along with a slip of paper.

"Go do what you have to do. Pick this up on your way back. It's ready, and they'll drop it in the truck bed. It's right around the corner, but if anyone asks, you went up to Scarborough to pick it up. And there was traffic. I got you about two hours."

His eyes widened. "You don't have to do this, Van."

I disagreed. "It's your family, Simon. Go. Fast. Before he sees and sends someone else. I happened to cross paths with you, and I asked. Got it?"

His expression was filled with relief. "Thanks, man. I owe you."

He hurried away as Liv and Jordan arrived. I watched her approach, my vision focused entirely on her. She was in jeans with a large plaid shirt on top, the sleeves rolled up. Steel-toed boots on her feet and a hard hat topping her golden hair completed the package.

She was sexy as hell.

I narrowed my eyes as she got closer, not bothering to hide my amusement.

Jordan went past me with a wink, heading to the trailer. Liv stopped, smiling up at me.

"Hi."

"Nice shirt," I murmured, fingering the material. "Looks rather familiar."

"It should. It's yours."

"Wearing it like armor against the enemy, Liv?"

"I was thinking more like your arms around me, but whatever works." She lifted the collar, inhaling. "It smells like you. I smell like you. I like it."

I was torn between being touched by her words and being turned on.

"*Jesus*, Liv. You say shit like that, and you expect me to act professionally? All I want right now is to drag you over to the closest building with some privacy and fuck you," I hissed out.

She winked, her mood light and happy. "Maybe later."

She moved past me, purposely brushing against my arm. Her fingers flicked against my hand, quickly squeezing it, then she moved away. I turned my head and watched her until she disappeared around the corner. I would give her a few minutes before I followed her to the trailer.

I need those few moments for my dick to soften.

Damn tease.

The meeting went well, even though I knew how Nolan made the deadlines he promised. He drove his crew hard, with the main incentive being they got to keep their job. With construction work down overall, many of them had no choice. I had noticed several new faces already, and I assumed when it came to how he ran his operation, that was the norm.

Jordan went to check on a few things, and Simon came into the trailer. He handed me my keys.

"Everything good?" I asked.

His eyes spoke volumes, but his words were short. "Yes, sir. I handled it all."

"Thanks."

"You sent Simon?" Nolan asked.

I feigned indifference. "He was the one I saw first. I didn't think you'd mind."

"No, it's fine."

We went into the building, checking out the work. The progress was fast, and soon we would be moving into the next step of rebuilding and outfitting. I ran my hand along the walls.

"Nice work. Your crew does nice work."

"Yep. It meets my standards or they're gone." Nolan eyed Liv. "My standards are high. In every aspect of my life. I only accept the best."

She didn't react. She turned and walked away. I wanted to laugh and tell him she *was* the best and he was a narcissistic asshole, but I refrained.

We walked toward the fence. The sound of my name being called made my stomach drop when I saw who was shouting it.

Elly and Mouse were by the fence, waving frantically.

Beside me, Liv gasped quietly. I stepped forward, hoping to cut them off, but Mouse broke free, rushing toward me. I met her halfway, scooping her up and carrying her back toward Elly, hoping neither Nolan nor Elly noticed the other person and I could get them out of there.

But Mouse only laughed and stretched out her arms. "Mommy! Come with me and Mr. Van! Grammie is gonna make us all supper!"

Nolan stiffened and turned to Liv. She moved past him, hurrying toward us. Elly's expression was shocked, and she froze, staring at Nolan. At the fence, I stood Mouse beside her.

"Why did you take me away, Mr. Van?"

I swallowed down the truth. "You can't be in here without a hard hat, Mouse."

Liv arrived, her face pale.

"Mom."

Panicked, Elly looked at her, then Nolan, who was heading our way. "We wanted to surprise you. Take both of you to dinner. I wanted to see these buildings you've been talking about." She blinked. "I didn't know…"

"It's okay, Elly," I urged. "We'll explain. Why don't you take Mouse, and we'll meet you?"

Elly's gaze swung to mine, and she must have seen my panic. She reached for Mouse's hand. "Good idea."

But it was too late. Nolan arrived, his voice cold. "Hello, Eleanor."

Mouse, the ever-friendly, sweet little girl she was, looked up, already smiling and ready to meet a new friend.

"Hi!"

He glanced down, his face contorting. I knew what he saw. A miniature version of her mother, the only difference the eyes she inherited from her father—him—gazing upward.

"Hello."

"I'm Sammy. But Mr. Van calls me Mouse." With those words, she wrapped an arm around my leg. "He made me the best bookcase in the whole world, and we have tea parties together!"

Nolan looked at me, then Liv, realization dawning.

"Oh, really?"

"Sammy, hush. Go with Grammie." Liv said, her voice shaking.

Nolan bent one leg, kneeling close to Sammy. "No, it's fine, Olivia. Tell me, *Mouse*, what else does *Mr. Van* do for you?"

I knew in that instant we were fucked.

FIFTEEN

Van

Elly's teacup hit the saucer with a clatter. Liv reached over, patting her hand. "Mom, please calm down."

"I didn't know." Elly stared at Liv. "Why didn't you tell me?"

Liv sighed, running a weary hand over her face.

"I planned on telling you tonight, Mom. I didn't want to upset you while you were visiting Aunt Jane." Liv's shoulders dropped. "Bad decision, I guess."

Elly sighed, resting her head on her hand. "What have I done?"

I leaned forward. "Stop this—both of you. As far as we know, nothing is going to happen. He saw Sammy. Talked to her for a few minutes and walked away. That's it. It's not as if he didn't know about her."

Even as I spoke the words, I knew I was lying.

Liv shook her head. "He's going to cause trouble. Now that he's seen her, he's going to do something. Even if it's verbal. It's the way he works."

I glanced down the hall to make sure Mouse was still in her room. All three of us had done our best to act normally. I had ordered pizza, knowing Elly wouldn't feel like cooking, and the treat would distract Mouse from the lack of conversation. She was happily playing in her room, waiting for dinner to arrive.

"He signed his parental rights away," I insisted. "He can't do anything aside from asking some questions which you don't have to answer. He has no claim on her."

"I know he has no interest in being a father, but he can make my life miserable for the next while." She met my eyes. "Yours too. He saw how Sammy was with you, Van. He knows we're more than coworkers."

I covered her hand with mine. "I know. I don't care, though."

She looked over my shoulder. "He's going to start with his remarks. He doesn't want us, but he doesn't want me to be happy either. He'll belittle me every chance he gets, the same as when we were together. Remarks about my clothes, hair, weight. He'll question every decision. He'll question your decisions. Say things about when we were a couple. Tell you all the things he found wrong with me." She snorted. "Tell you how I didn't meet his high standards."

I tilted my head at her words with a frown. "He can go fuck himself." I looked at Elly with a shrug. "Sorry."

"Not a problem. I agree," she said.

I hunched closer. "Liv, I don't give a rat's ass about what he says or thinks. His thoughts mean nothing to me at all. I hate the fact that what he says might hurt you. But if you think they'll sway me in any fashion, you're wrong."

She nodded, not meeting my eyes. I looked at Elly and she stood.

"I'm going to check on Sammy."

"Hey," I called softly when Elly left the room.

Liv looked up, and I tugged on her hand, bringing her onto my lap. "Nothing," I repeated, "Nothing he says matters."

"He's awful," she whispered. "I don't want him near Sammy."

"I don't want him near either of you."

"Not much choice right now."

"We can ask Bentley to pull you from the project."

"Then he still wins. I love this project, and I want to see it through. If I let him chase me away, he still wins."

"Then you aren't alone with him. We won't give him the chance to say or do anything."

She pushed off my knee and paced, rubbing her temples.

"In theory, that's great. But it won't work, Van. There are times I will be alone with him. In fact, I have to be. You can't shadow me all day and be effective in your role. And I can't let him know how much he affects me." She pushed off me and paced the kitchen. "He has never been physical. There are only words. I'm not the same young, insecure girl I was six years ago. I can ignore him now because he means nothing. I'll deal with it, and you have to let me." She leaned against the counter. "And you have to deal with it too. We both have to see this through. It's six weeks until his part of this project is done, right?"

I hated she was right about this, but I knew she was. If I shadowed her, it gave that asshole more ammunition. We both had to ignore it.

"Yes."

"Then for six weeks, we handle it. We don't react. We don't engage unless it is work-related." She lifted one shoulder. "He's the typical bully on the playground. The one who knows your knee is sore, so that's where he'll hit you. He'll look for the weak spot, and he'll keep pushing at it until he gets a reaction. Don't give it to him."

I nodded grimly. Not punching him in the face was going to be an exercise in restraint for me.

She approached me, standing between my legs and laying her hand on my chest. "His opinion or thoughts mean nothing anymore, Van," she repeated. "You do. Your positive words and support mean everything. He can't change that."

I lifted her hand and kissed the palm. "I'm here, Liv. There is nowhere else I want to be and no one else I want to be with. You amaze me, and I *adore* you."

"I've never been adored before."

"It's only the tip of the iceberg of how I really feel," I confessed. I wanted to tell her I loved her, but I didn't want it to be because of this shit situation. I wanted to tell her when the time was right and we could explore it. When we were both ready.

Her eyes glowed. "I adore you right back," she whispered. "I'm right there with you."

I held her face and kissed her. "Good."

The buzzer sounded, and I stood to go get the pizza. "Six weeks. We can do this."

She sighed. "Six weeks."

It took him three days to get under my skin. He was, as Liv described him, insidious. His remarks were snide and nasty, yet never said directly to Liv or me, instead muttered observations or offhand sentences. I tried to hold back, but at times, I couldn't. He hated my responses, but he'd hate my fist in his face even worse.

"Jeez—does she own anything feminine?" he muttered eyeing Liv as she crossed the pavement, her steel-toed boots hitting the ground in easy strides.

"She doesn't need it. She's sexy enough wearing my shirt." I smirked.

Nolan stomped away.

"Olivia is late again." He glanced at John. "It happens a lot. I wouldn't allow it."

Jordan saved me from responding.

"Liv is with another client. When she is done with them, she'll arrive and give you the same undivided attention she gives them. It's one of the things BAM admires most about her. If we don't have an issue with it, neither should you. Let's carry on."

Nolan scowled and shut up. Then I noticed his remarks began to change in their direction.

"Who is looking after your daughter while you're working late—again?" he asked one night at a meeting.

"My mother has her," Liv replied shortly.

"Hmmm," he muttered. "That must be difficult for her. Never having a set schedule. Kids need that."

Liv's eyes narrowed. "Since when did you become an expert on what kids need?"

He lifted one shoulder and dropped it.

Until the next time.

Jordan, Liv, and I were talking about another project we had on the go, discussing time frames and laughing about the fact that Bentley never stopped.

Nolan leaned against my doorframe.

"Do you have to work so much because of your student loans, Olivia? Did you ever pay those off, or are you still ignoring them?"

She turned, her eyes flashing. "I never ignored them, Nolan." She sneered his name. "I had only finished school when we met, then I had other priorities. Unlike some people, I don't turn my back on my responsibilities." She paused. "And I don't believe it's any of your concern."

"That depends."

"On?" she demanded.

Again, he lifted his shoulder and shrugged. Liv turned back and look at Jordan.

"Sorry. Where were we before we were so rudely interrupted?"

I curled my hands around the arms of my chair in order not to punch Nolan. It took everything in me to stay quiet and ignore the way he baited her.

Then there was the day Elly fell ill with another headache. Liv was in an important meeting with a supplier, and the woman at the day care wasn't available to stay late, so I offered to go and get Sammy.

"But you have a meeting at five. They're bringing the wood samples for you to compare. I can reschedule."

I sighed. "No. You need to be at your meeting. Nolan is usually gone by four. I'll go get her, and she'll be fine. She can be my assistant for an hour—she'll get a kick out of walking through the building with me and measuring things. I'll buy her a hard hat of her own—she'll love it. My meeting will only take an hour—maybe less."

"What if he sees her?"

"So he sees her. He knows about us, Liv. We said we weren't going to let him dictate our actions, and we won't. I don't care if he sees me with her. I won't let him near her."

We went back and forth until she grudgingly agreed.

Nolan stayed later than usual and saw me lifting Sammy from the back seat of my truck. I avoided the trailer, slid the hardhat on her head, lifted her onto my back for a "piggy ride," and hurried to the building I was getting ready to start on. His crew had moved onto the next one, so it was empty and safe for Mouse to be in with me.

As we waited for the samples to arrive, I kept her busy. She held the tape measure for me as I worked. Told me how pretty the room would look in pink. Asked a million and one questions about the building, what I did, and told me how she was gonna draw and build stuff when she got big too.

I ruffled her hair.

"I bet you will, Mouse. You'll be great."

"I'm hungry, Mr. Van."

I pulled a KitKat from my pocket. I had a sandwich for her in my trailer, but I didn't want to take her there. This would suffice until I was done. I was certain Nolan would be gone by that time.

I was wrong.

He appeared in the doorway, staring at us. Mouse looked up and grinned, her innocent belief that everyone Mommy knew was a friend once again shining through.

"Hi!"

"Hi. What have you got there?"

"Mr. Van gave me a KitKat for a snack. It's a secret," she giggled, holding a finger to her lips. "Don't tell Mommy."

"Anything else he does you aren't supposed to tell Mommy?" he asked, his words so insulting, I was on my feet and heading his way before I could think. I pushed him into the hall and pulled the door closed behind me, ready to punch him.

It was only his self-satisfied expression that uncurled my fist.

I glowered at him, my voice cold and low so Mouse couldn't hear me.

"Shut your fucking mouth."

"Are you going to make me?" he sneered.

"You'd like that, wouldn't you?"

He shrugged. "Not my fault you took what I said the wrong way."

"I took it the exact way you meant it. You're a fucking bastard."

He crossed his arms. "Is that a fact?"

I stepped forward menacingly. "You say shit like that again, Nolan, I swear, I will take you out."

He smirked. "I was wondering, Van. Why the hell would you be so interested in another man's daughter?"

"She is Liv's daughter." I stressed her name. "No one else's."

One eyebrow rose.

"Immaculate conception? Is that what Olivia told you?"

"Sperm doesn't make you a father."

"Neither does fucking the mother after the fact."

"Shut. Your. Face," I growled, my hands once again curling into fists.

He stepped closer, his voice taunting. "Go ahead. I think you'd like to take a swing at me. God knows I want to wipe that holier-than-thou look off your face."

I leaned into him, our faces inches apart. Hatred poured from my words as I snarled at him. "Then let's go outside. I'll let you take the first swing. But trust me, it'll be the only one you get."

We were locked in a staring contest when Simon came up the steps and cleared his throat, breaking our standoff.

"Am I interrupting?"

I stepped back, common sense dissipating my anger.

"No. I was making sure Nolan here understood something."

"And I was saying out loud what I think," he replied.

"Think whatever the fuck you want to. Keep it to yourself. Stay the hell away from me, Liv, and Sammy," I uttered in a low voice.

He stormed past me, purposely pushing his shoulder against mine. I refused to let him see the twinge of pain it caused me.

I turned and watched him walk away.

I had a feeling the ugly situation was about to get worse.

Liv

I steeled myself as I entered the trailer. I hated meeting with *Nolan,* and I especially hated these last-minute meetings he requested, but it was part of my job. I admit it was easier when Van or Jordan were there, but he still found ways to get his cutting remarks in and I hated the smug look he got when the guys would appear. He knew why, and it gave him more pleasure to insult me in front of them. I did my best to ignore him, and I tried not to let it upset me. That seemed to anger Nolan further and his words became even sharper, desperately trying to find a weak spot on me he could hit. I, in turn, refused to let him find it.

Nolan was at his desk, and as usual, everything was in order. Papers piled neatly, folders stacked, pens gathered together in a cup holder, and the surface of the desk clean. His hard hat and boots were lined up precisely by the wall. A cup of coffee sat to his right, a paper coaster protecting the desk. I tried not to roll my eyes at his useless touch—it was so Nolan.

He always insisted on order both at home and in the office. My "messiness" had been a source of irritation for him many times. He hated my "scribbles," as he called them, on the table. The way my hands were often dotted with markers, or the fact that I stuck pencils in my hair. How he kept his desk so dust-free and tidy in a construction site was beyond me, but I pitied anyone who messed up his area. I glanced toward the other office Van used. It, too, was piled with papers, but they weren't in order. Blueprints were pinned haphazardly to the wall in order of importance. Pencils lay in various spots, and half-filled cups sat in others. A spare hard hat sat on the edge of the desk. The two variances said so much about the two men. One real and involved, living and breathing his work—the other nice to look at, without much happening otherwise.

I pulled back the visitor chair in front of Nolan's desk as far as I could without being obvious and sat down, pulling out my tablet for notes. I drew in a long breath to calm myself and met his frosty gaze.

"Nolan."

He inclined his head. "Olivia."

"You wanted to meet? Something about questions you had?"

He pursed his lips. "More about some thoughts I've been having."

"All right," I said, getting my stylus ready. "What kind of thoughts?"

He lifted his coffee cup to his lips and took a sip, carefully setting it back down on the desk. "It's more a personal thing."

Every nerve in my body tensed. The blank smile on my face froze.

"Personal?" I repeated.

He leaned back, regarding me. "I've been thinking about my life. Things I want to change, that sort of thing."

His words made my stomach clench.

I bent down and slid the tablet back into my bag to give me a moment to calm down. I sat up and crossed my legs. "Oh?" I managed to get out, my hands clasped into fists at my sides.

He nodded, already enjoying my discomfort. I forced myself to relax.

"It's always a good thing to reevaluate at times," I offered.

"Exactly." He studied me. "Sometimes what we want changes."

I shrugged. "That's great. But I really don't see what it has to do with me. Unless it's about work, we have nothing to discuss."

"That's where you're mistaken, Olivia."

"Oh?" I asked, digging my fingers into my legs.

"I made an error in my past, and I want to correct it."

I already knew what he was going to say. I felt it in my gut, and I steadied myself before replying.

"And that is?"

"I want to get to know my daughter."

"Forget it," I snapped.

He narrowed his eyes. "I'm her father."

"No. You're her sperm donor. You signed away your parental rights."

"I was young. Scared. I wasn't ready. I made a mistake."

What bullshit.

I stood. "Sometimes we have to live with our mistakes. This is one of those times, Chris."

"Nolan," he corrected. "I prefer Nolan."

I barked out a humorless laugh. "Why? Because a new name makes you a different person? You're the same, self-centered, nasty person I knew years ago. Nothing has changed except you don't hide it as well. You treat people like shit, *Nolan*. Your employees, your clients, everyone. Unless you deem them important in your eyes, they're beneath you and you treat them that way. If you think I'm going to give you the chance to get your claws into *my* daughter, you can forget it. I will not subject her to your cruelty or your treacherous words that would destroy her self-confidence. You can forget it."

"She's my daughter too. I have rights."

"You have nothing!" I yelled, suddenly furious. "You threw her and me away as if we were garbage. You called her an *it*. As if she was nothing. You wanted me to abort her! You had no interest before, and you have none now—you're only doing this to get at me!"

"I'm doing this because she's my daughter and she needs a father. That's me."

"What the hell do you know about what she needs?" I seethed. "You haven't been there for her—not once. Not when she was colicky, not when she cut her first tooth or took her first step—never. Being a father isn't just biological."

He stood, leaning on his desk, anger rolling off of him. "But your boyfriend is? I see him sniffing around, acting as though she belongs to him. Like you belong to him. He is nothing. She carries my DNA, and I'm going to be part of her life."

I gaped at him. "That's it, isn't it? The same old Chris. You want what you can't have. You saw how much she loves Van and it pissed you off. He's pissed you off. The fact that you can't get to me anymore pissed you off. So now you want to take that from him. Destroy my life and hers." I shook my head. "You don't give a fuck about her. This is another one of your little games. Well, it's not going to work. You signed away your rights, so it's too late."

I grabbed my bag and spun on my heel. His voice stopped me before I reached the door.

"I've already contacted my lawyer about having my rights reinstated."

Panic seized my chest, but I refused to back down.

"It's rare that it's allowed." I knew it, because I had checked.

He shrugged. "Rare, but it happens. Once I tell my story and prove what I have to offer, I think I have a good shot."

"What you have to offer?" I repeated with a laugh. "A biting, critical tongue and an overzealous need for perfection?"

He crossed his arms. "When my father died, I became quite wealthy. I have a steady job, a boss who thinks I walk on water, a house with a yard, a housekeeper, and the means to provide my daughter with the best education and care money can buy." He paused. "I'm also engaged to a woman who wants kids and will love Samantha as her own. Together, we can provide a stable, loving home with two parents." He tilted his head, studying me. "As opposed to a single mother who requires the backup of her boyfriend and mother to make sure her daughter is looked after. Who is barely able to meet her financial obligations, has no car, no savings toward Samantha's education. A woman who dresses like a dyke and hangs around construction sites likes she's one of the boys, choosing to work erratic hours before going home to her rented accommodation and her neglected daughter."

The air flew out of my lungs in a long gasp.

Everything he said was true but taken out of context. But I knew what he was doing—already building a case against me. Making himself sound perfect, and me unstable. I refused to let him see how terrified his words made me feel.

"You are such a bastard," I hissed. "I will fight you every step of the way."

He leaned against his desk. "I've already instructed my lawyer to petition for visitation."

"Over my dead body. You will lose."

He picked up his cup, taking a long sip, not at all worried about my reaction.

"We can do this one of two ways, Olivia. You let me see her, get to know her, and we arrange something legally between us, or I fight you. I have the means, the best lawyer money can buy, and the time. I can make this as ugly as possible, or we can work together, and nobody gets hurt."

"Except Sammy. Nothing good will come from her spending time with you."

"It's going to happen. You know what I'm like. When I set my mind to something, I don't give up. You fight me, you risk legal bills you have no means to pay and losing your daughter completely."

I couldn't believe this was happening. "You threw us away. You made this choice."

He smiled, a cold, evil one which made me shiver.

"Not when I tell the story, *Livvy*." He sneered Van's nickname for me with so much venom, I could feel the hatred in his voice.

He stood, crossing his arms. "Van Morrison is not going to get to play daddy to my daughter. You're going to lose, and if you fight me, I'll make sure you lose big-time."

His words made me feel ill.

"When I'm done, you'll be lucky to see her on weekends," he threatened.

I refused to let him see how terrified I was. How his words were affecting me. I picked up my bag and headed for the door. I paused before I walked out. "Bring it on, Chris," I said, my voice filled with loathing. "I'm not the only one with something to lose here."

I walked out before I collapsed.

He had found my weak spot and hit it so hard, I was bleeding.

SIXTEEN

Van

I wrote down the last of the measurements and snapped the cover shut on my notebook. "Okay, I'm going to double-check all this, then order all the millwork for the building." I clapped Simon on the shoulder. "Thanks for the help."

He grinned. "No problem. I hope I get a chance to help with the installs. I love that part."

I had discovered Simon shared my love of woodworking. He showed me some of his work he had pictures of on his phone, and I could see he was a real craftsman. He told me he often did jobs on the side, and if I could arrange it, I planned to hire him to help once the contract with WIN was over.

Which couldn't come fast enough. Not beating the shit out of Nolan was getting harder every day. Between the way he ran his crew and his snide comments, I was ready to blow. Liv was so anxious, the dark circles prominent under her eyes and the stress she carried evident in the tense set of her shoulders. It was killing me. But he was a smart bastard. His remarks were either muttered to himself or done in such a way he could defend himself, passed off as "teasing." My hands were tied about how he ran his crew since he was getting the job done, and I had no control over his jurisdiction. John was rarely on-site, and when he was, Nolan was smart enough to behave.

It was driving me crazy.

I shook my head to clear it and turned, running my hand over one of the intact window casings. "I want to reproduce all this as close to original as possible. It's going to be gorgeous when we're finished."

Simon stepped beside me, admiring the beveled edges and intricate cuts. "It will. Your boss has an eye for detail and unique opportunities." He laughed humorlessly. "Nolan would have bulldozed these places to the ground and rebuilt."

The words were out before I could stop them. "Nolan is a short-sighted, narcissistic asshole."

He guffawed, and I had the decency to look ashamed. "Sorry. I know he's your boss."

"He is. That is all he is. My boss. I work hard and earn my paycheck. I don't owe him anything more than that. He doesn't deserve anything more than that, frankly."

"Have you thought of leaving?"

"Only every day. I apply for every job that comes up, but there isn't much these days. Building has changed. So much is prefab off site and brought in and put together like a jigsaw puzzle." He pushed his hard hat up his forehead, wiping his brow. "I kinda miss the old days of building from the ground up and being proud of the work I've done. Now they just need strength and to be fast." He shrugged. "I do what I have to and put up with Nolan because WIN pays well, and I have to think of my family. I don't have to like it—I only have to put in the hours and go home to what really matters."

"He isn't easy on you."

"No, he isn't. But to be honest, I've worked for worse. John runs a good business. No cutting corners or shoddy workmanship allowed. I'd rather put up with the likes of Nolan's attitude than risk my life with negligent operators or be forced to build shit, if I'm being honest."

"I can understand that."

"That's why I do some small side jobs. I get to indulge in what I love doing and it helps make the Monday-to-Friday gig bearable," he explained. "This one is actually great. I'm enjoying working on this one with you, Van."

I was about to respond in kind, when I saw the trailer door fling open and Liv rush through it, her steps fast. Nolan appeared in the door and shouted something after her, but with the distance, I didn't know what it was. I knew, however, it wasn't good.

"Shit," Simon swore. "Is he at it again?"

Wordlessly, I turned and jogged down the stairs, needing to get to Liv. I grabbed a spare hard hat as I went and met her partway across the pavement.

"You need to be in a hard hat, Liv," I muttered as I placed it on her head. "What the fuck did he do?"

She was so pale, I was sure she was going to faint. Ignoring the looks and not giving a shit about the unwritten rule we had, I wrapped an arm around her waist and steered her toward the building. She was shaking, her body vibrating so hard, I was surprised she could walk. As soon as I got her into the building, I pulled her into the closest apartment, shut the door, and yanked her into my arms. She gripped my waist, burying her face into my chest. I tugged off the hard hat and stroked the back of her neck for a minute as I murmured quiet reassurances.

"I have you, Liv. It's okay. Whatever it is, it's okay."

A long shudder went through her, and I tightened my grip, pressing her into my body.

"Did he touch you?"

If he had, I was going to kill him.

"No," she whispered.

"Was he being an insulting asshole again?"

She lifted her face, her eyes dry but panicked. "He wants to take Sammy away. He says he's going to fight me."

My response was instinctive and honest.

"The *fuck* he is. No one is taking your daughter from you, Liv. Not in this lifetime."

"He's hired a lawyer. He's going to try to get his rights back. He-he wants visitation."

I slid my hands up her neck, cupping her cheeks. "I don't care what he wants. Our girl is staying where she belongs. With us. He doesn't get her. Do you understand?"

"How am I going to fight this?"

Her heartbreak and pain bled from her eyes.

I held her face tighter. "You're going to fight it with me. And we're not going to lose." I wrapped her back into my embrace. "I won't allow this to happen, Liv. I swear to you."

She fell forward, my words giving her what she needed for now —strength.

I held her, then tilted up her chin.

"Tell me everything he said."

Listening to her repeat the conversation with Nolan, I became enraged. His remarks were insulting, degrading, and all lies. Liv grabbed my hand as I swung around, determined to cross the site and teach him a lesson he would never forget.

"Don't, Van. It's exactly what he wants—you going off in a rage and attacking him. It would only add to his story and give him more ammunition against me," she pleaded.

She was right, but I had to hit something. Take out my wrath. Liv gasped as my fist plowed through a piece of drywall, the sound exploding in the room.

"That fucking bastard—I swear I'm going to kill him," I raged.

She was at my side instantly, inspecting my hand. She clucked at the scraped flesh and rapidly bruising skin.

"Look what you've done," she admonished.

"It was the wall or his head. The wall, I can fix. His head, I can't."

She met my gaze. "This isn't your fight."

"The hell it isn't."

She sighed, the sound a painful shudder of the air leaving her lungs. "Are you sure I'm worth it?"

I held her chin with my good hand. "Absolutely."

Her phone rang. She ignored it, and it pinged a few seconds later. Mine did the same.

"We can't talk about this here."

"Tonight," I agreed. "Do you need to go home?"

"No." She shook her head. "I have work to do, and I need to stay busy."

I pressed a kiss to her forehead in admiration. "You are the strongest person I know, Livvy."

She looked up, her eyes telling me everything she couldn't say at the moment. Fear, panic, and worry filled them, but she refused to give in to it right now. I was so proud of her.

"Let's get through this afternoon, and we'll figure out our next step tonight."

"Mom is down with another bad headache."

"Okay. After Mouse is in bed."

She nodded and moved toward the door.

"Liv, avoid him until you leave. Do not give him a chance to reengage. I'll make sure to keep an eye on you."

She paused. "Control your temper, Van. I know how his mind works. He's counting on you losing it. That's why he keeps baiting you."

"I won't give him the satisfaction."

"Okay. I'll work in here for a while." She slipped out and I followed, watching her walk upstairs to do the measurements and sketches she wanted to work on today. Simon passed me in the hall.

"There was a little accident in unit one," I muttered.

"I'll fix it now."

"Thanks."

"I hope everything is okay."

I glanced toward the staircase. Liv's body language said it all. Nothing was okay.

But I would make sure it was. No matter what.

How Liv held it together all day was a mystery to me. How I

managed to make it through the rest of the day and not beat the shit out of Nolan was a miracle. We met in our usual Friday afternoon session, Jordan's presence a buffer for all the tension in the air. John made an unexpected appearance, which put Nolan on his best behavior. Updates, schedules, and issues were addressed. Liv's responses were short and quiet, mine direct and blunt. John was pleased with the progress, as was Jordan.

"We might finish ahead of schedule," John stated, pleased. "I guess I had better get your bonus ready, Nolan."

"Does the rest of the crew get a bonus?" I asked. "Or do the rewards stop at Nolan the same as everything else does?"

Jordan lifted his eyebrows at my unusually snarky question. John lifted one shoulder. "I leave it to Nolan. He decides who is deserving."

I snorted quietly. "Well, I guess that answers my question."

Liv nudged my leg. Nolan glared at me.

"Got something on your mind, Van?"

I leaned back in my chair. "Nope. It was a simple question. Always interested in how other people run their crews."

"I run my crews just fine," Nolan snarled.

I shrugged. "Never said anything different."

"You insinuated," he insisted.

Jordan spoke up. "I think that's enough. It's been a long week for everyone and we're ahead of schedule. Let's leave it at that and wrap this up."

I stood. "I'm done."

Nolan stood, his hatred for me blatant in his gaze. "So am I."

I barked out a laugh, heading for the door. "You got that right."

Liv said nothing but picked up her bag, following me. Nolan spoke.

"We'll talk more next week, Olivia."

She stopped and turned. "I'm happy to discuss the project with you anytime, Mr. Nolan. If there is anything else you want to talk about, you'll have to book an appointment. With my lawyer."

With that bombshell, she walked out ahead of me.

I wanted to kiss her, but I refrained.

She worked the rest of the afternoon on designs, spoke with people on the phone, and solved problems with her assistant, sitting in an empty apartment while I double-checked my order. She was calm, in control, and efficient.

Only I saw the turmoil in her eyes.

We picked up Mouse, and I made dinner for my girls. I decided mac and cheese was in order, and I made it extra cheesy and gooey, much to the delight of Sammy. Liv barely ate, but Sammy was so happy, she never noticed. She talked nonstop, filling us in on her day, and asking about going to the park on the weekend and her need for a bacon and grilled cheese sandwich before we did.

I noticed how Liv's eyes followed her. The way she sat closer than normal and listened with an intensity born of fear. I cleaned up the kitchen while Liv gave Mouse a bath, taking extra-long with her. They cuddled on the bed as I read to them both, giving Liv the chance to hold Sammy close and stroke her hair.

"You're so cuddly today, Mommy," Sammy observed. "You're hugging me extra hard."

"Because I love you extra much." Liv's voice caught.

"I love you too, Mommy." Sammy's eyes met mine. "I love you too, Mr. Van."

"Right back at you, Mouse. And I told you last week you can call me Van if you want."

She rubbed her nose, looking thoughtful. "You call me Mouse because it's a special name, right?"

"Yep."

"I like calling you Mr. Van because it's special too."

"Okay."

Liv's lip trembled, and I knew it was hitting her. The whole awful day and the situation that was happening. I stood, shutting the book.

"I'll leave you girls to say good night." I bent down and kissed Sammy. "Sleep good."

"I will!"

I left the room and headed for the kitchen to make a pot of coffee. I had a feeling we were going to need it.

I was on my second cup when Liv appeared. She looked exhausted, her shoulders drooping, and eyes heavy. She paused in the kitchen, shaking her head no at my offer of coffee. She turned and headed back to Sammy's doorway, leaning on the frame.

I drained my cup and followed her, standing close and observing Mouse as she nestled under the covers, her doll clutched tight, sleeping dreamlessly.

I knew she would probably be the only one getting any sleep tonight.

Liv began to shake. The tremors started slowly and grew. I could feel the rate of her heart picking up as her emotions began to overwhelm her.

I slid my arm around her waist, pulling her back to my chest.

"Shh, Liv."

"What if he wins? What if he takes her away? How am I going to deal with this, Van?" she whispered, her voice raw.

"He won't. I promise."

Her breathing became harsh. "You can't make me promises like that."

I tugged her back to the living room, turning her to face me. The pain in her face made my chest ache.

"We're going to get all the information we need, and we're going to fight this, Liv."

"I don't have the resources. He knows that." Panic began to overtake her. "How can I fight him? He's right—he has everything on his side!"

Tears formed in her eyes, her earlier strength now depleted. She was falling apart in her panic, and I realized I needed to let her. She needed to give in to the fear before she could face it.

I pulled her into my arms. "Let it out, Liv. It's okay."

She began to sob. Her tears bothered me because of the way she cried. Silently, her body shaking so hard from the force of her cries, yet no sound coming out. I knew she was used to handling everything on her own, hiding her fears, and not showing the world anything but a brave face.

But I wasn't just anyone. She needed to know that.

I lowered my face to her ear.

"I told you earlier I've got you. I meant it. You and Mouse are safe with me. Nothing, and no one is going to hurt either of you. Especially not some lowlife from your past who thinks he can waltz in and take what's mine. Both of you are mine now, and I will protect you with everything in me. Know that, Liv. I have you." I paused a beat, knowing I had to say it. "I love you."

Her body stilled, and she looked up at me. Her cheeks were wet with tears, the pain and worry etched into her eyes. I wiped away the tears. "I love you," I repeated, hoping my declaration would give her some strength. "And I've got you. We'll figure this out together—you don't have to handle this alone. You don't have to handle anything alone ever again, okay?"

She buried her face in my neck, fresh tears pouring down her face. But this time, I heard her cries—quiet and raw, but loud enough for me to hear. She was allowing me to feel her pain.

Between her sobs, I heard the words I would hold on to the rest of my life.

"I love you too, Van."

I held her and let her cry herself out. Her body slumped into sleep on my lap, no doubt from the exhaustion and stress of the day. I sat quietly, my head lifting at the sound of light footsteps. Mouse came around the corner, clutching her doll. She stopped when she saw me holding Liv, a frown marring her face. She hurried forward.

"What's wrong with Mommy?"

"Mommy had a bad headache, so I was giving her some snuggles. She fell asleep."

"Oh." She stepped closer, patting Liv's leg with her little hand. "Grammie gets bad headaches too. Are you going to look after her tonight the way Mommy does with Grammie?"

"Yep." Wanting to prepare Mouse for finding me here in the morning because there was no way in hell I was leaving Liv alone tonight, I added, "I'm going to stay the night and make sure she's okay."

She furrowed her little brow. "I sleep in the guest room at Grammie's, and Mommy sleeps beside me." She eyed me. "We don't have a guest room, and I don't think you'll fit on my bed."

I chuckled. "I'll sleep on the sofa, Mouse."

Her face brightened. "You can sleep beside Mommy. She has a big bed!"

I nodded. "That's a good idea, Mouse. Then if Mommy needs me, I'll be right there."

She bobbed her head in agreement. "Okay." Once again, she looked dubious. "I don't have any pajamas to lend you. They're too small and won't fit you."

This kid was going to be the death of me with her caring attitude and the way she fussed—the same as her mother.

"Probably not. But I can sleep in my clothes, and I'll go home and change in the morning. We can make breakfast before I go—maybe pancakes."

Her eyes brightened. "Mommy loves pancakes. Maybe that will make her feel better?"

"I'm sure of it."

"Okay, I'll go back to bed."

"Did you need something, Sammy? I can get it for you."

"I woke up and thought I heard a noise. I wanted to ask Mommy, but it must have been you humming."

"I was humming?"

"Yes. It was nice. You can keep humming if you want. I liked it."

I hadn't even noticed I was doing so. I knew my mom used to hum to me when I was upset as a kid, and I must have unconsciously done it to help Liv relax.

"Sure, Mouse. If you like it, I will. Sure you don't need anything?"

"No." She turned to go, pausing before she disappeared down the hall. "I like you here, Mr. Van."

"I like being here, Mouse."

She bobbed her head. "Good. You can talk to Mommy about living here all the time if you want. Or we can live in your house. I'd be okay with that."

I stared after her, her words surprising me, yet somehow not.

An idea began to form, and studying Liv's sleeping form, I wondered how hard she would fight me on my plan.

I decided to find out in the morning.

SEVENTEEN

Van

I woke up cramped and stiff. I was across Liv's bed, Mouse curled around me on one side, Liv on the other.

Not long after I carried Liv to bed and lay down, holding her close, Mouse had appeared, climbing up beside me.

"I can't sleep, Mr. Van."

"What's wrong, kiddo?" I asked quietly, not wanting to wake Liv.

"I don't know." She furrowed her little brow. "Mommy never gets headaches. Only Grammie. Is Mommy sick?"

"No, Mouse. I promise. Mommy is okay. Sometimes grown-ups have bad days and they get extra tired. That's all."

She mulled over my words and tilted her head. "Like when I spill my juice and can't find my boots?"

"Yes."

"Oh. So, tomorrow will be a new day, like Mommy says to me?"

"Exactly."

She huffed out a sigh. "Okay. But I don't want to go back to bed. Can I stay here?"

I lifted my arm, and she slid in beside me, burrowing close. She was asleep in less than five minutes, her breathing becoming deep and even. Liv clutched me tightly, even in her sleep, and my mind was full, going over what I needed to do. It was past four when I finally drifted off to sleep, uncomfortable but refusing to move. I held both of my girls. They needed me and I wasn't letting them down.

Blinking, I met Liv's gaze. It was tired but calmer than last night.

"Hey," I murmured.

"Hi."

"You okay, baby?"

"I'm better. I can't believe you stayed all night. I can't believe I slept."

"You were exhausted."

"You must be in agony. Me and Sammy on you all night? Did you get any sleep?"

"Some." I smiled at her. "I need to move, if I'm being honest."

She slid away and came to the other side of the bed, gathering Mouse in her arms. I stood, stretching and bending my back, trying to ease the aches. As Liv settled Mouse back into her bed, I used the bathroom, then headed to the kitchen. I poured a cup of cold coffee and heated it in the microwave.

Liv shuffled in, and I wrapped my arm around her, pulling her close to my chest as I sipped the warm liquid.

"I can make a fresh pot."

"No, this is fine."

"I'm sorry about last night."

I set down the coffee and cupped her face, forcing her to meet my eyes. "Don't you dare apologize for that. It was hardly a surprise you broke down after the shit Nolan put you through yesterday. Frankly, I'm surprised it hasn't happened before now."

She wrapped her hands around my wrists. "Thank you for being there for me."

I brushed my lips over her head. "There is nowhere else I would have been."

Her voice was quiet. "Did you mean it, Van?"

I knew what she was referring to. "Yes, Liv, I meant it." I held her gaze. "I love you. I've loved you for weeks, but I've been holding it in. I thought it might help you somehow if you knew."

Her sigh was ragged. "It does. I love you too."

I kissed her. "That's a good thing."

"What am I going to do?" she whispered.

"Do you trust me, Liv?"

"Yes."

"Enough to let me do something?"

"As long as that something doesn't involve you hitting Nolan."

"Not physically. But what I have in mind will deliver a punch, but I need your permission to do it."

"You have it."

"Okay. We're going to meet with the BAM boys this morning."

Panic filled her eyes. "Why?"

"They need to know, and they need to hear it from us." I wasn't looking forward to telling them. They weren't going to be happy, and I wished I had confided in them before now.

"It's personal."

"Not anymore. Working with an ex is one thing. He is threatening your future and your well-being. It is something completely different. We need them on our side."

She swallowed, staying quiet as she thought about my words.

"But it's Saturday."

"I know. I already checked, and they've agreed to see us. We need to do this today, Livvy. I don't want to wait until Monday."

"Okay."

I squeezed her hand. "Okay. But first, I promised Mouse pancakes."

Bentley, Aiden, and Maddox listened to what I had to say. Jordan sat at the other end of the table, a quiet support for us. Liv sat beside me, her hand clasped in mine under the table. I could feel her tremble as I spoke, telling them everything, leaving nothing out. When I finished, I sat back and squeezed her hand.

For a moment, there was silence. Then Bentley leaned forward, his hands folded on the table. He regarded us for a moment.

"I'll start off with this. Your relationship is private. I have no objection to it whatsoever. There's no company policy about dating within the office, so you've broken no rules. To be honest, the two of you work so well together, I'm not surprised it's carried over into a personal relationship." He held up his finger. "But to be clear, if this doesn't work out, I expect you both to act professionally."

"Not an issue," I replied. "Since it's not going to happen."

"Understood. Now the second part is more troublesome." He ran a hand over his face. "I wish you had told me of your past relationship with Nolan, Liv. I realize it was personal, but a heads-up might have been helpful."

Jordan spoke up. "I knew the situation, Bentley. I have been watching it closely. Liv and Van have been completely professional in their dealings toward each other and Nolan. I can't say the same for his behavior—especially lately."

Bentley's gaze swung his way. "And you chose not to say anything because?"

Jordan met his eyes directly. "Because Liv and Van both assured me they had it under control. There are many times we work with people we dislike. As I said, I have been watching the whole thing closely. Even Van will admit, Nolan is a complete ass, but he is getting the job done. If he hadn't pulled this, we wouldn't be here."

"But here we are."

"I never expected this to happen, Bentley," Liv assured him. "Not in a million years. Nolan walked away from us and has never expressed any interest. I thought I could handle myself, work the project, and he would be gone again."

Bentley pursed his lips, looking angry.

"From what Van has said, you *have* handled yourself, Liv. It sounds as if he's the one with the issues." He looked between us. "Toward both of you."

Aiden spoke. "What if we pull Liv and Van from the project—assign someone else? Then they don't have to deal with him on a daily basis. Would it make things easier?"

Liv and I shook our heads.

"We aren't running, Aiden. If we did that, it would show him we're scared."

"Van is right," Maddox stated. "Nolan is a bully of the worst kind. He wants them to run. He wants the upper hand."

For a moment, the room was silent. I knew they were upset over this news, and I hoped they would give me a chance to explain further. Especially Bentley. He trusted me, and I didn't want his trust to waver. I was grateful when he spoke again, showing he was concentrating on the problem at hand.

"What do we do?" Bentley asked. "What do you need from us?"

I leaned forward. "We don't expect you to do anything. I'm going to get Liv a lawyer, and we're going to fight this all the way. We needed you to know because it could cause friction between WIN and BAM."

The three partners looked at each other, then Aiden addressed us. "If you expect us to do nothing when one of our own is under attack, you're sadly mistaken."

Liv began to protest, and Bentley silenced her. "Samantha is your daughter, Liv. You've raised her on your own. Given the new feelings I've discovered since becoming a father, I can only imagine the terror and anger you're feeling at the thought of Nolan being part of her life if he's the terrible person you describe him as being. If someone were a threat to Addi, I would move heaven and earth to eliminate them." He leaned forward, tapping the table with his finger. "You aren't going to lose your daughter, Liv." He met my gaze, his determined. "I won't allow it."

I sat back, relieved. I needed to hear those words. We needed the clout of BAM behind us, and now we had it.

Bentley stood, directing his attention to Aiden. "Call John and arrange a meeting today—and tell him Nolan needs to be there as well for part of it. I want all of the cards on the table. If he doesn't agree to my terms, the contract is being canceled. I don't care about the ramifications. And get Reid on this. I'll call Hal Smithers—he's a shark in family law. I'll get him on retainer."

Liv rose to her feet, her voice quivering. "Bentley, I..."

He shook his head, and in an uncharacteristic move, pulled her in for a fast hug. "Not needed, Liv. We're family, and you know how I feel about family." His gaze was intense as he stared at us. "Don't ever keep me out of the loop again, understand?"

I stood. "It was my call."

"We'll discuss it later. Right now, we're going to focus on solving this issue."

He left the room quickly.

"Shit," I muttered. "He is pissed."

Maddox rubbed his chin. "He is, but he'll deal with it later. He knows what's most important now and that's dealing with this issue."

Aiden reached for his phone. "I'm a little pissed too, to be honest. If you had told me, I might be ahead of the game already. I need to make some calls. You okay with Reid being part of this, Liv?"

"Yes, although I'm not sure why he has to be?" she asked.

I covered her hand with mine. "Reid will find everything out about Nolan. *Everything,*" I stressed. "Even things he's forgotten."

"Oh, ah..."

Maddox looked kindly at her. "He's completely trustworthy, Liv. You're safe with him." He flashed a wide smirk. "I probably can't say the same for Nolan."

I chuckled.

Liv's fingers pulled at the seams of her jeans. "I can't afford the likes of Hal Smithers."

"I can," I said calmly.

She frowned, and I slid my hand around her neck, rubbing the tense muscles. "Remember the royalties I told you sit in the bank, Liv? There are millions of them. I only use the money for important things. I bought my house, I made my father retire, and I take care of my parents. And now, I'm taking care of you."

"I can't—you can't," she sputtered.

"I can. Don't argue. You and Mouse are the most important things in the world to me."

She stared.

"Hal's a friend of Bentley's," Aiden drawled. "His office is in one of our buildings. He lives in one of our condo towers. He'll do right by you, Liv." He winked. "I'll make sure he doesn't break the bank either, Van."

I met his gaze. "I wouldn't care."

He nodded. "Good man." He glanced at his phone. "Bentley's already reached out. Hal will see you later this afternoon."

Overwhelmed, Liv buried her face in her hands, her shoulders shaking. Jordan, Aiden, and Maddox left, pulling the boardroom door shut behind them to give us privacy. I pulled her into my arms and held her close.

"I told you that you wouldn't be alone."

"I had no idea," she hiccupped.

I tilted up her chin. Her usually bright eyes were dim and filled with worry. "We're fighting this together, okay?"

"O-okay," she sniffed.

"I need to ask something from you now, Liv."

"What?"

"I need you to go home, pack up some things, and come stay at my house. I want you and Mouse close."

"Why?" she breathed out.

"Because I do. It's simple. He's threatening you. You're going to fight back—something I don't think he expected. It'll make him angrier, and I need to protect you. My house has an alarm, and I'm there."

She rubbed a hand over her face. "Won't it give him even more ammunition? That I'm living with my boyfriend?"

"He's living with his girlfriend."

"Fiancée. I'm sure he would argue the difference."

I studied her and lowered my face close to hers, dropping my voice. "Is that what you want, Liv? I'll take you down the street right now, pick a ring, and we can go to city hall."

Her eyes flew open wide. *"What?"*

I warmed to the subject. "It will cancel out most of his arguments right there. You move in. We'll get married. Mouse will have a stable home with two parents already. Hell, I'll build a spot for your mom, and she can come move in too. A house filled with people to care for Mouse. He can go fuck himself."

Liv looked shell-shocked. When I grinned at her with an exaggerated wink, she relaxed.

"Too much?" I asked. I had been teasing—mostly.

"A bit."

"Okay. How about you move in with me?"

"Temporarily."

I tucked a piece of hair behind her ear. "For now. But in all seriousness, I would feel better."

"Are you sure?"

"Yes."

"Okay."

I was surprised. I had been certain she was going to push back. Refuse and tell me she didn't need any protection. It showed me how anxious she was over the situation.

"My dad and I will move Mouse's bed and bookcase over later, so she has familiar things in the house," I offered. "Your mom has Sammy until tonight so we can get this all handled today."

"It seems like a lot of work for a few weeks. Why don't I use one of the beds from the warehouse?"

"Nope. Both will go in the truck in minutes. Mouse will be happier. You pack whatever clothes and stuff you need. We can get anything you forget later."

She huffed but grudgingly agreed.

I didn't bother to tell her it wasn't for a few weeks. I had a feeling once this was over, I wouldn't let them go.

Hal Smithers closed the file and glanced up at Liv and me. He was younger than I expected—younger than me. His brown hair was short, his beard trimmed, and his suit expensive. There was an air of confidence about him, his gaze direct, and his demeanor intense.

He was perfect.

He tapped the file. "I'm not going to lie and say this is open-and-shut, but I'm going to make this very difficult for him. Very, very difficult."

"Can he really do this?" I asked, aghast. "Waltz back into their lives after all this time and demand to be part of Sammy's life?"

"Oh, he can demand anything he wants. It's my job to make sure he doesn't get it." He sat back. "He signed his rights away. He has a huge uphill climb to get them back."

"He said he is going to ask for visitation."

He shrugged. "Again, he can ask for anything he wants. A judge will decide if it's in Samantha's best interest. Since he hasn't had any contact, provided any support either financially or emotionally in her lifetime, it's a pretty *big* if. I'll fight it and use his past behavior against him."

Liv shuddered, and I slipped my arm around her shoulders.

"From now on, Liv, you don't talk to him about Samantha. I would prefer you not have any contact with him." He studied her. "I know it's your job, and this project means a lot to you, but you need to decide which is more important."

"Sammy," she replied immediately.

"Then figure it out."

"I was thinking maybe Liv could do the design work but send an assistant to meetings and to do the on-site checking until WIN is off the project," I offered.

He thought it over and nodded. "It might work." He met my gaze. "What about you, Van?"

"I can handle myself."

He snickered, the sound without humor. "From what I've been told, this guy excels at getting under your skin. Can you really?"

"I'll move my stuff from the trailer. I'll work out of one of the empty apartments. I'll only communicate for business reasons, and I won't be alone with him. I won't give him the chance to get to me."

He huffed a sigh. "I'll be honest. This complicates things, but I understand you have a job to do. But one wrong move can affect this case—you understand?"

"Yes."

"As soon as I get the papers from his lawyer, I'll respond. I'll try to get this before a judge privately and nip it in the bud. Hopefully we'll get one of the judges I have in mind on the case." He paused, flipping open the file. "Aiden tells me he has Reid digging into Mr. Nolan's background."

"Yes," I replied.

He smirked. "I would kill to poach Reid away from BAM. If anyone can find anything to use against Nolan, it'll be Reid."

"I still don't know why Chris is doing this," Liv stated. "He didn't want her before. He has never liked children. He wanted nothing to do with her."

"Revenge. Anger. Jealousy. To be a prick." Hal made some notes in the file. "I've seen it all."

"What should we do?" Liv asked, her voice quivering.

He sat back, regarding us. "Stick to your schedule. Live your life. Make sure Samantha is taken care of. Don't engage with Mr. Nolan, no matter what occurs. Let me handle this."

"Can he win?" I asked, my voice tight.

"It's rare it happens in cases where the rights have been voluntarily signed away. But it can occur." He addressed Liv. "From what I see, your daughter is happy, well-cared-for, and thriving. There is no reason a judge would take her away from you. If I do my job right, we'll shut this down as quickly as possible. But on the off chance he wins, you will have to prepare yourself that he might be part of her life. We would demand supervised visitation and a limited amount of contact, at least to start. It's not as if she'll suddenly be living with him on a part-time basis."

"I don't want her with him at all. He's a terrible person," Liv protested. "He would destroy her the way he tried to destroy me."

"That's what we need to show the judge. Did you confide in anyone? Were there witnesses to the way he treated you?"

Liv sighed. "My mother. I didn't have a close friend. Chris sort of cut them all off. And I was ashamed, to be honest. He made me ashamed."

"Typical."

He folded his hands on his desk. "Leave this with me. Let's see what Reid comes up with. I want you to write it out. All of it. Any detail of your time with him—especially when he found out you were pregnant. Anything you think of—you never know what could be significant."

"Okay."

He stood. "I'll let you know when they make the first volley."

I shook his hand, watching as he reached for Liv's shaking palm. He met her worried gaze. "I'll do everything I can, Liv. Trust me—you're in good hands with me. I eat people like Mr. Nolan for breakfast and shit them out before lunch. I will break him."

Her lips curved upward in a tremulous smile. "Okay."

I met his gaze. "I look forward to it."

EIGHTEEN

Liv

Sammy bounced on her bed, her eyes bright.

"I love my room!" she crowed. "My bookcase is perfect here!"

"Calm down, Sammy. No more bouncing on the bed. I don't want you to fall," I murmured, sliding some clothes into the dresser Van had brought into the room for her.

She sat on the edge, looking around the room. "Is this forever, Mommy?"

I turned from the dresser, glancing around the room. How Van had done this, I had no idea. Her bed was here. Her bookcase. Toys, dolls, and books. A few pictures. Even her table and tea set. Drapes had been hung to match the cushion Van's mom had made. A bright rug covered the floor.

I had brought Sammy and my mom back to Van's place. His parents were there, helping Van. My mom and Lila bonded over Sammy. Dinner was ready. Sammy's room set. All I had to do was unpack the two suitcases I'd had ready and Van had added to the truck. It was as if the house was waiting for us. It was lovely and somehow overwhelming at the same time.

Sammy had been in her element. Nanna Lila, Poppa Joe, plus Grammie, all glued to her words. Van, who sat beside her, made sure she ate and let her sit on his lap after dinner was done. His muscular arm held her safe as he chuckled at her stories. Looking around the table, I felt the love, and more than once I had to swallow the thickness in my throat. Van's eyes met mine, his slight nod and

226

understanding gaze making my chest warm. Our parents left not long after dinner, Joe and Lila insisting on driving my mom home. I had a feeling I would be seeing lots of them together.

Van cleared his throat from the doorway. "We don't know how long it's for, Sammy. A few weeks until they fix the apartment for sure."

We had told her a pipe burst and we were staying at Van's while it was fixed. When she found out her bed and bookcase were already there, she had been excited. Add in the touches from Lila, and it was perfect for Sammy.

"Oh, okay. I like forever, though."

Van grinned, his eyes crinkling the way Sammy loved. "I like it too, Mouse. We'll see how it goes, okay?"

She clapped her hands. "I'll be good!"

He kneeled beside the bed, his tone gentle and loving. "You're always good, Sammy. You're one of the best kids I know. It's a grown-up thing, okay? Not you."

She flung her arms around his neck and said something in his ear. His expression grew tender as he held her close, a small bundle in his massive arms.

"Me too," he whispered back.

I had to blink away the tears in my eyes as I turned back to the dresser. I loved the way he was with her. Her friend, protector, and father figure, all in one giant package. Gentle and sweet with her and those he loved, but fierce and stern with those who threatened them.

I wiped away the moisture and turned around. "Okay, kiddo. Bath time and then bed. It's late."

She didn't argue, and as soon as her bath was done and she was tucked in, she was asleep. I watched her for a moment. Van stepped behind me, wrapping his arm around my waist. "We'll leave the bookshelf lights on," he murmured. "And I added a night-light in the hall in case she wakes up and is confused. We'll leave the doors open."

I leaned back into him. "You're so good to us."

He pressed a kiss to my head. "I'm just getting started, Liv." He drew me to the door. "Now, it's your turn."

Twenty minutes later, I was in the huge tub in Van's en suite. He had filled it and added bubbles, turning the lights down low, and had soft music playing. He'd even left a glass of wine on the edge.

I leaned back with a sigh, letting the warm water soothe away my tension. Van came in, set a thick towel by the sink, bent over and pressed a kiss to my forehead, then turned to leave.

"Stay," I asked.

He settled beside the tub, entwining his fingers with mine. "Okay, Livvy?"

"Yes. Considering the day it's been, more than okay. I don't understand how you did all you did and..." My voice trailed off.

He chuckled. "My parents helped. A friend helped, and we loaded Mouse's bed, bookcase, and other stuff in about ten minutes. My mom did the rest—the rug and drapes, and she and Dad set it up. The dresser was in the other room. None of it was a lot of work, so relax."

"Did you-did you talk to Bentley or Jordan?" I asked.

He studied me. "Do you really want to talk about it now?"

"Yes."

He huffed out a long breath. "Jordan said the meeting was tense but fine. John wasn't happy about the past relationship either, but given the story Nolan had told him about Sammy, was very supportive of him. Bentley laid down some very strict demands, and John agreed to them. John's a smart man—this is too lucrative a contract for him to lose. Being part of a BAM project is huge for his status. If Bentley canceled the contract, it would hurt him, even if he sued BAM. With the reputation BAM has, his business would be toast." He smiled tightly. "The three of us will have very little interaction from now on. Especially you and Nolan. It's not really necessary, and Kim or someone can handle any meetings if needed."

"What about you?"

"I will attend meetings with Jordan or Aiden present. Most of our communication will be via text or email. He'll get as little chance as possible to get personal with me."

"Have I jeopardized your job, Van?" I asked, worried.

"No. I talked to Bentley this afternoon. We had a frank face-to-face meeting, with Aiden and Maddox there as well. He'd calmed down and it was fine," he assured me. "I think Bentley's impression of Nolan helped. He was pretty full of himself in the meeting at the start. It didn't last too long once Bentley finished with him."

"Oh." I wasn't sure what else to say. I felt terrible for what was happening, yet at this point, I couldn't fix it.

Van rose up and lifted my chin. He bent close and brushed a kiss over my lips. "I know what you're thinking, Liv. To be honest, I think Nolan going after you and Sammy was something that was going to happen, regardless. My gut tells me this was planned. Even if we had gone to the boys with the info and WIN hadn't gotten the job, this would have happened. This way, we can keep an eye on him and try to figure out why. Even Bentley thinks that way." He stroked my cheek. "Everything is fine, okay? Our jobs are safe. You and Mouse are safe. You're right where you should be." He stood. "Well, almost."

"Almost?"

He looked down at me, his dark gaze intense. "I want you in my bed, Livvy. Soak for a while and finish your wine. Once you're relaxed, come to me, and I'll help you relax a little more."

I felt a rush of desire from his words. "I'm actually done in here."

"There's no hurry."

I offered him my hand. "I want to be with you, Van. I need you."

He pulled me up, the water splashing over the edge of the tub in his haste. He lifted me as if I weighed nothing, wrapping the towel around me. He ignored the water streaming from my body and carried me to his bed, kissing me the whole time. He tasted of coffee, cinnamon, and mint. Of Van. I wound my fingers into his hair, moaning into his mouth as he laid me on the mattress. He stood over me, his breathing hard and fast.

"You are so beautiful," he murmured, stroking my skin, trailing his fingers over my collarbone. "So soft and pretty. I love how you look in my bed."

I clasped his hand, bringing it to my lips and kissing his knuckles. "I want you in the bed with me."

He pulled his shirt over his head, his toned and muscled torso bare in the dim light. I watched with hooded eyes as he slowly unbuckled his belt and kicked out of his jeans, leaving him in only black boxers that clung to his muscled thighs. He cupped his growing erection, meeting my gaze.

"Is this what you want, Livvy? My cock?"

"Yes," I breathed out. "I need you inside me, Van."

He slid his fingers inside the waistband of his boxers, back and forth, a wicked expression on his face as he teased me.

"What's the magic word?" he asked, his voice low.

"*Please.*"

He pushed down his boxers, his cock springing free. Long, heavy, and swollen—I ached for it. For him. I held out my arms.

"Make love to me, Van. Make me forget. Just for a while."

He moved between my legs, his chest pressing to mine. He held himself over me, his weight resting on his forearms. He skimmed his cock along my center and I lifted my hips, wrapping my legs around his waist.

He dropped his face to mine, our lips barely touching. "I'm here, Livvy. Right here, baby. I've got you."

A tear rolled down my face and he kissed it away. His mouth covered mine, and for long moments, there was only the feel of his lips on me. The taste of him as his tongue stroked and tangled with mine. The way his body covered me, the hard planes and sinewy muscles firm under my touch. He slid into me, stilling as we were joined, a low groan deep in his chest.

"The way you feel around me, Liv..." he whispered as he began to move—long, unhurried glides of his hips. "There is nothing like it. There never will be. Promise me I can have it all the time. Promise you'll be here."

I was already rushing toward the edge. It was as if he knew my body and how to drive me to ecstasy quickly and took great pride in doing so. I gripped at his back, whimpering in need.

"More," I pleaded, my voice shaking as I grasped his shoulders and pulled him in tighter. "I need more, baby."

With a long hiss, he began to move in me vigorously, hitting the spot only he had ever found, and I broke. I cried out, his mouth covering mine to stifle the sounds as my orgasm rushed over me, powerful and intense. I shook with the force of it, my body spasming around him. His release followed, and he drove himself as deep as he could, stilling, pouring himself into me until he was spent.

He collapsed on me, his weight substantial and welcome. For a moment, there was only the sound of our heavy breathing. He rolled, pulling me onto his chest. The sheets were wet from the bathwater, our skin sticky from our exertions, and my hair a tangled mess from his hands. A trail of water led from the bathroom to the bed, and the comforter was on the floor, getting wetter by the second. Neither of us cared.

He pressed a kiss to my head. "Welcome home, Livvy."

I nestled closer. He was right. With him, I was home.

Van

The next ten days were a juxtaposition of emotions. We were both tense at work, the hours dragging by. I struggled to keep my temper in place, and Liv worried constantly. I kept in touch all day, and I missed having her around the site, even though I knew it was for the best.

The evenings were the exact opposite. Since the band was still taking a break, my entire focus became Liv and Mouse. I loved having them with me.

Sammy's laughter and endless chatter filled the rooms, and I realized how lonely my house had been before she was here. Aside from music, I lived a solitary life. I began to long for the end of the day, knowing what waited for me when I walked in the door. There was no longer only silence and hours to fill with my own company.

Instead, there was a little girl who could hardly wait to be hugged and tell me about her day, and her beautiful mother who greeted me with a kiss and filled the house with the delicious scent of dinner. My parents often joined us. So did Elly. There were lazy evenings filled with games and movies. Quiet moments of reading to Mouse and watching her fall asleep. Having Liv beside me at night. Playing my guitar to help her relax. Making love to her every chance I got. It would have been perfect except for the toll the situation was taking on Liv.

She tried to hide it, but she couldn't. She barely slept, and her appetite was minimal. She was pale and wan-looking, her cheeks sunken from the weight she was losing. She tried so hard to keep things normal for Sammy and only broke down when we were alone. I often found her in the bathroom, weeping into a towel, trying to hide her fears even from me. I would gather her into my arms and carry her to our bed and love her until she forgot everything, lost to the passion we had between us. But it only lasted briefly, and I knew she would slip from our bed and watch Mouse sleep, pace the house endlessly, and worry while I lay alone, unable to relax and sleep until she crawled back into our bed in the early hours of the morning, her body curling around mine for warmth. Only then did we doze fitfully until Sammy would bound in a short time later, wanting her morning cuddles.

For the first time ever, I found myself short-tempered at work, easy to rile, and fast to criticize. More than once, I had to walk away from things when I realized how fast I was losing control. The lack of sleep and worry were eating at me, and I felt helpless. Watching Liv fall apart was killing me slowly.

Things came to a head when Hal informed Liv that Nolan had filed the paperwork to have his rights reinstated and was asking for immediate visitation. Luckily, Hal had the visitation request struck down until the judge could review all the paperwork and meet with both sides. It bought us some time, but I had a feeling it was running out.

I sighed, my head falling back as I waited for Reid, Hal, and Liv to arrive. We were having another meeting, so that we could all get on the same page, and I had arrived at the office early, waiting in the boardroom. I startled as I felt the touch on my arm, my eyes flying open. Sandy was there, holding a cup of coffee.

"You look as if you could use this."

"Thanks."

She offered me a smile. "You are going to get through this and be stronger, Van."

"At what cost?" I asked. "Liv is about ready to collapse and I'm losing ground every day." I ran a hand through my hair. "Dealing with Nolan daily is a strain." Even with our limited contact, he managed to get under my skin with his offhand comments and snide remarks.

"Worrying over Liv is killing me. Thinking of Nolan spending time with Mouse makes me ill." I shook my head. "I wish I knew the why behind it. Then we could figure out how to stop it."

Reid walked in, laptop in hand. "I may have the answer to that question."

Sandy bent close, patting my cheek in her motherly fashion. "This is going to work out, Van. You have too many people working on it for it not to happen."

She left, holding the door for Hal and Liv. I held out my hand, pulling Liv into the chair beside me. She looked like the walking dead today, the circles evident under her eyes, their golden color dim and clouded.

"What do you have, Reid?" Hal asked, getting underway fast. I had seen the worried look on his face as he observed Liv, and I was grateful for him not wasting time. I was also grateful Reid knew how serious the situation was. He didn't joke around, instead opened up his laptop and began to talk.

"I'm not going to get into how I found this, but I did some digging. What Nolan told you was right, Liv. He inherited money from his father. Quite a bit. But he also spent it fast. He bought a big house and paid cash. Same with two fast cars. And a bunch of other things. He makes a good living, but aside from the house and cars, he isn't really solvent."

"What does that have to do with Sammy?" she asked.

"That's what I'm trying to figure out. Obviously, he isn't after you for money—" he lifted one eyebrow "—no offense."

"None taken."

"But interestingly enough, his fiancée, Breanna, is a very wealthy woman in her own right. Far more affluent than Nolan. And she is a spoiled only child, who will inherit a great deal when her father dies. From everything I have gathered, she is, ah, well, a handful. Beautiful to look at but demanding, exacting, and selfish."

"A perfect match for Nolan," I murmured, internally shuddering. A nightmare for Sammy and Liv.

Reid nodded, looking at his keyboard. He glanced toward the closed door, then at Liv and Hal and finally met my gaze.

"I know you asked me to find out what I could about Nolan and his life and keep it legal, Hal. I did that. But I couldn't find enough."

Hal held up his hand. "I'm not sure I want to hear this."

Reid leaned forward, his voice serious. "Yes, you do. I did some hacking. Nothing big and nothing that can be traced to me or any of you. I did it all off site too—nothing will come back to BAM."

I was both grateful and horrified. We all knew Reid's story. If he was caught hacking, he could go back to jail. "Reid," I protested. "You can't do that."

He held up his hand, a frown marring his usually happy face.

"I am not going to sit by and let this happen. I know Sammy. I know what a great life she has and now that you're together, she has a chance at a family. I am not going to sit by while the system steps in and fucks it up because some conceited asshole decides he wants to play daddy and they let him. My childhood screwed up my life and I'll be damned if I let it happen to someone I care about. I won't let her life be destroyed by the system that should protect her." He jabbed his finger rapidly on the wooden table. "I know how badly the system can fail."

For a moment, the room was silent.

"What did you find?" Hal asked, his voice calm.

"I looked through their texts and emails. He wants to get married. She wants a child. 'Someone to play with,' as she calls it. She's been at him about it for months." Reid paused before he spoke again. "Given what I know of Nolan, he wants her money. So in order to keep her and get her to marry him, he needs to give her that."

"So why not knock her up?" I snarled. "Leave Sammy out of this."

"He can't," Reid stated.

"Why not?" Liv asked, confused.

"I did more digging. He was sick a couple of years ago. Late-onset adult mumps." Reid sat back. "It left him infertile."

"Holy shit," I muttered.

"I kept wondering how this tied back to Sammy. I did more checking and cross-referencing. Unlike you, Liv, Breanna likes to call attention to herself. I found an email to a friend where she refers to an argument she and Nolan had where she informed him she wanted a baby with him now—or else. The next week, your design and you were featured in *Toronto Life*. I think he saw it, thought of Sammy, and figured out a way to solve his problem. I have no idea what story he spun to Breanna, but I'm sure he came across as the injured party." He drew in a breath. "I even found an email where he suggested to his boss they go after the BAM contract. It was to get to you. To get close to Sammy."

"I knew he had this planned," I said.

"So you're saying since he can't give her a child, he wants to take mine—the one he never wanted—so the two of them can play house?"

Liv asked, horrified. "He's not even doing this because he changed his mind? It's all for money?"

"Yes. As I said, she is spoiled. I don't know if he told her about his infertility and suggested Sammy, or how it happened, but there is no doubt he planned it."

I looked at Hal. "Can we stop him?"

"This is all theory," Hal mused. "It's still a long shot for him, but he is determined to fight. I can't do a lot with it since you obtained so much of this illegally. I need something concrete to shut him down and make the judge see the reasons behind this sudden interest."

He turned to Liv. "You haven't come up with anyone else you confided in?"

"No."

"No taped arguments or texts?"

She shook her head. "I hate texting—I always have. I don't think I ever texted him anything personal. I never taped any of our phone conversations. I never thought I would ever need it." Tears filled her eyes. "It's his word against mine."

Hal looked grim. "Don't give up, Liv. We've got a good judge. He already put aside the visitation and refuses to rush this. We have a week before our next appointment." He ran a hand over his face. "Long shot here, but did you ever have an argument in public about you being pregnant someone that might have overheard? A colleague or friend?"

"No. He was so ashamed of my 'situation,' he refused to see me except in private. And he was cold and distant. He lost it badly once..." Her voice drifted away, and her eyes grew wide.

I took her hand. "What is it, Liv?"

"I forgot." She stuttered. "I forgot—an-an email." She covered her mouth. "How could I forget that?"

"Tell me," I urged, ignoring everyone else but her.

"He was drunk one night and wrote me an email."

Hal leaned forward. "What did it say?"

"It was vile. He kept referring to Sammy as an it. He told me to kill *it*. Get rid of *it*. He wanted nothing to do with the bastard child I had tried to trap him with." Her eyes were bright with unshed tears. "He told me what a sorry excuse for a woman I was—he listed all my faults and said knowing it was a girl, she would be as weak and useless as I was. He wanted no part of her life or mine, and I was never to contact him again." She shuddered. "I changed my email the next day and had my lawyer send him the papers. I never heard from him again."

She wiped the tears off her cheeks. "I forgot about the email. It was so awful, I pushed it from my mind."

"Do you have a copy?" Hal asked eagerly.

"No. I deleted it." She slumped back in her chair.

"What device did you get it on, Liv?" Reid asked, his voice anxious.

"My cell phone. My emails went there. I couldn't afford a laptop while I was at school, so I used theirs, and I had a cell phone."

"Do you have the cell phone?"

Liv's brow furrowed. "I think so. I tend to keep that sort of stuff. I think the cell phone is in a box in my apartment. But I don't have the same provider anymore, and I deleted the email."

Reid leaned forward, eager. "Did you delete the provider from your phone?"

She thought about it then shook her head. "No. But when I changed providers, I got a new phone. I threw the other one in a box. I don't think I touched it."

"Can you trace the email, Reid?" I asked. "Even if the phone is dead?"

Reid's eyes were bright. "Yeah, if it was on the phone, I can find it." He paused. "Do you remember what his email was at the time?"

"Um, it was a Hotmail account. He refused to pay for email." She looked upset again. "I can't remember what my email was, Reid."

Reid grinned. "It's fine, Liv. I don't need it. I need you to find me the cell phone."

"Okay."

I glanced at Hal. "If she finds them, and you can recover it, what happens?"

Hal leaned back in his chair. "I nail that bastard to the wall with his own words. Then I take back my words. This *will* be open-and-shut—by the asshole himself."

I stood, holding out my hand. "Come on, Liv. We need to find that phone."

NINETEEN

Van

"Think, baby," I encouraged her.

Liv ran a hand through her hair, the strands tangled from her constant worrying. "I can't remember," she cried, tears pooling in her eyes. She had been crying constantly for over an hour, her panic clouding her memory.

I tugged her onto my lap in the middle of the chaos surrounding us. We'd gone through every drawer and shelf in her closet, the kitchen, even the bathroom. No cell phone.

"Okay," I soothed, stroking her hair. "You threw it in a box."

"Yes."

"Did you live here then?"

"N-no." She hiccupped. "We moved here when Sammy was two."

My heart sank. Had she thrown it out when she moved?

"But I saw it after we moved. I added another phone to the box. I thought I should chuck them both, but I put the box on the shelf and forgot."

"Okay, good. Good job remembering that, Livvy." I pressed a kiss to her head. "Have you seen it since then?"

She sighed, and I let her think, rubbing her back in long passes.

"Sammy," she breathed.

"My parents and Elly have her. She's fine."

She pushed away. "No! Sammy...she loved to play with my phone when she was little. She loved to push the numbers. I gave her

239

a phone to play with." Her eyes grew round with the memory. "I gave her the phone!"

I stood, pulling her with me. In Sammy's room, we split up, going through shelves and drawers. I had no idea how much stuff a little girl could have. I discovered lace, ribbons, hair things, doll clothes, little bits and pieces everywhere I looked, but no cell phone. In desperation, I shoved my hand under her old bookcase, encountering something soft. I pulled it out, staring at the little cat purse. It was thick and I opened it, pulling out the small cell phone.

"Liv?" I held it up. "Is this it?"

Her hands covered her mouth, but she nodded. I tried to open the case, frowning as it stuck.

Liv swallowed. "She dropped it," she said, her voice raspy. "In the tub. I remember now. She dropped it, and I threw it in some rice to dry it out. She must have dug it out and brought it in here. I gave her the other one to play with instead, but she lost it." She met my eyes. "It's probably unusable now. All this is for nothing." Her shoulders drooped.

"Hey," I called.

She lifted her head.

"Don't forget who we're talking about here. It's Reid. If anyone can get something out of this phone, it's him. Don't give up hope yet." I stood, digging my cell phone out of my pocket and dialing Reid's number.

He answered on the first ring. "Find it?"

"Yep. But there's a problem. It took a bath. I don't know..."

His chuckle interrupted me. "Bring it to me. Let me work on it."

"On my way."

"I'll be at the office."

"Okay."

I looked at Liv, huddled on the floor, pulling at her hair, unable to cope with more stress. She was breaking. I could see it happening right before my eyes. If this didn't work, and the bastard got his rights back, I didn't know how she was going to handle it. And I didn't know how I was going to handle watching her snap.

I crouched in front of her. "Don't give in, Livvy. I know how strong you are. Find your strength for Mouse. For me. Don't give in to the fear. If you do, he wins regardless, because he is destroying you. Don't let him." I held up the phone. "I'm taking this to Reid. He'll do everything he can, but if it doesn't work, we'll fight. Together, we'll fight. But I need you to fight with me."

She drew in a long breath. Then another. Her shoulders straightened, and she held up her head. She slid her hand into mine and squeezed. "We fight."

I pulled her into my arms and held her, praying it wouldn't come to that.

For two days, we waited. I knew not to bother Reid. Aiden had informed me he was locked in the server room, BAM on the back burner as he worked to help Liv. When I offered my thanks, Aiden shook his head.

"Family, Van. This is about family."

I stared at the ceiling, unable to sleep. Liv was dozing, only finding a little rest because I had made love to her again, tiring her out physically so her body would force her to sleep—even if it was only for a short time.

It was just past three a.m. when my phone buzzed on the nightstand. I grabbed it, anxious when I saw Reid's number flash across the screen. Liv sat up, instantly awake. I hit speaker.

"Tell us," I said.

"Bang, bang, Hal's big ole silver hammer is gonna come down on his head," Reid sang. "Bang, bang, Hal's big ole silver hammer is gonna make sure that claim is dead."

It was corny, badly sung, and off-key. And the best rewrite of an old Beatles song I had ever heard.

I began to laugh. Big guffaws of relief. Liv giggle-snorted, tears falling down her cheeks.

"We got him," Reid said. "Hal's already on it."

I calmed. "I owe you, Reid. I owe you a debt I can never pay."

His voice was as serious as Reid ever got. "Just love that little girl and look after her. Keep her safe."

"With my life," I vowed.

"Then we're even."

I wasn't allowed to be present at the meeting between the lawyers, their clients, and the judge. Hal explained each side would be allowed to present their argument, then the judge would decide if there was a case—and whether it would move forward or be decided today. It was in an office building, not the courthouse, which made it less scary for Liv.

"They encourage parents to work together if they feel it is in the best interest of the child." Hal patted his briefcase. "After today, the judge won't feel that way. Nolan's story that he was young, scared, and not thinking straight is going to be shot to hell when I present this email and all the corroborating facts." Reid had dug up dates and timelines, Liv's statements, and put it all together for Hal.

Hal smiled. It wasn't a pleasant smile, but rather the kind which happened right before the monster ate you. "I'm going to insist he go first. I'll let him hang himself with his lies." His teeth flashed again. "Then I'll refute every word."

Despite his reassurances, leaving Liv to face this without me was difficult.

I worried. Liv was calm, but I knew how fearful she was—terrified that something would happen. I drove her to the building and waited downstairs, alternately pacing and sitting with my head in my hands. My parents and Elly had Mouse, treating her to a day off school and spoiling her, all anxious for news. I knew, regardless of the outcome, Liv would need to get to her fast once this meeting was over.

Bentley and Maddox checked in on me, sending encouraging emails. Jordan had spoken to me the night before, offering his support and telling me to take whatever time I needed away—he assured me it was covered.

Unable to stay still, I went outside, walking around the side parking lot, needing the fresh air.

Hearing my name being called, I glanced up, surprised to see Aiden.

"What are you doing here?"

"You're here for Liv. I'm here for you."

"I'm fine."

He squeezed my shoulder.

"I know, Van," he encouraged, "I'm only here to keep you company."

"It's been a while." I indicated the building with a tilt of my chin.

"These things take time. You got this."

"Reid got this, you mean," I said, worried. I knew I had to keep him out of this, no matter what occurred.

"Yeah, the boy wonder has struck another blow for the good side," he mused. "He's turned into quite the defender."

"Thank God he's on our side."

Aiden chuckled. "You got that right. He's covered. Don't worry. I couldn't be prouder of him if he were my own brother. I love that kid."

The side door of the building was flung open so hard, it slammed into the exterior wall. The noise startled me, but not as much as the sight of Nolan marching down the stairs, his face red and livid. He was talking to his lawyer, gesturing in anger. He was cursing and blaming the world for everything and anything. He hurled insults at his lawyer, who threw up his hands and stormed away, leaving Nolan on his own. He caught sight of me and rushed forward, his fist raised, screaming obscenities. I fell back into a fight stance, ready to defend myself and hoping he enjoyed the punch. It was the only one he would get.

"You think this is over?" Nolan shouted.

Except, as he rushed forward, Aiden stepped in, and with one well-directed swing of his fist, knocked him to the ground. Nolan lay there, stunned and not moving.

"Yep," Aiden drawled. "I heard the fat lady sing. It's over."

For a second, I gaped, then I grabbed his arm. "Aiden—what the fuck? He was coming for me! What did you do that for?"

Aiden shook his head, looking nonchalant. "I didn't do anything, Van. I slipped, and my elbow knocked into his chin."

"The hell you did," Nolan growled, shaking his head. "I'm going to sue you. You and your fucking company."

Aiden leaned down and grabbed him by the collar. "Let me help you up." He jerked him upright, the air escaping Nolan's mouth in a hiss. Aiden leaned close. "Bring it on, you asshole. I've been waiting for this moment. You mess with my family? I mess with you." He pushed Nolan away, who fell, cursing, to his knees.

Nolan scowled, inspecting his hands. "I am going to ruin you," he spat.

A security guard appeared. "Is there a problem?"

Nolan pointed to Aiden. "He attacked me."

A voice to the left startled me. "I saw the whole thing. Mr. Callaghan is telling the truth. He slipped the first time, accidentally hitting Mr. Nolan, and Mr. Nolan stumbled afterward."

I gaped at Simon.

Why was he here?

Nolan glared at him. "You're fired."

Simon waved him off. "I quit this morning. I can take a lot of things, but I won't work for a man who would try to take away a woman's daughter." He turned to me. "I came down to offer my support, Van. Looks as if I got here just at the right time." He straightened his shoulders. "I'll testify if I have to."

Aiden nodded. "Thanks."

"Me too." I offered.

Nolan struggled to his feet, wiping his mouth, glowering at Simon. "You'll never work in this town again."

Aiden tilted his head. "I wouldn't be so sure of that."

Nolan spun on his heel, stalking away. The security guard looked at us and walked away with a shrug. I tried not to chuckle. He looked about sixteen and not equipped to handle spilled milk, much less break up a fight.

"Aiden," I began.

He waved off my words. "Go get your girl. I hafta call Bent and break it to him. He's gonna yell. And he is gonna make me pay for breaking the contract." He grinned. "But man, so worth it. It felt good. I didn't like that scumbag." He clapped Simon on the shoulder. "I might be looking for a smart man to head up a current project working with Van. I heard you're a hard worker. I'll need a crew immediately. Know anyone?"

They walked away, and I hurried inside and up the stairs. Liv sat in the hall, Hal standing next to her. He was leaning down, talking, when they heard me approach. Liv was out of the chair, running toward me. I caught her in my arms, letting her sob into my chest. She was shaking with relief, the adrenaline rush hitting her hard.

I looked at Hal, who followed her.

"It's over, Van. No reinstatement of rights. The judge was very clear. Nolan couldn't disprove his own words. He doesn't have a snowball's chance in hell now, next week, or next year. We've shut him down."

Keeping one arm around Liv, I offered him the other hand. "Thank you," I said, the only words I was able to push through the tightness of my throat.

He shook my hand. "Let me know when you want to proceed with the other matter we discussed. I'll do it pro bono. Consider it a gift." He smirked. "I heard a bit of commotion happened outside. Everything all right?"

"Yep. It's all good."

He winked. "I'll be in touch."

I encased Liv back in my embrace.

"We got her, Liv. Our girl is safe and staying with us."

She lifted her face, relief and happiness radiating from her eyes. It had been so long since I had seen her beautiful eyes shine at me that way.

"I need to see her."

I wiped the tears from her face. "No more crying. It's over. He can't touch her or you."

"I know."

I held out my hand. "Come on, Livvy. I'll take you to her. Everyone will want to celebrate, then we're going home and having a celebration of our own."

She spoke as we headed to the stairs. "I guess we can go back home now. To the apartment"

I stopped and looked at her. "The apartment isn't your home. You're already there. With me."

"What are you saying?"

A conference room emptied out, the hallway getting busier. I stepped closer to her as people jostled and hurried by, not paying any attention to us.

I wrapped my arm around her waist. "Stay, Liv. You and Mouse. Stay with me. You've made the house a home, and if you go, it'll be empty again. I'll be empty."

Her eyes grew big. They became nervous, but then she smiled. "You want us? You really want us?"

"Forever."

"Okay, then."

I picked her up, holding her tight. "Okay, then."

"Mr. Van, can we do this every night?" Mouse asked, grinning widely. Marshmallow and chocolate stuck to her face, bits of graham crackers littered down the front of her shirt.

I chuckled and slid another marshmallow between two crackers, offering it to Liv. She preferred it without chocolate. Although, I informed her quite sternly, then it was no longer a s'more.

But she could have it anyway she wanted as long as she looked the way she did tonight. It was amazing what a couple of nights rest and the absence of stress could do for a person.

She was happy, smiling. Relaxed.

Finally.

Sandwiched between her and Sammy, I was more content than I thought possible.

"It's only for special occasions, Mouse."

Her frown disappeared as I handed her another treat.

"Besides, you don't have an outdoor fireplace at your apartment." I pointed out.

"Oh." Her frown returned.

I set down my skewer and tapped my chin. "Unless..."

Her eyes grew round with anticipation. Her mouth opened in a big O, waiting for my next words.

"Unless you and Mommy wanted to live here—with me."

She blinked. Looked at Liv then back at me. Her voice quivered. "Forever?"

I pulled a small box from my pocket and opened the lid. A tiny ring sat inside, the world's smallest diamond twinkling in the light. "If I give you this ring and you say yes, it's forever, Mouse."

Sammy squealed, and no matter how often it happened, or how much I braced myself for it, I was never ready. My eardrums shuddered with the sound. But her little arms around my neck and her excited kisses on my face made up for it. Liv watched us with an indulgent look on her face.

"Really?" Mouse cried. "We can live here with you? Like a family?"

I set her on my knee, facing Liv. "Yes, I want you and your

mommy to live here with me and be a family." I drew in a deep breath. "My family."

"Can we, Mommy?"

"Yeah, baby. If that's okay with you."

Sammy looked up at me, her dark eyes pleading. "Can I call you something besides Mr. Van?"

I ran a hand through her hair. "Sure, Mouse. You want to try just Van?"

She shook her head. "Can I—can I call you Daddy?"

My gaze flew to Liv's. Her eyes widened, but before she could speak, I did. Mouse had given me the perfect segue.

"I'd like that, Mouse, but on one condition."

She frowned. "I don't know what that is."

I chuckled. "It means, if you call me Daddy, then Mommy—" I pulled out another small box, extending it toward Liv "—has to call me husband."

I barely noticed Mouse's squeal this time. All my attention was on Liv. Her gaze went from the box to my face, then back to the box. Her hands clasped at her chest and her mouth opened, but no sound came out.

I leaned close. "I love you Olivia Rourke. I love Samantha. Let's move on from the past of being alone and live life together. As a real family." I reached out and cupped her cheek. "Accept my ring, Liv. Accept me. Live with me and be mine."

For a brief moment, there was silence, then she said the best word in the world.

"Yes."

I claimed her mouth hard and fast, pulling her into the circle of my arms. I kissed Mouse on the nose and hugged them tight.

I had them both.

My girls.

EPILOGUE

A year later

I folded the newspaper and drained my cup of coffee. Crossing the room, I refilled my cup, leaning against the counter and surveying the main floor.

It had changed a great deal in the past while. I had always liked the simple lines of the room, but it had lacked something. Liv had changed all that. She'd added color and texture, moved the furniture around so it was a comfortable grouping. Added pieces and made the house feel like a home. My favorite addition was the chaise lounger which sat by the fireplace. I had taken it from the cabin, with Bentley's blessing, and restored it. It held a lot of great memories for us.

But it was Mouse's additions which really changed it.

My world used to consist of blue and gray. Dark woods and smooth textures.

It now contained a lot of pink. And lace. Little girls, Sammy especially, liked lace.

And the damn horrid glitter was everywhere.

Every room contained something of Sammy's. Her hair things, ribbons, favorite toys. Her tiny shoes were scattered around the house like decorations. I found stuffed toys everywhere I went—even the workshop where Sammy spent a great deal of time with me.

And I loved every damn thing about it.

With a sigh I pushed off the counter and looked out the patio doors. I'd finally added the hot tub, and in the middle of the yard was a small aboveground pool. Sammy was like a little fish and spent much of her waking hours in the water on hot days. I loved climbing in with her and cooling off after a long day, listening to her never-ending stories of what occurred while we were apart for a few hours. To hear her tell it, the hours were endless, and I had to admit, some days, it felt that way to me. She was growing too fast, and I hated missing a moment of it.

I glanced toward the mantel, the additions on the bookcase, as always, making me happy. The two framed collages highlighted the two most important days of my life.

One was from the day I married Liv. Right here in our house—the place she made a home. We had the ceremony in the backyard under the trees, festooned with lights. The day was simple, surrounded by our closest friends and family. There'd been lots of laughter, music, food, and love. So much love. It was the exact kind of day we wanted.

Mouse tripped down the aisle, scattering flowers, and talking to everyone as she went. She paused by Bentley, who was holding his daughter on his knee. She patted Addi's leg and admired the sparkly shoes on her tiny feet.

"Ooh—where'd you get those shoes for Addi, Mr. Bent? Can you tell Daddy? I bet he'd buy me a pair."

Everyone chuckled, and to make sure I married Liv today and not next week, I held out my hand. "I will, Mouse. But you need to come to the front."

She glanced back at the shoes, then the ones on her feet. They were plain white with only a few sparkles on the bow, and I knew they no longer pleased her.

"We'll order some online as soon as we're done here," I pleaded, desperate enough to bribe her, even if it got me in trouble with Liv.

That did it. Wreathed in smiles, she dumped her basket of petals and hurried to the front. She wrapped her arms around my leg, gazing up at me. "I love you, Daddy."

Everyone in the crowd melted. I did as well.

It didn't matter that she was supposed to stand to the left. I didn't care if the petals were a mound of color on the carpet runner laid out for Liv. Bending, I picked her up and kissed her nose, then settled her on my hip. "Good job, Mouse. Let's watch Mommy now, okay?"

Liv was a vision in a pretty pale blue dress that swirled around her knees as she walked toward us. Her hair tumbled past her shoulders, and her smile was brilliant. But she was taking too long, and I met her partway down the aisle, bending to kiss her.

"You are so beautiful," I murmured against her mouth.

"And you are so off-script," she teased.

I tucked her hand into mine, and we finished the walk as a family. I never put Mouse down, and I never let go of Liv's hand until it was time to exchange rings. And as soon as it was done, I wrapped my hand around hers, refusing to let go.

I still held her hand every day.

The second frame held the adoption certificate Hal had helped me acquire. Sammy was officially mine. Liv took the picture of Mouse and me. I was holding her with an indulgent grin as she gazed up at me, her hands on my face as she talked.

Mouse talked constantly.

That day, it was only the three of us. Me and my girls celebrating our little family—now legal and binding. No one and nothing could take her from us.

I sat down on the sofa, remembering those awful days wondering if we would lose her.

Nolan had tried and failed. In his selfish attempt, he had lost everything. John, the savvy businessman he was, offered Bentley a deal once he heard the real story. He fired Nolan, rehired Simon and allowed him to run the crews and finish the project. He avoided the bad press, kept his name attached to BAM and their good publicity, and cut all ties with Nolan. Once the project was finished, BAM hired Simon, who also brought along a handpicked crew. He had become one of my most trusted foremen and a valuable employee for BAM.

Nolan lost his job, his fiancée walked, and the last we heard, he sold everything and disappeared. I wasn't upset by any of the news. Good riddance.

I startled when Liv's arms came around me. Her sleepy voice made me smile.

"Why are you up so early?"

I tilted up my head, and she pressed a kiss to my forehead.

"Hey, baby. Couldn't sleep. Did I disturb you?"

"No, but I woke up and my heating blanket was gone. I was cold, and I didn't know where you were."

I patted the sofa. "Sit here, Livvy. I'll warm you up."

She slid over the back of the sofa, curling up beside me. I tucked her feet under my legs and draped a blanket around her shoulders. She frowned as she studied me.

"Are you okay?"

I ran my hand over her head, sliding my fingers through her thick hair. "Yeah. Just thinking."

"Are you nervous?"

I huffed out a sigh. "Yeah, I guess I am."

"It's going to be fine, Van. We're going to meet him. Get to know him a little. Let him know us. See if we think it will work."

"I know. It feels so...big. I don't want to disappoint him." I looked at the file sitting on the coffee table. "I think he's had enough disappointments."

She cupped my cheek. "It is big. And I love that so much about you. But today is very casual."

I chuckled. "It doesn't feel casual to me."

She leaned forward, pressing her mouth to mine. "I know, baby. Another reason I love you."

"Yeah?" I asked. "Care to share more reasons?"

"I could show you."

I quirked my eyebrow. "Here?"

She smirked. "Sammy is at Mom's. We have the house to

ourselves. It's still early, and we don't have anywhere to be for a few hours."

I slid my cup onto the table and turned to her. "Oh, I have someplace to be, all right." I pushed her back into the cushions, covering her with my body. "Inside you."

She wrapped her leg around me, drawing me close.

"Get at it then, Van."

I tugged at my collar. It felt warm in the room. I glanced toward Liv. She looked calm. Why wasn't I calm? I tugged again, and she leaned toward me.

"Van, relax."

"What if he doesn't like me? His file says he has a hard time with new people."

"Just be patient. Be Van."

"I don't know what that means," I muttered, using Sammy's favorite phrase.

She laughed and cupped my cheek. "Yes, you do. You do you better than anyone. He is gonna love you."

The door opened and our caseworker, Angela, came in, smiling brightly at us.

Liv and I had decided to adopt another child. We had gone through the interviews, passed all the requirements, and were now ready for the next step. We had agreed we wanted an older child. One of the ones who was harder to place. I was shocked when I saw the number of kids waiting to find a family. The babies and toddlers were easy to find homes for most of the time, but as Angela explained, once they were no longer cute and cuddly, older kids were hard to place permanently.

We had looked at tons of profiles, both girls and boys, but somehow, when I saw the picture of this kid, my heart had kicked in. Together, we studied his file, and my chest ached the entire time. He was eight years old. His parents were killed in a car accident that he survived over a year ago. He was left with a limp that still persisted. He needed glasses to read. He stuttered at times. With no other family, he was put into the system. He'd had three foster homes and one attempt at adoption, but he hadn't bonded with anyone and the last family found his constant quietness troublesome and felt they weren't equipped to deal with his issues. His photo told me his issues. He needed love and understanding and a place to feel safe. He needed a home. I wasn't a fool—I knew it wouldn't be easy, but something about this kid made me want to make the effort. At least meet him and see what happened.

And the kicker?

His name was Reed.

I met Liv's teary eyes.

"Yeah?" I asked.

She nodded in agreement, and I kissed her head.

"Okay. I'll make the call."

Now we were here to meet him.

"Okay, he's here," Angela informed us. "I'll introduce you and you can visit."

"Does he know why we're here?"

Her expression became sad. "He knows there is a chance you want to adopt him. He's been through this before. He's a great kid, but a bit hard to get through to at first. His foster family is awesome, but he needs to find a real home and family. I think, in the right place, he'll blossom." She sighed. "He has so much potential, but he needs the right family to bring it out."

I shared a glance with Liv. We knew all about potential. "Okay."

We stood and followed her into the next room.

My heart broke at the sight of the child standing next to the window.

Slight of frame, he had wild and curly dark hair. It needed a trim. Heavy glasses sat on his nose and he pushed them up constantly in a nervous gesture. His clothes were too loose and hung on him, his sneakers worn and old. As we drew closer, his light brown eyes were apprehensive. His hands twisted and tore at the sides of his jeans. But he thrust out his chin and met my gaze, his bravado reminding me of Liv. His eyes widened as I moved closer, and he watched every move I made.

I stopped when I was close enough and smiled at him. "Hey."

He said nothing.

Liv bent down, holding out her hand. "I'm Liv Morrison. This is my husband, Van."

Still, he said nothing. To my horror, his chin began to quiver, and I took a step back.

"It's okay, little man. If I scare you, I can go stand over there. You can talk to Liv for a bit, okay? She's really nice."

I began to move away, and he spoke.

"No!"

I froze. "Okay."

"Are you—are you a giant?" His voice was low and raspy, as if it wasn't used often. I wanted to change that.

I laughed and lowered myself to one knee. "You know, you're not the first person who has asked me that question. My daughter said the same thing the first time I met her."

"Your d-daughter?"

"Yeah. Her name is Sammy—I adopted her. But no, buddy, I'm not a giant. I'm just really tall."

"I want to be t-tall." He pushed his glasses up his nose.

"You probably will be when you grow up."

He edged closer. "Really?"

I nodded sagely. "I was about your height when I was your age."

"Wow," he muttered.

Liv crouched beside me. "Would you like to visit with us for a while?"

He paused and my heart sank. I thought we were doing pretty well. Maybe my size was too much for him?

He looked past me. Angela was still in the room, waiting to see what happened before she left us alone.

He pushed his glasses back on his nose again. "Y-yes."

"Good," I replied. "That's good. We'd like to talk with you for a while."

"Remember what I told you?" Angela called to him.

His eyes went round, and once again, his chin trembled. "I was supposed to be p-polite and say my-my name," he sniffed. "The way you did."

"That's okay," I assured him. "We can start again. We have do-overs in our house all the time."

"Yeah?" he breathed out.

"Oh yeah."

I held out my hand. "Hi, little man. I'm Van and this is Liv."

He rubbed his hand on his jeans and lifted it toward me. "H-hello."

I closed my hand around his. It felt small within my grasp, and he trembled. But again, he lifted his chin.

"My name is Reed Armstrong."

I shook his little hand. "Hello, Reed."

Two hours later, I didn't know how I was gonna leave this kid behind. I was on the floor, my legs stretched out with him on top of my thighs. Liv was beside me and we were answering Reed's never-ending questions. I discovered, once he relaxed, his stutter was less frequent, his voice lost the raspiness, and his grin was brighter than the sun. And there was nothing quiet about him.

He wanted to know all about Sammy, our house, and the park. How I got my muscles. If I could drive the big trucks the way he saw when he watched TV shows on construction. If I had a hard hat. When I told him about my friend Reid and how he worked with computers, his face lit up.

"Can-can I meet him? I love computers."

His face became sad, and his eyes clouded over. "I had one... before. My dad and I used to play games on it."

"You miss your parents, Reed?" Liv asked gently.

He hung his head. "Yes."

"You can talk about them, you know. Tell us all about them. It's okay."

"They died."

I rubbed his arm, hating the fact that he was so thin. He needed some of Liv's home cooking.

"We know. We're sorry. And we're sorry you were hurt."

He rubbed his leg. "I walk funny now. And s-sometimes I talk funny. Kids laugh."

"People sometimes laugh when they don't know what to say."

"They say I'm w-weird."

"Hey," I said, waiting until he lifted his head again. "We don't think you're weird. We like you. And you know what else?"

He shook his head.

"My friend Reid won't think you're weird. He would love to show you his computers."

It was the first time I saw the kid in him.

"Awesome!" he crowed.

He was fascinated when Liv pulled out her pad and drew him a picture. He watched her constantly as she moved.

"She's so pretty," he whispered to me in an awed voice.

"Yeah, she is," I agreed, ruffling his hair.

He pushed up his glasses again, and I held out my hand. "Can I see those, Reed?"

He handed them to me, and I frowned. They were old and obviously used, but I realized probably the best that could be done given the budgets in the system. But I carefully worked the arms a little and slid them back onto his nose. "Better?"

He nodded. His gaze drifted over to the box beside me and I chuckled. "You want another Danish?"

"Please."

I opened the box. "Help yourself, little man."

He munched away, and I met Liv's eyes. I could see she felt the same. She stood, brushing off her jeans. "Excuse me."

My eyes followed her to the door, knowing she was going to go and talk to Angela.

I had the feeling my family was going to expand.

A week later, we brought Sammy to meet Reed. Within minutes, they were on the floor, talking. His dark head bent low over her bright hair as they each chose a Danish from the box, then ate their snack. Liv sat with them, teasing and laughing.

Beside me, Angela shook her head. "I can't believe how he has responded to you."

"We want to move forward. Take him home."

"It won't always be this easy," she warned.

I looked at the three of them. "I know, but it will be worth it."

Another year passes...

The front door burst open, and Reed rushed in. "Dad!"

I looked up from the sofa. "Hey, big guy. What's up?"

He hurried over. "Look!"

I groaned. "Another computer?"

Reid strolled in, grinning. "Me and my buddy built it over the last couple of weeks. He did most of it himself."

I ruffled my son's hair, knowing he hated it. Or at least pretended to. "Good job."

"You should see the games it has on it. It is wicked." He turned and fist-bumped with his buddy. He took off upstairs, and I knew he would be playing for as long as we allowed.

My son had two favorite people in the world aside from us.

Number one was without a doubt, Reid Matthews. When we

first brought our Reed home, it had been difficult. Despite our great start, he had been terrified of being rejected again and had pushed us away, constantly testing us. Reid understood his fears and could relate to him on a level we couldn't comprehend. He became his friend and confidant, bonding over computers, pizza, and a lot of private conversations. With Reid's help, we had broken down Reed's barriers, and he had come to trust us. Trust the love and know he was part of our family. The respect and admiration I already had for Reid grew by leaps and bounds watching him help my son.

My gratitude was, and always would be, endless.

His second favorite person in the world was Aiden. As awed by his immense size as he was by mine when we first met, Reed was fascinated when I took him to watch Aiden work out. Crouching to his level, Aiden spoke to him man-to-man.

"Van tells me you have a weak leg."

Reed nodded, backing into me, his fingers grabbing on to my pant leg. I rested my hand on his shoulder, letting him know I was right there for him.

"Kids pick on you?"

"S-sometimes," Reed whispered.

"You know, growing up, I was so small, I got picked on all the time. Smaller than you."

Reed looked up at me, doubtful.

"He was," I confirmed. "I've seen pictures."

"I can help make your leg stronger." Aiden told him.

Reed released my pants, shuffling closer to Aiden. "You c-can?"

"Yep. It'll take some hard work. You'll spend lots of time with me and Van here in the gym. You okay with that?"

"I like the g-gym."

"Okay. We'll make you strong. Once you're bigger, you remember never to pick on anyone else, okay? You always stick up for other kids."

"Okay."

Aiden grinned, his dimples deep. His voice lowered. "You know what else Van told me?"

Reed shook his head.

Aiden stood and reached for a box. One I recognized. Aiden flipped open the lid.

"That you love lemon Danishes too."

They'd been fast friends since that moment.

But nothing compared to his love for Sammy and Liv.

To Sammy, he was a big brother. Fiercely protective, ever patient, even when she insisted on tea parties and hats. She made him laugh and act like a kid. They watched movies, had popcorn fights, argued over the last piece of cake, or who left the door open. He adored her, and she returned the affection tenfold, smothering him in her kisses and cuddles—even when he didn't want them.

His love for Liv was endless. She was the softness and light he needed. The comfort he craved and the intense care he required. She made it her mission to get him healthy. Gone was the thin frame, and his appetite now rivaled mine. I wasn't sure how we'd manage to fill him up once he became a teenager. The baggy clothes, worn sneakers, and used glasses were a thing of the past. We had his eyes tested and proper frames fitted, and he no longer struggled with the glasses sliding down his nose. Liv worked with him, infinitely patient, and helped him catch up at school. She met with his teachers, helped with his homework, and soothed his worries.

As he grew more comfortable, his stutter began to fade. When he was tired or upset, he would falter, but it, and other symptoms of his trauma, began to disappear.

And for me, he was my little buddy. My little man and my best friend. He sought me out for advice. Asked me countless questions about the world. He came to me when Sammy drove him to distraction, knowing I would understand since "I was a guy too," and "Dad, I just can't today."

We rode our bikes together. Baseball became our thing, and we took in as many games as possible, often with Reid and Aiden coming with us. I began to teach him how to play the guitar. He was a natural at it, and there were times we lost hours to simply playing tunes together. He loved to come with me to practice, and the guys in the band always made him feel welcome and let him jam on occasion.

He loved to work with me in my workshop. Sundays were his favorite day since my dad came over and the three of us hung out, working on our latest project. Never having a grandparent before, he loved the extra attention and perks, and he learned fast from Sammy how to work them.

It made me laugh.

We did so many things as a family. Movies. Bowling. Cheering him on at soccer, attending dance practice and recitals for Mouse, celebrating birthdays, weekend trips away, family game night. Our life was full.

And tomorrow, I would add a third frame to the mantel, and add another important day to my life.

He was already ours. My son. But tomorrow, he would officially be a Morrison.

"You ready?" Reid asked, bringing me out of my thoughts.

"What? Oh yeah. Liv has it all under control. We're going to the courthouse in the morning, signing the papers, and having breakfast as a family, then everyone here tomorrow afternoon to celebrate."

He grinned. "I got the video done."

Providing all the pictures we'd taken over the past year, I'd had Reid create a video, documenting Reed's life with us. It was a surprise for everyone.

"Liv is gonna love it."

"I know."

"He is a great kid, Van."

It was my turn to grin.

"I know."

The house was full, the party spilling into the backyard. All of our close friends and family were here. BAM was well represented, including Simon and his family. His wife, Cathy, and Liv had become close friends, and we saw them often.

Bentley, Aiden, Maddox, Reid, and their families mingled with Elly, my parents, my bandmates, Hal, and a few other close friends. Sandy and Jordan were in attendance, their story still new and evolving. It was good to see the light back in Sandy's eyes and see how happy my friend was these days. They were a great couple.

I realized it was much the same gathering as at our wedding. We didn't need quantity when it came to our life. We preferred quality.

Reed stuck close to either Liv or me. It had been an emotional day for all of us, but him especially. Adopting him had brought up a lot of unresolved issues around his parents' death, and we'd worked through them, not proceeding until he was ready. Calling us Mom and Dad had come easier. His parents had been Mama and Papa, so the titles didn't bother him as much as much as changing his name. He worried about how they would feel and if he would forget them.

It was Liv who came up with the compromise. She sat us down one night with an idea.

"Reed, you have no middle name. I checked with Hal, and we can arrange to add Armstrong with ours. You could be Reed Armstrong Morrison. That way, you have both of them. I think it sounds like a great name. What do you think?"

He launched himself at her, winding his arms around her neck and sobbing. I rubbed his back, smiling at my wife. She always knew what we needed and, somehow, managed to make it happen.

Hal took care of the legal end, and now Reed carried our name with his.

I looked around the room with a smile.

Friends and family filled our home.

Love filled our hearts.

It was my dream brought to life.

I met Liv's gaze, her beautiful eyes soft with emotion.

She was my dream.

Today my family was complete.

And because of her—I was complete.

Thank you for reading Van.
Want a little more?
Sign up for my newsletter and receive an additional bonus epilogue

Melanie Moreland Newsletter

https://www.subscribepage.com/bonusepiloguevan

ACKNOWLEDGMENTS

~Thank you~

As always, I have some people to thank. The ones behind the words that encourage and support. The people who make these books possible for so many reasons.

To my readers—thank you for taking a chance on this series. Your love of BAM makes me so happy!

Lisa, thank you for your keen eyes and guidance. Your comments make me smile and you make my words better.

My beta readers—Beth, Janett, Darlene, Trina, Melissa—thank you for your feedback, support, encouragement and eyes.

Carrie, Beth(yes you again), Mae, Eli, Suzanne, Jeannie, Freya— I love you and am honored to call you friends. You humble me.

Peggy, thank you for your support and keen eyes.

Deb, your role has changed, but you are a part of my team and always valued. Much love.

Flavia—your hard work and support is so appreciated. Thank you for all you do.

Karen, my wonderful PA and friend. Every book, every day, you continue to amaze me with your support and love. I ask so much of you and you surpass it every time. This Canadian author is beyond grateful, eh. I look forward to many more adventures with you!

To all the bloggers, readers, and especially my review team. Thank you for everything you do. Shouting your love of books—of my work —posting, sharing—your recommendations keep my TBR list full, and the support you have shown me is so appreciated.

To my fellow authors who have shown me such kindness, thank you. I will follow your example and pay it forward.

Melissa—your covers make my books shine. Your teasers and banners are epic. Thank you!

My reader group, Melanie's Minions—love you all.

And, as always, My Matthew. My everything. Love you forever.

BOOKS BY

New York Times/USA Today bestselling author Melanie Moreland, lives a happy and content life in a quiet area of Ontario with her beloved husband of twenty-nine-plus years and their rescue cat, Amber. Nothing means more to her than her friends and family, and she cherishes every moment spent with them.

While seriously addicted to coffee, and highly challenged with all things computer-related and technical, she relishes baking, cooking, and trying new recipes for people to sample. She loves to throw dinner parties, and enjoys travelling, here and abroad, but finds coming home is always the best part of any trip.

Melanie loves stories, especially paired with a good wine, and enjoys skydiving (free falling over a fleck of dust) extreme snowboarding (falling down stairs) and piloting her own helicopter (tripping over her own feet). She's learned happily ever afters, even bumpy ones, are all in how you tell the story.

Melanie is represented by Flavia Viotti at Bookcase Literary Agency. For any questions regarding subsidiary or translation rights please contact her at flavia@bookcaseagency.com

Connect with Melanie

Like reader groups? Lots of fun and giveaways! Check it out Melanie Moreland's Minions

Join my newsletter for up-to-date news, sales, book announcements and excerpts (no spam): Melanie Moreland's newsletter

Visit my website www.melaniemoreland.com

facebook.com/authormoreland

twitter.com/morelandmelanie

instagram.com/morelandmelanie

Made in the USA
Monee, IL
13 October 2020